HONEST SECRETS

Payback Mountain– Book Two

Diane Benefiel

PRAISE FOR USA TODAY BESTSELLING AUTHOR
DIANE BENEFIEL

Solitary Man

NATIONAL READERS' CHOICE AWARD WINNING NOVEL

"I am in love with this story. I devoured this book and didn't want it to end. The chemistry between the characters and the plot kept me wanting to read late into the night. This is my first read from Diane Benefiel but definitely not my last. I can't wait to read more from this amazing author. Thank you Diane Benefiel for getting me hooked on your books!" ~ CJ's Book Corner

"Ryder was exactly who Brenna needed in her life, and trust me when I say you will love him because yeah he really is that good of a guy. Solitary Man is my first book by this author and it will not be the last. I really think you all will enjoy this one as much as I did it is one I do recommend." ~ I'm A Sweet And Sassy Book Whore

"I really enjoyed this book and there were a few twists and turns that kept me completely involved in the story. This is the first time I have read this author and it definitely won't be my last!" ~ Sassy Southern Book Blog

PAYBACK MOUNTAIN SERIES

Dangerous Secrets

"I couldn't resist this compelling tale of a wrongly convicted man and the woman who never stopped loving him." ~ Sue's Reviews

"This is a fast-paced story, steamy and action-packed with likable characters. The story line is engaging and pulls the reader right in

with detailed world building to make it feel like you are right there with them." ~ Di Kecap

"Benefiel has written a great first book in her new series. The suspense was good with plenty of action. The romance was well done with plenty of realistic conflict between the characters. I'm looking forward to the next in the series." ~NancyJ

THE JAMESONS U.S. MARSHALS SERIES

Hidden Betrayal

"As someone who never pre-orders ANYTHING, I put my order in a WEEK before it came out. Know why? Because I just didn't want to wait! Not to give away any spoilers but this is my favorite book from this author yet, in no small part because Mikayla is my favorite type of heroine. Right from the get-go, she's absolutely determined to meet everything on her terms. I loved the dialogue between her and Linc--with her saying, "I didn't stay back because *I* was handling it." Yes, he's a hottie with a protective streak, but she's certainly no little woman. It really WORKS. In the end, 10/10. Can't wait to pre-order the next one too!" ~Amelia

"An exciting, romantic read with a sexy hero and a determined heroine who is hell-bent on doing things her own way. The romance heats up as the plot thickens. Linc and Mikayla need to work together to survive, but along the way, the sparks start flying. You need to read this!" ~danube eichinger

Hidden Judgment

"Don't buy this book if you want to get anything done!! I couldn't put it down! I laughed, I cried, I felt all the emotions that a brilliantly written romance novel brings. I am anxiously awaiting the third novel in the series!" ~Sandy Morris

"I couldn't put this book down. I thoroughly enjoyed the story line and the characters. Diane Benefiel does a great job bringing her characters to life, and weaves a compelling story. Looking forward to the next installment of this series!" ~Becca E H

Hidden Loyalty

"5 EXPLOSIVE STARS!! This book was explosive and had me flipping pages. I love law enforcement and this one was perfect....Seth was hot and bossy, Bella kept him on his toes. This was my first book by this author and it will not be my last." ~Rhonda

"I really loved this book, and enjoyed reading the sparks fly out of control between these two characters who have both so clearly been suppressing their true feelings for one and other.
But beyond the romance Benefiel also addresses Bella's troubled past and creates a strong but nuanced heroine. The connection between these protagonists is instantaneous and will have readers anxiously awaiting the steam between the two when they finally get together. Loved this book!" ~ Pri R

HIGH SIERRAS SERIES

Flash Point

"Diane Benefiel takes us on a story filled with mystery, suspense, and action as we try to solve what is going on in the small town of Hangman's Loss. Flash Point is a story that will have you flipping the pages and wondering who is the behind the attacks against Hangman's newest resident and why." ~ Sarah Reads

*"**Flash Point** really surprised me. It's not what I was expecting but I really enjoyed reading it. It's a fun easy read that captured me from the start."* ~ Coffee Chat

Dead Giveaway

"Diane has written yet another winner in her High Sierra series. Murder witness and 'person of interest' Gwen flees with her godson to Cameron's uncle Eli. Gwen and Eli have no use for one another but come together for Cameron's sake and to find the true murderer...and in the process find their way to one another. My evening with Gwen and Eli couldn't have been more delightful, and I look forward to the next installment of the High Sierras." ~seniorphotog

*"I loved this second book in the High Sierras series. This is a story of two people who are attracted to each other, but reconnecting under the worst of circumstances. I discovered Ms. Benefiel's books and have loved the careful way she draws you in to the story with characters that make you feel as if you are reading about friends. I am really looking forward to the next High Sierras book, **Already Gone**."* ~paytonpuppy

Already Gone

"This series has only gotten better and better! Seriously, there's something that really speaks to my heart about Maddy and Logan, and Hangman's Loss FEELS like a small California town tucked away in the Sierras. They're such a power couple! I read this book in just a couple of days--totally sucked me in. It's that perfect blend of fun, sizzle, and suspense! I just want to live in Maddy's life forever but since I can't--I can't wait for the next book!" ~Katharine Montgomery

"A wonderful story about second chances. The minute you start reading, you will be instantly hooked. The author weaves a tale of drama and romance that keeps you enthralled and turning the pages. Maddie is feisty and Logan is her brooding and over protective suffering hero. The sparks fly every time they see each other. Eventually they give in and realize that they are perfect for each other and have always been. This is a great story right up to the last word." ~Simatsu

Burnover in Rescued Anthology

"Sweet, Sexy stories featuring furbabies and helping to save lives, it's a win win for all." ~Kara's Books

"8 stories by 8 outstanding authors. In these stories, there is a tattoo artist, two firefighters, two sheriff deputies, a famous furniture maker, a veterinarian, and a country music singer, and I loved them all. Then add in that each story has a dog or puppy that is rescued, along with a story of love and romance, it is a winning combination." ~Susan D

Deadly Purpose

I loved everything about this book, and it made me want to check out the other books in the series! The immediate suspense drew me in, and the High Sierras setting was perfect, as was the mysterious stranger Meg finds in her cabin. This novel had a well-written, exciting, and descriptive narrative that kept me glued from start to finish. Without giving away spoilers, the author has crafted one exciting, romantic ride, full of twists and turns. I highly recommend this book and can't wait to see what the author comes up with next. ~Sebastian Moran

This book took me by surprise. I didn't expect to get so caught up in this book that my whole day was spent captured in its pages. It has been a long time since I couldn't put a book down but Deadly Purpose did this to me. I loved every page. ~WildfireJane

Clear Intent

"I'd been waiting on this one awhile!! I truly loved the story! I laughed, cried and got so frustrated I couldn't see straight! I'm now hoping there will be more from Hangman's Loss, I don't want to see this series end! Thank you for a very wonderful getaway!! I highly

recommend this complete series!!!! Wow! Just Wow!!" ~Linda Helms

"I've looked forward to every book in this series and have enjoyed each one, loving the characters as it feels you walk with them through exciting, scary situations and sigh as relationships become beautiful. This was an exciting story with almost nonstop action and heart stopping dangers. All of my favorite people in Hangman's Loss are together to help Jack, Dory, Adrian and the town through crisis." ~JLocke

Break Away

"Oh man did I love this book. It was well written and has a great storyline. It's emotional and has a nice amount of suspense. I really need to go back and read the first six books in the series. Now saying that, this book definitely reads as a standalone. I haven't read the first six books, but I never felt lost or like I am missing anything with this story. You will obviously have some small spoilers since the books are all connected. ~CrazyBookLover

"Break Away is Diane Benefiel's seventh book in the High Sierra series and is definitely a second chance at romance. Zoey had a high school crush on Levi, and when he returns home after many years, she realises her feelings have not diminished. I'm a sucker for the sexy, broody bad boy vibe, and Levi has it in spades! But the storyline also has emotion, danger and a powerful attraction that is not only undeniable, but totally unavoidable too. These characters have great chemistry and the romantic suspense plot is well written and a real page-turner." ~Arch_Angel

www.BOROUGHSPUBLISHINGGROUP.com

HONEST SECRETS
Copyright © 2023 Diane Benefiel

ISBN 978-1-957295-37-4

It seems appropriate to dedicate this book about sisters
to my sisters, Ellen and Sandy.
You've known me the longest
and I can't imagine my life without you.

ACKNOWLEDGMENTS

Thank you to Kevin for his infinite patience while I spend so many hours tapping away at my computer. Also, thank you to Michelle, the most patient editor/publisher in the known universe. My books are better because of you.

HONEST SECRETS

CHAPTER ONE
Emery

Emery sipped her chardonnay and closed her eyes, willing herself to relax when she heard her phone ding. She wouldn't look. She wouldn't look. Damn. She looked. Then wished she hadn't. Nothing could sabotage her calm like her mother.

She scanned the message and uttered a strangled groan. Yay, neither of her twin sixteen-year-old brothers, who ran wild as if raised by feral wolves, were in the hospital bleeding out. The adventuresome twins, with identical bright blond hair and brown eyes, were her heart. Their coloring came from their mother, while Emery's blue eyes and dark reddish-brown hair must've come from her father.

The father she'd seen only in photographs she'd dug up on the internet.

The twins were fine, but her mom had bought dog food for the local animal shelter, paid for a weekend at a motel for a homeless woman and her kids, and had to have the CV joints replaced on her car. Or maybe just the boots over the joints replaced. Her mother wasn't exactly clear. But the upshot was she didn't have enough money to pay the mortgage, and could Emery please send a little to help her get through the month. A little being five hundred dollars.

Emery felt like bricks had been added to the weights already balanced on her shoulders. Dustin, Emery's stepdad, was out of town for a gig—he played drums for a grunge band and remained steadfast in his optimism for a resurgence in the genre's popularity.

Her mother, Delilah, promised they'd repay the "loan" once he got paid.

Right. And Emery believed in the tooth fairy and the Easter bunny.

She set down her phone with a mental note to reply later. Closing her eyes again, she visualized herself floating on a raft down a slow-moving river, the sun warm on her face, and birds singing from the trees. She tilted her head to stretch her neck muscles one way, then the other. She needed to add lazy river rafting to her bucket list.

"Hey there, I'm Jen. Are you ready to order?"

Emery jolted at the chipper voice, her lids flying open. A waitress stood by Emery's table with an iPad and an expectant smile. Her red polo shirt had the bar's Easy Money logo stitched over the left chest area.

Refusing to be embarrassed at being caught looking like she was ready to nod off, Emery scanned the bar menu. "I'll take the chicken parmesan dip with Italian bread." Making a meal of an appetizer was her go-to.

"Excellent choice. I'll bring that right out."

Another sip of wine, a cleansing breath, and Emery felt herself unwind a tiny bit more. Enough anyway for her to take in the atmosphere of the bar and be glad she'd forced herself to go out.

Being around people was a thousand times better than sitting in her hotel room stewing over the upcoming meeting with her new boss tomorrow. People in their infinite varieties brought limitless entertainment. The waitress was doing the flirty thing college girls do with their hair, flinging it while laughing, eyes sparkling at what a couple of college-aged guys were saying.

The bartender was downright yummy with dark hair curling over the collar of his shirt and long-fingered hands working a tap to fill a glass with beer.

She studied the other patrons, making a game of guessing who were regulars and who were visitors to the charming mountain town of Sisters, California.

A silver-haired couple with sturdy walking shoes entered the bar, stopping to peruse historic photos of the town hanging on the wall. Visitors, she decided. She pegged the thin man sitting on a stool at the end of the bar, a ball cap pulled low over his forehead and his eyes glued to the baseball game on the TV over the bar, as a regular. He yelled obscenities in reaction to someone scoring, drawing a sharp look from the yummy bartender, who handed the guy what looked like a soft drink.

A woman came into the bar from a back door wearing short shorts, blonde hair in a frizzy ponytail, and a clingy yellow top cut so low Emery had to watch to see if there might be a wardrobe malfunction. The name "Cyndi" with a heart dotting the "i" was spelled out in sparkly letters across her breasts. When the woman made straight for the bar, Emery decided: a regular.

"Ooh, Owen," she leaned over the bar, "don't you look yummy." Ha! Called it, both on Cyndi being local and the bartender being yummy. Cyndi leaned farther, stretching the material of her top tighter. Both baseball guy and yummy bartender Owen seemed momentarily paralyzed, gazes locked on the luscious display perilously close to revealing nipple. To his credit, yummy Owen recovered first and jerked his gaze heavenward. Paralysis still had Baseball Guy in its grip. He'd given up watching the game in favor of a prodigious set of boobs.

"What can I get for you, Cyndi?"

"Surprise me with something sweet. I've had a heck of a day." Cyndi's voice was a high-pitched coo like a baby doll's.

"You got it."

Emery was impressed. Never in her life had she garnered the kind of male attention Cyndi drew. Obviously, she aimed for sexy, but achieved a kind of sweet too.

Movement at the back entrance had Emery shifting her gaze, and this time she let out a low, wheezing breath. Bartender Owen was yummy, but the two men walking into the bar made this place hottie central. She tagged one of the guys as dark, dangerous, and delicious. The other was every cowboy fantasy she'd ever dreamed of come to life.

Cowboy romance novels were her kryptonite. If this guy were on the cover, women wouldn't be able to buy the book fast enough.

Long and rangy, he had killer shoulders and a loose-limbed walk that made her think he'd spent the day in the saddle. The black hat resting low over his brow added an air of mystery. She couldn't see his eyes, but the jaw under golden stubble looked strong and firm. Denim jeans worn white at the stress points rode low across his hips, held up by a belt with a wide silver buckle.

His dark chambray shirt bore a smudge on the back of one shoulder and the sleeves were rolled above his elbows to reveal tanned forearms corded with sinewy muscle. Emery sat perfectly still. If she squirmed in her seat like she wanted to, she'd go off like a rocket.

He pulled the cowboy hat off his head to hang it on a peg on the wall and revealed tousled hair that even in the low light gleamed with every conceivable shade from nut brown to burnished blond streaks. She knew women who spent a fortune and hours in a salon chair to attain that look, but she'd bet money this cowboy got his as a gift from the sun.

"Ooh, Shane." Same opener, different guy, Cyndi surged forward to engulf the hot cowboy in a hug. Emery sighed with envy.

On top of the looks, his name was Shane. She *loved* the name Shane and had ever since she and her grandma had watched the classic movie *Shane*. Kudos to this Shane for making it a one-armed hug, his gaze never straying lower than Cyndi's chin.

Emery barely noticed when the waitress set the bubbling hot plate and bread basket in front of her. Watching the regulars of Easy Money was more entertaining than her favorite reality TV show.

Cyndi beamed at Shane, then turned under his arm to aim a dimpled smile at dark, dangerous, and delicious. "Who's your pal?"

"Gage is a friend. He's working at the ranch." Of course, Shane's voice was low and rumbly.

"Ooh, Gage is such a manly name." Cyndi batted her eyes.

Gage gave a half smile that didn't get anywhere close to reaching his eyes, but he extended his hand. "Pleased to meet you, ma'am."

Cyndi fluttered a hand over her bosom that might actually be heaving. "Oh my. Do I ever love hunky men with manners." She extended her hand daintily. "I'm Cyndi." Emery thought Cyndi would swoon dead away when Gage flashed white teeth and revealed his own dimples. "Why don't I join you gentlemen and we can get the evening started."

"Gage and I have some business to discuss, so maybe later, Cyndi." Shane's smooth response made Emery think he'd anticipated her request and had a diversion ready.

"Oh poo. That's no fun." Cyndi gave a pretend pout and with obvious reluctance moved back to the bar. "That's okay, I'll hang over here and flirt with Owen."

"Hey, what about me? Why don't you ever flirt with me like you used to?" Baseball Guy's comment had an edge Shane must have noticed, because he gave him a narrow-eyed stare that was clearly a warning.

Cyndi sniffed. "Bobby, we kissed a time or two back in the day. But things are different now. If you took care of yourself like you did then, maybe women would look your way. But nobody wants to cuddle up with a guy who doesn't bathe regular, especially one who's out on bail pending trial."

Baseball Bobby's expression turned ugly, but Cyndi's attention was already on Owen, on whom she bestowed a broad smile. "Besides, Owen's more to my liking."

Shane and Gage took stools at the opposite end of the bar only feet from Emery's table. If she kept ogling, Shane he'd catch her at it, so she gave a resigned sigh and pulled her tablet from her bag with a firm self-directed order to focus. Tomorrow was a big day, starting with the morning meeting with the vice president of Norris Group, her boss's boss, and going over her notes would help her feel more prepared.

"Bobby Finley, you put your hand on my ass again and they'll be calling you Stumpy, because that's all you'll have left."

Bobby had scooted over several seats and was now leaning against the bar, staring at Cyndi's cleavage.

"What the fuck, Cyndi? You put out for every asshole who walks in this bar."

"How dare you say that about me. I like sex. I'm not ashamed to say it. But I'm picky about who I share myself with. And you," she waved a hand in front of her nose, "smell."

Bobby clenched a fist and Emery worried he'd strike Cyndi.

"Back off, Bobby. Like a dozen feet off," Owen uttered the warning in an uncompromising tone, his muscley arms braced against the bar.

Bobby turned on Owen with a snarl. "I'm getting fucking tired of you thinking you can tell me what to do. I was talking to Cyndi, not you, asshole." Turning back to Cyndi, Bobby said, "C'mon. We're going out back to talk." He took her elbow and pulled her off her stool.

Emery thought Bobby was definitely lacking brain cells. In this place, if Cyndi had any trouble she couldn't handle, there were several men who looked willing and able to help her out.

"Let me go." Cyndi twisted her arm in Bobby's grip, but he held tight. She tugged harder. "Ow, you're gonna give me a bruise."

Shane pushed off his stool, followed by Gage.

"Leave her alone, Bobby." Shane's gravelly tone cut through the room like a knife.

"Shut it, asshole. This is between me and Cyndi."

Bobby gave Cyndi's elbow a jerk. She jerked back, teetering on her heels before breaking free. Her ankle twisted under her and she stumbled. Gage caught her with an arm under her shoulder. "Ow, ow, my ankle."

Bobby's face contorted. His expression ugly. "You're faking it. Your ankle's fine. Let's go."

Bobby made another grab for Cyndi only to come to an abrupt stop when Shane caught him by the shoulder.

"You need to leave." There it was again. That rumbly, low voice.

Bobby knocked Shane's hand away, his face flushing. "Like hell. I'm tired of fucking assholes getting in my fucking business, acting like they're fucking better than me."

"You became my fucking business when you stole and slaughtered one of my calves."

Bobby's expression turned crafty. "You don't know if I did that."

"You and I both know you did, and leaving the gutted calf on my neighbor's property was not only criminal, it makes you a bigger asshole than people already assumed you are."

"Guess that'll be up to a jury of my peers when I go to trial, *asshole*. Now leave me and Cyndi alone."

"Cyndi told you she doesn't want you bothering her. You put your hands on a woman when she doesn't want them there and I'll get in your fucking business every time."

That, exactly that, made Emery's heart swell in her chest. She was all for women taking care of themselves, but there was nothing wrong with a man having her back. Shane's deep voice held a warning she thought Bobby would be wise to heed.

But he wasn't. Under the bristly stubble, Bobby's face was turning increasingly redder. "What are you, the hands police? You can't tell me what to do."

"Cyndi told you to leave her alone. That's what you're going to do."

"I'll do whatever the hell I want, and some asshole cowboy ain't about to stop me."

Bobby raised clenched fists in a fighting stance, bouncing on the balls of his feet, and Emery stifled a giggle. He looked ridiculous, like a Victorian pugilist.

He bobbed and weaved in front of Shane, then launched himself. Arms flailing and head lowered, Bobby charged like a billy goat.

Shane grunted as he caught Bobby in a headlock and staggered back, heading for Emery's table.

Panic replaced amusement when she realized both men, off balance and reeling, were coming straight at her. She felt like she was watching a slow-motion fight scene in a TV western. She grabbed her wineglass and jumped to her feet moments before the men hit her table with a crash.

The dish holding her chicken parmesan dip skittered across the floor, leaving a cheesy, gooey mess topped with chunks of bread. She'd been so focused on the unfolding drama, she hadn't even taken a bite.

Bobby twisted free and landed on the floor, face down in the bread basket. Shane had tried to pivot, but momentum had him slamming into her.

Her wineglass went flying, chardonnay raining down on her hair and clothing as his long arms circled her.

She braced for impact as she felt herself going down, but before they hit the floor, Shane pivoted so she landed on top of him. He gave a grunt that sounded ripe with pain while she landed sprawled over six-foot plus of solid male.

She struggled to breathe, which she thought had more to do with her landing on a hot cowboy than from impact.

Shane lay still, one hand cupping her butt. And since her mid-thigh skirt had hitched up, his long fingers were perilously close to *down there.* To add to what had to be quite a picture, she lay nestled between his spread legs, her best parts aligned perfectly with his.

His gaze locked with hers and all the air seemed to vanish from the room. She stared into eyes that matched his hair, dark brown rimming gold. She could do a deep dive into those eyes and never need to come up for air.

His gaze dipped to her lips, then lower to her breasts crushed against his chest. He seemed to realize his hand was inappropriately placed and yanked it away. "Goddammit. Sorry."

Emery couldn't say she was sorry. Yeah, her dinner was now splattered across the floor and her shirt was soaked with wine, but a few millimeters of clothing was all that separated her from being skin to skin with a gorgeous cowboy.

She dipped her head and hoped he didn't notice her taking a whiff because, yep, he smelled of sunshine and hay.

On top of that, literally, she was in an excellent position to attest to Shane's awesome muscle tone. Shoulders, chest, abs, some, ahem, other places—all nicely firm. Hard, even.

It wasn't polite to notice, but how could she not when he was pressing gloriously against the most sensitive part of her body? Heat surged and it took every ounce of self-control not to bite him on the neck.

So really, she'd be okay staying right where she was for as long as he was inclined to lie on the floor beneath her. But the commotion around them was beginning to register.

She turned her head to see Owen haul Bobby to his feet and frog march him to the back door. "That's it for you. Don't come back to Easy Money until you clean up your act. That'll start with an apology to Cyndi."

Owen slammed shut the door and cut off Bobby's angry response.

Since Shane's breathing seemed shallow, Emery shifted to move off him.

She pushed against his chest and he gave a strangled groan.

She froze. Gold flared in his eyes.

She barely managed to stifle a groan herself because the lovely pressure of his erection, which she was well aware had been incessantly growing more substantial, sent the heat already searing through her into meltdown.

Jean-clad legs appeared. She looked up to find them attached to Owen. He reached a hand down.

With a regretful sigh she let him take her elbow and help her up. Gage stuck out a hand to Shane, who clasped it and allowed himself to be pulled to his feet.

"Shit." Jaw clenched, he sucked in a breath.

Was he regretting her being pulled off him as much as she was?

"That bull got you bad. You crack a rib? You're in more pain than you let on." Gage's brows dropped over his gorgeous dark eyes.

She hoped the low light hid her blush. While she'd thought Shane's moan had been caused by her lying on him like they were engaged in a sex act, his groans and shortness of breath were due to an actual injury.

"I'm fine." His gaze locked on Emery, making her feel like he was still touching her. "Sorry to take you down like that. I—"

"Ooh, Shane, honey. Did a bull get you in the ribs? Let me take a look. You know I'm a nurse." Heeled sandals hooked on her finger, Cyndi limped to Shane and plucked at his shirt, which had come untucked from his jeans.

A flash of smooth skin over rippling muscles had Emery swallowing abruptly to keep herself from drooling. Then she saw the angry bruise in a rainbow of colors below his ribs and gave a sympathetic wince.

"Oh, poor baby. Owen," Cyndi turned to the bartender who was righting Emery's chair, "be a dear and get Shane an ice pack." She turned back to Shane. "Have you taken any pain meds, honey?"

Shane pushed his shirt down. "I'm good, Cyndi. I don't need an ice pack." His attention returned to Emery. "You okay?"

"Yeah. I landed on you so I didn't really, you know..." The reality of exactly how she'd landed on him had heat stealing into her cheeks.

"I'll pay to replace your meal. Sorry to ruin your evening."

"It's on the house. I already took care of it," Owen interjected.

Jen wheeled a bucket with a mop through a swinging door behind the bar.

Owen gestured to Emery. "Let's get you to another table and I'll clean up this mess."

Emery pulled the material of her top away from her skin. "Could you put my dinner in a to-go container? I'll take it back to my hotel."

Owen took the mop and sent Jen to the back with the to-go request.

"Oh, you poor thing," Cyndi said. "You're new in town and dropped in for a nice evening and look what happens, you end up in the middle of a brawl. That Bobby Finley has a lot to answer for. I'm Cyndi by the way. Our yummy bartender is Owen, the hunky cowboy is Shane, and our sexy friend, who I only met tonight, is Gage."

Emery was good with people. She chatted easily, liked listening to people's stories. Basically, she played nice with others. But this situation was more than a little awkward, clearly due to the sudden overwhelming and intense attraction she felt for Shane.

The effect left her tongue tied. She was *never* tongue tied. Her mother liked to say Emery came out of the womb talking, and hadn't stopped since.

"Um, I'm Emery." Could she maybe not start a sentence with "um"? It made her sound like a moron.

Shane's mouth lifted at one corner and her mind went perfectly blank. He was hands-down the most gorgeous man she'd ever met. But more than that, there was a moment on the floor when they were a few short steps from having sex, she'd felt a connection, like he really *saw* her.

Granted, she'd been sprawled over him like one of those weighted blankets, but there'd been a moment. At least on her end.

His speculative gaze made her wonder if he knew exactly what she'd been thinking. "Owen has employee shirts in the back if you want to change."

"Oh, thanks, but I'll head home and change. Well, not home, but to my hotel. I'll head to my hotel." She stifled a relieved sigh when Jen returned from the back with a paper bag.

"Here you are. There are napkins and utensils so you're good to go."

"Thanks." Emery reached for her backpack, which Owen had placed on the seat of her chair. "I'd really like to pay for my dinner."

Jen put her hand up like she would decline when Shane cut in. "Not a chance. I'll settle with Owen later."

"Well, thank you." She gave a little wave as she edged toward the door. "Nice to meet you all."

She thought she'd make her getaway, but Shane moved past her to open the door, and then stepped through onto the boardwalk. The evening had cooled considerably from the earlier warmth of the late September day. Laughter carried from couples walking on the boardwalk across the street.

"Are you parked in back?"

"No, I'm on foot."

"Where are you staying? I'll walk you back."

"No thanks."

More than anything what she wanted now was a hot shower. She'd need to wash her hair and rinse her top, then she planned to burrow under the covers.

Burrowing in her own soft bed with its cushy decorative pillows and beautifully stitched quilt was her number one choice for comfort, but the hotel bed would have to do. And while there she'd work very hard to put her reaction to the hot cowboy out of her mind. She knew all too well how dangerous over-the-top responses to men could be.

Blocking off her reaction was particularly hard when Shane was standing directly in front of her and didn't look like he planned to move. His hands rested on his lean hips, and his brows were drawn down in a scowl. "Look, I get you don't know me, but I want to make things right."

"This wasn't your fault." Staring into his amazing eyes gave her a little shiver. "You were doing the right thing. That guy was being obnoxious."

"Yeah, he was." He thrust his fingers through his hair in a gesture of frustration. "But you're the one who paid the price. Sure I can't give you an escort? I'd like to make certain you get to your hotel safely."

She raised a brow. "Is Sisters such a hotbed of criminal activity a woman can't walk two blocks to her hotel alone?"

"Doesn't matter where you are, you need to be smart to be safe."

She shook her head. "I'll be fine."

If she stayed in Shane's orbit any longer, his gravitational pull would suck her in and she'd end up biting his neck like she'd fantasized about.

She gave a little wave and forced herself to start walking.

"Bye."

CHAPTER TWO

Emery

Emery pulled open the door of Three Sisters Bakery and breathed in the mouthwatering aroma of coffee and cinnamon. She wished it was Sunday because then she could indulge in a full-on bakery item. Being only Friday, her sweet tooth would have to make do with something much less satisfying. If she treated herself more than once a week, the pounds piled onto her already curvy curves.

She scanned the room, looking for the man she was supposed to meet. Though they'd never met in person, she'd seen pictures of Vance Norris. She was more than a little nervous about the meeting. He was vice president of the Norris Group and son of the president, Leon Norris. Norris Group had acquired Northwood Development, the company she worked for, and everyone in their Sacramento office was jumpy because of recent rumors of a potential staff shake-up.

She sighed with relief. She'd arrived ahead of him.

"Hi there, I'm Rico. Welcome to Three Sisters Bakery. What can I get for you this morning?" The man behind the counter was tall and thin, and was either born that way or didn't indulge in his products.

She ogled the bakery case. "Oh, wow. Those cinnamon rolls look amazing."

"I can assure you they are, and were baked fresh this morning."

With one last longing look at the cinnamon rolls, she held strong and said, "As much as I'd like a cinnamon roll, I'll have the fruit and yogurt and the orange spice tea." She preferred coffee, but since she only liked her coffee heavily creamed and heavily sugared, coffee was another once-a-week indulgence.

She took her breakfast to a booth. She had only a minute to collect herself before the door opened and Vance Norris walked in. He was tall and fit with wind-tousled blond hair, and was dressed in khaki slacks and a golf shirt.

Given his attire, she could've gotten away with something less professional, but since this was their first meeting and she wanted to make a good impression, she wore a pencil skirt matched with a trim blazer over a lacey cami top.

He scanned the room much as she had until his gaze settled on her. He gave her a slight nod before turning his attention to Rico at the counter. In less than a minute he was carrying coffee to the booth, a briefcase in his hand. As she rose, he gave her a once-over, lingering a beat too long on her cleavage. Ew.

"Hello, Mr. Norris, I'm Emery Marino."

She thought he would shake her hand but instead, he leaned in to give her a hug. "Hello, Emery. Call me Vance." His lips spread in a slow, appreciative smile that showed perfectly even teeth so blindingly white she'd wager he used a whitening kit regularly. "We'll be working together, closely together, so let's not get stuck on formalities."

They slid into the booth on opposite sides of the table. Emery sat straight in her seat while Vance lounged against the corner, one arm draped along the back cushion, the other across the table. She squelched a sigh at the obvious male-dominance move.

"So, Emery, tell me about yourself."

Time to focus. "I'm the sustainability project manager for Northwood Development, now part of the Norris Group. Which, of course, you know. My job is to—"

Vance held up a hand. "Stop right there. I want to be clear. Northwood Development is currently one small part of a much larger company. It's been absorbed into the Norris Group so that's who you work for."

"But I thought—"

"Obviously, you thought wrong." He flashed his perfect smile again.

"Right. Well, my job is to find ways to mitigate the impact of housing developments on the environment and to develop strategies to promote sustainability in our residential communities. For example, we—"

"Wait," he interjected, chuckling. "You're eager. And that's good in some circumstances." He winked while giving her a sly smile that made her stomach roll. She kept her best professional expression in place despite the alarm bells clamoring in her head. "I asked you to tell me about yourself, not about your job, which, you'd have to agree, is pretty boring. Do you have a boyfriend? I don't see a ring."

Her back went poker straight. "Mr. Norris, my relationship status can't be of any interest to you or the company. My understanding is I was sent to Sisters to work with you on a development project the Norris Group is pursuing."

"Feisty. I like that."

She *hated* when men said that. Men were confident or assertive while women were "feisty." Which was code for behavior women would display in the bedroom. Ugh. She tried not to let her aversion show.

"And remember, it's Vance. I was simply being friendly." He gave a good-natured shrug like, *Hey, a guy can try, right?* "But if your feathers are so easily ruffled, we'll stick to business."

"I'd prefer that."

"Fine, but your loss, by the way." He sat up and opened his briefcase and withdrew a laptop. "Okay, sharpen your pencil, girl, because I'll be throwing a lot at you." He cracked his knuckles and wagged his fingers.

She gave a weak smile when he seemed to expect a reaction to his theatrics.

"Here it is. Big picture: the Norris Group is dedicated to a complete reimagining of Payback Valley and the town of Sisters. It takes a person with vision to see past the dusty antique stores and old-timey farms to understand the vast potential here. I'm the man with that vision."

Emery schooled her features not to give away her instant dismay. She'd enjoyed what she'd seen of the town. Sure, Main Street had an eclectic collection of businesses, but she'd found them appealing because they weren't the same stores with the same merchandise as every other town with a strip mall. Plus, they didn't have the same chain restaurants you found in most places in the state. Or the country, for that matter.

She spoke, realizing she needed to choose her words carefully. "The shops I saw were fun. The boardwalk is charming and there's a nice variety of retail outlets. There seemed to be something for everyone, and it's obvious the community takes pride in making the town shine."

He shook his head. "You're wrong, which is why I'm in charge." He smiled as if to soften the criticism. "Besides being low class, what's here is dated and boring. Norris Group envisions a community renaissance with all that entails. Our plans will incorporate high-end residential, retail, and recreational development and opportunities.

"The homes we build will appeal to the sophisticated buyer who'll bring a panache the region is currently lacking. This development marks a full-scale revitalization of the area. Ultimately, I see us getting rid of the little mom-and-pop businesses to bring in the kind of retail experience our buyers expect with specialty boutiques, venues for expert craftsmen, and upscale outdoor apparel. Think Jackson, Wyoming, or Aspen, Colorado. As Sisters evolves, our clientele will evolve along with it. We already have one project in the works for the south side of the valley. It's hit a couple speed bumps but we're getting that sorted out."

"What sort of speed bumps?"

He waved a hand like he was flicking away a pesky fly. "There's opposition we're in the process of neutralizing. People are upset over us bulldozing a bunch of old trees. It's ridiculous. Too many locals have no vision. They're rather provincial in their mindset so it's not surprising. Meantime, we've purchased fifty acres on the north end of the valley and plan on acquiring another couple hundred acres. That's the project you'll be assisting me with."

"Is the local opposition you mentioned specific to the property in the south valley, or is it in opposition to development in the area in general?"

He again waved a dismissive hand. "Doesn't matter. These local yokels are stuck in the past, yammering on about preserving the rural feel of the area. They don't want anything to change in their little valley. What they don't think about is how they'll be able to sell their property for an excellent return, or how they'll benefit from the jobs that'll come with development."

He'd dodged her questions, and his responses made her wonder if he understood what he was up against. People who'd built their lives in the valley probably wouldn't want to sell their properties. Even if they got a good price, they'd still have to find a home somewhere else and with property values rising everywhere, that wouldn't be easy.

Vance continued expounding on his plans and she forced herself to tune in.

"I'm tasking you with the job of assisting me in what we're currently calling the North Bench development." He tapped a few keys, then turned his laptop so they could both see the map on the screen. "There's a farm here with prime access from Mill Creek Road." He hovered the cursor over the left side of the screen.

"My initial concept was to acquire the farm for this project, but the owners have refused to be reasonable even when presented with an offer well above market value. I think they'll eventually come around when the neighboring properties are transformed and their business model becomes an anachronism."

Emery sipped her tea and fought her rising concern. Vance's proposal went against everything she believed in as well as the core values of Northwood Development, which had worked to integrate their projects into an area. They certainly never sought to displace existing residents or change the character of a community.

"This," Vance moved the cursor again, "is the land we've acquired. It's north of a property known as Lone Pine Ranch in an area locals refer to as the north bench because the hills flatten for about half a mile before rising again.

"We're calling this Phase One and plan to build a luxury development of high-end homes with Payback Mountain providing a dramatic focal point to the north and with commanding views of the valley to the south. The views alone will bring top dollar. This," he moved the cursor, "is Lone Pine Ranch. The farm would have been the best option, but Lone Pine Ranch is an excellent second choice."

He sipped from his coffee mug before continuing. "The land is prime for development, with the added bonus that it also fronts Mill Creek Road, which will provide the primary access point for the Phase One development. The owner hasn't been friendly, so we need to find the right inducement to get him to sell. Once the acquisition is complete, we will gain four hundred acres, enough to add a commercial element, two golf courses, a private lake with recreation opportunities, and town houses. We'll work with the county to change the zoning so we can add a retail element. We're planning those amenities for phases two and three."

Emery studied the map with a frown. "Have you done an environmental impact report?"

That, too, was waved off to pesky-fly land. "That will come, and whatever the report says, we'll deal with it. Part of your job will be figuring out strategies that'll allow us to do what we want for as little cost as possible. No good developer lets environmental laws get in the way."

Her jaw threatened to drop open at his cavalier response, and at the idea that rules put in place to protect the environment could be so casually dismissed. She leaned forward to study the map displayed on the laptop screen.

"There's US Forest land north of the fifty acres you already own, so with private property on the remaining borders, unless you can acquire the ranch you mentioned, you're landlocked."

"Phase One requires an easement across a small border area of Lone Pine Ranch where there's already a dirt road. We've offered a generous incentive for the owner to agree to sell us that portion, and if he doesn't want to do that, then at least allow an easement so we can access our land. But again, as with other local hicks, he's shortsighted and obstinate." Vance's gaze shifted to her cleavage before moving up to her face.

His expression turned speculative. "Your first task is to get the rancher to cooperate."

Privately she thought if the owner wanted to preserve his ranch, he should do everything he could to prevent Norris Group from getting a toehold. She cast a wary glance at Vance. "You think I can somehow convince the owner to agree to an easement?"

"Oh yeah. Your job is to meet with Keller, the owner of Lone Pine Ranch. Get him to agree to the easement so we can start Phase One. He's already expressed opposition so you might have to use *all* your charms." Vance waggled his eyebrows.

Who in all of human history ever thought waggling eyebrows was in any way appealing or sexy?

"Once you've established a rapport and he's agreed to the easement, you can work on getting him to accept the fair price we offered for his ranch. He's refused every request we've made to sit down and negotiate. I'm sure he thinks if he holds out long enough we'll come back with a better offer. But I didn't get where I am today by accepting no for an answer. With the right incentive, he'll come around."

She shifted uneasily. Vance couldn't really be suggesting that she offer herself as the incentive. She wasn't for sale, and Vance suggesting she was, or that she'd do it or anything like it, was disgusting and probably unlawful. Never mind the owner was probably a family man with a half dozen kids and an adoring wife.

"It sounds like dealing with the landowner is a job for your lawyer."

"My lawyer already approached him and Keller turned him down flat, said he wouldn't talk to him again. Bastard's unreasonable. I have confidence you can convince him to change his mind."

He used the cursor to point to a road on the map. "See this dirt road? It cuts across this section of the ranch and winds up to the property I acquired. First things first, we need Keller to agree to an easement so we can improve that road and use it to bring in the heavy equipment needed to start clearing the land."

Emery shook her head. "I don't understand why you think I can convince him of anything. My job is to help mitigate negative impacts of development, to establish things like wildlife corridors and find innovative ways to cut down on carbon emissions in both the construction process and the operation of the home once it's purchased by the homeowner.

"On the acquisition side, I can give advice on environmental concerns over a property. First thing I'd have done would have been recommending against purchase of a landlocked property."

She peered closer so she could read the name of a stream. Pointing at it, she said, "This stream, Rock Creek, crosses the ranch and feeds into Mill Creek. It's potentially habitat for a protected frog species. If I'm right about that, protections for an endangered species will stop all development."

His gaze iced over. "This is *my* project. One I'm overseeing from beginning to end. When this is successful and Sisters is the upscale destination for the elite clientele I envision it to be, I'll be able to push my old man into retirement and the Norris Group will be mine.

"I made the decision to purchase that land because I know, given time, I can get the rest of what I want." He jabbed a finger at the map on the screen. "No fucking rancher raising a bunch of cows is getting in the way of a project this important. And no way in hell will a couple damn frogs keep me from building on my land. There are always ways around environmental protections. I'll deal with all that. What I need you for is to deal with the rancher."

"What you're asking me to do isn't in my job description and I won't do anything illegal or unethical."

His clipped words fell like hard stones. "Toughen up, sweetheart. Your job description is what I say it is. Get used to it. That sustainability shit was your old job. I told Gerald I needed someone to work with me on this project and we decided on you.

"Requirements were female and a looker. So guess what, sugar? You just got yourself a promotion." His expression turned calculating. "You get Keller on board, and you can expect a nice bonus. Fail and you're done with Norris Group and you'll never work in the industry again."

A surge of anger threatened to choke her. "My degree is in environmental sustainability. I like my current job."

"Maybe that job will still be there when we're done with this project. Convince that fucker Keller to stop dicking around and give me that easement, or better yet, get him to agree on the sale price for his shitty little ranch, then we'll talk about your job."

"You believe I'll be able to convince him to give up his home and livelihood?"

He leaned forward. "Yeah. Do *whatever* you need to do. Be creative. I don't intend to lose."

His gaze dropped to her cleavage, then lifted it to clash with hers. "Your job depends on it. Are we clear?"

CHAPTER THREE

Emery

Emery steered her car from the pavement onto the dirt road, driving slowly over washboard ruts. Sisters was only a couple miles up Payback Valley, but once she'd left town, she'd felt like she was stepping back in time. The wild beauty of the Sierra Nevada mountains appealed to her viscerally. The sky was so *blue*. A deeper blue than she'd ever seen. The granite peaks spearing into that blue, and the patches of snow at the highest elevations, contrasted boldly with the gray and pink stone while trees, dark green pines, seemed to be shaggy sentinels lining the ridges.

She'd grown up on the California coast in Santa Cruz where there was no dearth of gorgeous scenery, but this was a whole new level of beauty. She loved the ocean, but the mountains pulled at her in a way the ocean never had.

She rolled down her window and smelled the pungent aroma of pine. She drew the scented air deep into her lungs, then let it out slowly, hoping the process would help purge every revolting thing that'd come out of Vance Norris's mouth.

Her position at Northwood was her dream job. It balanced the elements important to her: preserving the environment while making sure people had homes to live in.

Everyone needed a place to live, and Northwood Development had been committed to attaining a carbon neutral footprint when providing people with homes. They were a leader in the industry for utilizing green building design, and her role had been important: to find ways to mitigate the negative environmental effects of their developments.

Everything from the construction process to the appliances they chose, to the roofing material they used, were all carefully considered to minimize adverse impacts.

The landscapes they put in place used native plants and drip irrigation. Every home they built was totally electric with solar panels, battery storage, and roofs made of recycled materials, and were wired so the homeowner could easily add a charger for an electric car.

She had been making a difference.

Now she knew the Norris Group had bought Northwood Development to "greenwash" what they were doing. She was horrified they'd glommed onto Northwood's reputation for supporting sustainability to make themselves look good while having no intention of honestly adopting Northwood's practices.

After meeting Vance, she'd returned to her hotel and called Gerald. The jerk had refused to pick up.

Now she understood why he'd called her into his office before she'd left Sacramento, and why he hadn't checked on her with a dozen emails and texts like he usually did. The coward knew what she'd face when she met with Vance.

Gerald Slater, the meek and mild middle manager, had never once stood up to his bosses, and she didn't know why she expected him to have grown a spine simply because the company had been bought by the evil empire.

He hadn't been a great boss before the Norris acquisition, but since Northwood had been bought out, Gerald's stress level had skyrocketed. Maybe something else was going on with him beyond the company being acquired, which made her suspicious.

She tapped the brakes when a chipmunk darted across the road before scampering into the brush. Down to her bones, she *knew* the Norris Group's three-phase plan should never be built.

Environmental concerns couldn't simply be brushed aside. Beyond those, to access the property they needed an easement from a reluctant landowner. Even if they did get the easement, having only one way in and out presented a serious safety issue in a fire-prone area. She found it baffling that they'd purchase a property with so many obstacles to development.

But after meeting with Vance, she figured his arrogance blinded him to the pitfalls.

How dare he suggest she use her "looks" to accomplish his goals, and to threaten her position. She *needed* her job. Like most college graduates, she had student loans to pay as well as rent and a car payment. Added to that was the not infrequent challenge of providing the "help" Delilah and Dustin needed to keep a roof over their heads, and to keep two sixteen-year-old boys fed.

Emery needed to look for another job. It'd be better if she could figure a way out of her current assignment and continue working for Northwood Development. *Norris Group*, she reminded herself. But that was looking less and less likely.

Her field was specialized and finding a position similar to what she'd been hired to do at Northwood would take time, and her family depended on her. She'd have to do her best to stay employed until she had something else lined up without selling her soul *or* her body.

Before meeting the rancher, and that was assuming he'd actually agree to a meeting, she wanted to take a look at the property. More than that, she wanted to follow up with the concern she'd had when Vance had shown her the map of the area.

She'd changed into jeans and a white tank topped by a red denim jacket, and her ancient Chucks on her feet.

She bumped along the road, the trail of dust raised by her car shadowing her.

This was the road Vance had shown her on the map, a stretch of which crossed Lone Pine property.

A pretty stream, Rock Creek, tumbled through a stand of tall pines, and the road took her over a wooden bridge. Her gaze sharpened. She'd been on the lookout for this kind of habitat.

She stopped on the far side of the bridge and got out of the car. Spying a narrow path along the creek, she set out.

Walking along with the call of birds carrying through the trees and the sun shining overhead had her spirits lifting.

Water cascaded over boulders and tiny fish darted in deep pools.

Close to the bank, fronds of delicate ferns unfurled in the dark shadows of tree trunks.

Emery felt the tension in her shoulders ease.

CHAPTER FOUR
Frank

Frank pulled his nondescript, older model sedan into the turnout on Mill Creek Road and watched the black Jetta turning onto the dirt road. No way could he follow and not be tagged. He parked in the shadows under the low-hanging branches of a bushy tree. The casual driver passing on the road wouldn't notice him. His job was to figure out what the woman was up to and report back. Fucking waste of time if you asked him. His boss was an asshole, and lately he'd been more of an asshole than usual. Something had been up with the guy, but Frank didn't care about that as long as his paychecks kept rolling in.

With his vehicle locked, he trotted across the pavement to the dirt road, then nearly doubled over with a hellacious sneeze. That one was followed by another he thought might rip out his lungs. Cursing the dust and the ragweed, and whatever else was hanging in the air, he set off at a jog.

There was a reason he lived in a city far away from shit that made his allergies go haywire. The sun reflected off the rear glass of the car up ahead. Even driving slowly, she kicked up a wide trail of dust. He sneezed again and wished he'd grabbed some tissues from the car. Glad he hadn't worn anything flashy, he kept sight of the car until the road curved and the car disappeared.

Frank tried to be as low-key as possible. He didn't carry a gun because a gun meant extra jail time if you were caught. His car, American made and gray, had been chosen to blend in. If anyone had reason to describe it, it matched millions of other cars just like it.

He'd left it behind because as the only other vehicle on the dirt road, it would stand out like a Lamborghini.

He sneezed again and wiped his nose on his sleeve, then rubbed his watering eyes. A minute later he rounded the curve and spotted the black car parked beside a bridge.

He saw a flash of movement, and then spotted her. The woman was on foot, taking off along a creek. Moving into the trees bordering the road and hoping like hell there was no poison oak, he moved as silently as he could to trail her.

He'd figure out what she was up to then head back.

The boss had been seriously pissed when he realized the woman's background included work on conservation and endangered species. Frank's job was to find out if she was sticking her nose somewhere she shouldn't and deal with her if necessary.

He followed the creek, misjudged a step, and his foot slid on slick moss and plunged into the creek where icy water filled his shoe.

"Fucking son of a bitch."

Why the hell wasn't there a sidewalk or something to keep people from slipping into the water? What the hell did taxpayers get for their money? Not that he paid taxes, but it was the principle.

Another sneeze sprayed snot and mucus over a five-foot radius. "Fuck this."

He turned around and headed back toward the road, his wet shoe squelching and leaving a muddy trail.

If the woman hadn't been aware of him before, he was making enough noise for her to hear him for sure.

If he had to deal with her, it'd be easier if she wasn't already on guard and suspicious she was being followed.

***

Emery

Emery walked along the creek, alert to the sounds around her. There was one she particularly wanted to hear. She climbed around a short waterfall, the water tumbling over large boulders and into shallow ponds ringed by maidenhair ferns. The trail was narrow and looked seldom used, which was likely the case since it was on private property. She paused, cocked her head to listen, then continued.

When a creaky groan caught her attention, she stilled, until the sound repeated. She brought up her phone and began recording. A blue jay made its distinctive call, and somewhere in the distance someone sneezed. Likely a hiker drawn by the beauty of the stream. Then she heard the creaky groan again and held her breath as it repeated. And repeated again.

Delight surged, and she knew she was grinning like a crazy person.

In college she'd done an internship with a biologist who'd led a team working to protect the endangered yellow-legged frog of the Sierra Nevada. While she hadn't been out in the field, she'd been tasked with sorting through recordings made by those who were. That creaky groan? She was positive it was the distinctive call of the same yellow-legged frog.

She held up her phone to scan the area as the recording continued, hoping the camera would pick up a visual of the frog.

Confident that even without visual evidence, she had captured the frog's croak. She added a geotag and timestamp to the video.

It paid to be careful.

She continued along the path, ears perked for more creaky groans.

The introduction of nonnative fish species, particularly trout, which preyed on frog eggs and tadpoles, as well as the impacts of pesticides and climate change, had decimated yellow-legged frog populations throughout the Sierra Nevada Mountain range.

If she'd correctly identified the sound, her finding would create a major obstacle to any development in the area that would disturb the frog's habitat.

When she got back into cell service range, she emailed a copy to herself and sent the recording to her professor to verify the identification.

She turned around and retraced her steps, the frog now quiet.

Once back in her car, she played the recording again. She couldn't help the grin splitting her face. A species on a trajectory toward extinction was continuing to survive despite so many obstacles.

The existence of the species in Rock Creek was good news for the frog, not so good for the Norris Group or even the rancher.

Emery twirled a lock of hair around her finger as she considered the implications.

She'd wait for verification from her professor, but if she was correct, development would be stopped, Vance's assertions aside.

Maybe she could find a way to work with the Norris Group to help them better understand the impacts of development in an environmentally sensitive area. Vance wasn't likely to support the idea, but there had to be others in the organization who might.

She could advocate for the company to abandon plans to acquire more land in the area. They may not like it, but with evidence of the frog in the creek, development in the surrounding area, including the fifty acres the Norris Group already owned, wouldn't go forward.

The rancher Vance had referred to as Keller was also likely to be unhappy, as his use of the land would be restricted.

She needed to stall. She'd talk with the rancher and explain the development plan. She was under no delusion she'd be able to influence him to agree to development any more than previous representatives from the company had. But if she at least engaged in the process, then maybe she could keep her job.

Once she got confirmation she'd found an endangered species in the area, the federal government would get involved and the project would come to a screeching halt. Not an ideal solution, but honoring her principles about sustainable development while remaining employed was the balancing act she had to maintain.

For a brief minute she thought maybe she could nudge Vance toward properties that weren't in environmentally sensitive areas, and to create developments that took into account they were all living in the age of climate change. She sighed as she dropped back into reality.

She started her car and continued along the road through the stand of trees. At least she had the beginnings of a plan she could live with and keep her job.

Dappled sunlight played across her windshield and she let the beauty of the mountains soothe her.

When she broke out of the trees, she stomped on the brakes to stare in wonder.

A wide meadow opened before her, the grass such a vibrant green it almost glowed.

The wildflowers were late for the season, and she imagined the colors were faded compared to their peak beauty. But still the shades of red, yellow, and white provided indistinct smudges of color like an Impressionist painting.

High in the deep blue of the early fall sky a hawk soared as it rode an updraft.

She pulled to the side of the road and stepped out of the car.

Bees buzzed in the warm air, and a breeze sent the blossoms dancing. The perfume of flowers tinged the pine-scented air, adding depth to a scene so incredibly beautiful it made her heart ache.

She wanted to live here.

She wanted to build a tiny cottage under the towering pines at the edge of the meadow.

Her cottage would have a little porch with cushioned chairs where she could sit sipping hot tea and watch the meadow change with the seasons.

Her rescue golden retriever, Tucker, would be her trusty companion.

And if she was lucky, there wouldn't be cell service and no one would ask her for five hundred dollars or insist she use sex to convince a landowner to part with his property.

She waded into the grass, trailing her fingers over the pretty blooms until she found a round rock and sat, tilting her face to the sun and closing her eyes. She didn't know how long she sat immersed in the smells and gentle sounds of the meadow, but eventually, feeling more peaceful than she had in a long time, she opened her eyes again.

Yellow butterflies chased each other over green grass that bent with the breeze. A grasshopper sat on a long blade of grass, bending the stalk under its weight. Puffy white clouds floated across the deep blue sky. Add the musical sound of the tumbling creek and the echoing cry of the circling hawk, in that moment her world was perfect.

A faint path disappeared into the grass, and she didn't bother stifling the impulse to follow it. The creek cut a narrow channel through the meadow and the path she was on followed it.

Telling herself she'd only meander a few minutes longer, she continued on, phone ready in case she had another chance to document evidence of the yellow-legged frog.

Maybe she could find work as a biologist for the Forest Service tramping through meadows looking for frogs.

The sound of rushing water intensified as the creek tumbled between folds in the hills sloping down from the mountain. The trail left the creek to follow the base of the hill.

She'd thought she was alone in her little slice of paradise until she heard an exasperated voice. "Get over here, you fucking bastard."

CHAPTER FIVE
Emery

Emery rounded an outcropping of smooth boulders and came to an abrupt stop, not at the rough voice, but at the huge black animal standing in front of her. A man on horseback sat maybe fifty feet away. She froze, afraid to move a muscle when the monster cow turned its head—and its horns—toward her. She didn't know if moving would provoke it, but she wasn't chancing it. The cow was watching her instead of the man on the horse. Staring right at her and blowing through its nose, it tossed its head and pawed the ground. She'd bet what was left in her savings account that wasn't a good sign.

The man uttered a string of profanity before saying, "Lady, take off the red jacket and drop it on the ground. Then slowly back away."

With her gaze locked on the cow, she did as ordered and shucked off her red denim jacket, then dropped it on the grass. Keeping her eyes on the animal, slowly she stepped back.

The cow bellowed. She yelped and scrambled backward.

The man, black cowboy hat clamped to his head, surged forward on the speckled horse while circling a lasso over his head. She recognized his low rumbly voice and the gilded hair visible under the black hat.

Yep. Shane.

The cow made a break for freedom and veered toward the creek. Man and horse anticipated its move and blocked it. The cow dodged in the other direction, and they blocked that move too. One last evasion attempt by the cow and Shane let the rope loose to circle through the air and drop neatly over the cow's horns and neck, then wrapped the rope around the saddle horn. The horse pulled back, keeping the rope taut.

Emery thought her eyes must be bugging out of her head. Shane and his horse worked as a perfect team against the cow, which looked disgruntled and let out a loud bellow, pulling against the rope as it again pawed at the ground.

"Emery." Startled he remembered her name, she jerked her head in Shane's direction. "Walk behind the horse to my left side. I want you up behind me."

Keeping an eye on the cow, she did as directed.

On the horse sounded a lot safer than on the ground. Shane nudged his horse toward her and reached down with a gloved hand, grasping her arm and effortlessly hauling her up behind him. The easy strength behind the move gave her a fluttery feeling low in her belly.

"Hold on to me. And whatever you do, don't let go."

She grabbed his shirt, knuckles rubbing against hard muscle beneath the fabric. Instant heat raced up her arms. Her reaction to him the previous night came roaring back. Finding herself up close and personal again heightened the feeling. Sneaking under her visceral response was the unhappy thought the meadow was probably on Lone Pine Ranch property, and Shane likely worked there.

He could even be the owner.

The horse moved and she tightened her grip. She'd ridden horses before. The pony kind tied behind other ponies going in circles at the county fair. When she'd been six.

The horse beneath her was doing some fancy footwork to fake out the cow. She gave an embarrassing squeal when the horse dodged. She started slipping and Shane's shirt pulled from his jeans as she held tighter, praying she wasn't about to be tossed in the air.

She thought he was focused on the cow until he reached back. "Give me your hand." She put her hand in his and he slapped it against his waist. "Both hands on my belt and hold on."

Slipping her fingers over his waistband and her thumbs under his belt, she did her best not to think about his shirt riding up and her knuckles rubbing softly against warm skin.

She peeked around Shane to see the cow staring at the horse with a look that could only be described as belligerent.

"C'mon, bastard, you've had your fun. Keep this up and I'll cut off your balls."

"Do cows have balls?" she spoke for the first time.

"No." Shoulder muscles flexed as he used the reins. "Bastard's not a cow."

"Oh. A bull?"

"For now."

He kicked and urged the horse into a bone-jarring trot. The bull had seemed to accept his fate and followed along. Shane pulled the reins and the horse slowed to a walk, its hooves making crunchy sounds in the sandy soil.

She glanced over her shoulder and eyed the big animal following docilely behind. "Would you really cut off his balls?"

"Actually, he only has one." She was trying to work that out when he said, "Unless we want a bull, male calves get their testicles banded when they're a week old. One of the bands must have broken and he grew one ball."

"Cows are castrated with rubber bands? I had no idea."

"Not cows, bulls. Cows are females who've given birth. Bull calves are castrated if they're not needed for breeding. Using bands is one method."

She'd thought about the cowboy she'd met the night before. Lying in bed in her hotel room, she'd fantasized about meeting him again. The hard body she'd been sprawled over so intimately on the floor of Easy Money had featured prominently in her fantasies.

Castration methods for cattle were *not* the conversation she thought they'd be having if they ever met again.

They rode on for a bit, her gripping his belt, him loose hipped in the saddle.

"Um, my car is on the road on the other side of the meadow. Now that you have the bull roped, maybe I can get my jacket. Do bulls really charge at the color red?"

"That's a myth, but Bastard's unpredictable. Who knows what set him off."

"Wait, is he a bastard, or is his name Bastard?"

"Both."

She laughed. "Right. Okay. But since you have him roped, is it safe for me to get my jacket and go back to my car?"

"We'll get your jacket and get you to your car once Bastard's where he's supposed to be."

"And where's that?"

"Up ahead. Almost there."

They left the meadow and were leading the bull along a path through scrub brush. Now, mostly on board with the program, Bastard followed behind them like a reluctant dog on a leash.

The sun felt wonderfully warm on Emery's shoulders, but she knew she'd start to burn soon. She was finding it hard to be too bothered. Riding on a horse behind a gorgeous cowboy under a beautiful mountain sky was the most exciting thing to have happened to her in far too long.

They came to a barbed wire fence and followed it.

"You got the bastard."

Emery peered around Shane's shoulder. A man with warm brown skin and a long white beard who looked as old as the mountains stood next to a mud-spattered utility-type vehicle. A section of the fence that had been pushed over had telltale tufts of black fur snagged in the barbs.

"Got yourself a woman too."

"Keeping Bastard, not sure about the woman."

"Hey," Emery interjected, "no one's keeping me."

She felt a tremor through Shane's body and thought he'd stifled a laugh.

He took his left boot out of the stirrup and twisted in the saddle to take her arm. He'd taken off his glove and the feel of his hand sent a jolt shooting through her like electric current.

"Put your foot in the stirrup and swing down." Once she had her feet on the ground, the sparks dulled as he released her arm. He pointed to the old man. "Go stand next to Harding and let me get Bastard back where he belongs."

Harding spoke, his voice surprisingly smooth. "Miss, step on this here wire to help me keep it layin' down so they can get past without gettin' all tangled."

"I'm Emery. Nice to meet you, Harding." The old man nodded in acknowledgement as he directed her on where to stand.

Keeping the rope short and tight, Shane led Bastard over the downed fence. When he was well away from the path to freedom, Shane loosened the rope to free the bull and urged his horse in a quick trot back over the fence, Bastard staring balefully after them.

Emery followed Harding's direction and moved off the wire as Shane swung down from his horse, leaving the reins trailing. He worked with Harding to right the fence.

The wood post had snapped, and Harding pulled a metal stake from the back of the utility vehicle while Shane hefted a sledgehammer. Wielding the heavy tool like it weighed nothing, Shane pounded the stake deep into the soil, bunched muscles stretching the material of his shirt across his back, and with his shirt untucked she was treated to glimpses of his tanned skin.

Both men worked to loosen the staples and pull the wire free from the broken wood post and cinch it to the sturdier steel stake.

Harding ran a hand down his beard. "Bastard's figured out he can just keep pushin' on the fence posts and eventually they'll snap. Then he can wander where he likes."

"He's looking for love. Tomorrow we're going to band that solo ball of his. That'll keep him from any amorous pursuits."

"That'll be fun." Harding's dry comment brought a grunt from Shane.

Emery was so caught up in watching the men work, she gave a yelp when something big huffed out a breath on her neck and tugged on her hair.

Harding gave a crackling laugh and she turned to find herself nose to nose with Shane's horse. He, she, *it?* Whatever, the animal, mostly white with brownish-orange speckles, was huge. But its big brown eyes looked friendly, and its nose velvety, so she raised a tentative hand to stroke, jumping back when it tossed its head.

"It's all on her terms, that one," Harding said.

A mare then. Knowing female horses were mares was the extent of her equine knowledge. "What's her name?"

"Birdie. She's the boss's darlin' and merely tolerates the rest of us. Good sign she nibbled your hair, though."

Emery withheld judgment. She glanced at Shane and when she caught him looking at her, she remembered she was wearing only a tank top. His gaze clashed with hers and the memory flashed—her, him, the floor, heat pressed to heat. His fingers oh-so-close to heaven.

He'd been affected; she'd felt the evidence. She'd bet he'd given their encounter some thought since then too.

"Is your last name Keller?"

He narrowed his gaze. "Yeah. So?"

Her shoulders slumped and she shook her head as he confirmed her suspicion. "Ah, nothing." Shane Keller was the rancher standing in the way of Vance's development. Well, him and yellow-legged frogs.

She'd have to talk with him, but that meeting wasn't happening when she was wearing her beat-up Chucks and a tank top displaying too much cleavage.

Not that she'd bring up having recorded yellow-legged frogs on his property. That still had to be verified. But if it was true, he'd be forced to make changes in his ranching practices.

Cattle in particular caused devastating erosion of streambeds throughout the state. Having interned on the frog project in college, she knew the last thing cattle ranchers wanted was an endangered species on their property that would restrict use.

"Thanks for rescuing me. That bull is scary. Sorry for trespassing." She backed up several steps. "I'll head back now, find my jacket. And my car." And maybe she could quit babbling.

"You know where you're going?"

She turned and looked back through the scrub brush. "I'll follow the footprints we made." She gestured in the general direction she thought they'd come from, hoping she was right.

"Nice to meet you, Harding. Um, thanks again, Shane. Bye."

The gleam in Shane's eyes made her think he was trying not to laugh.

She turned and kept her pace steady when what she really wanted to do was break into a run to get away from those knowing golden brown eyes.

***

Shane

"You gonna let her wander all over hell's half acres tryin' to find her jacket?" Harding spoke in his slow, deliberate way. "You don't think she could find herself more trouble while she's at it?"

"I'll get her. You got this?" Shane gestured to the fence. Bastard had come up to nose the new post.

Harding gave Shane a brief nod as he dumped the tools in the Gator. "Look at him, already testin' that post. Better get that ball done."

"First thing tomorrow."

Shane boosted himself onto Birdie's back, ignoring the ache from his bruised ribs, and nudged the horse to follow Emery.

He'd thought about her. Couldn't help but.

One moment he was taking a headbutt in his already-hurt ribs from that fucker Bobby Finley, and the next he had a beautiful woman spread over him, all long legs and knockout breasts.

And the most beautiful eyes he'd ever seen.

The punch she'd packed had hit him harder than the one from Bobby, and it pissed him off.

He didn't mind being attracted, but he sure as hell didn't want her taking up space in his head. He had enough on his plate without a woman complicating matters.

Coming up behind her, he eyed those long legs topped with just the right amount of curve to her ass.

The top she wore did nothing to protect her from the afternoon sun, but it sure did showcase the generous curves way up high.

The long fall of dark hair, hair he'd thought was brown, but in the sun realized had some red in it, was pulled back from her face with a clip thing that left most of it loose. He could admire the view and still wonder what the woman was doing on his property.

He brought Birdie alongside Emery. The creak of the saddle and the droning of insects were familiar sounds. He pulled the reins to stop the mare and took a foot out of the stirrup. "I'll give you a ride to your jacket and car."

She stopped, and apparently not one to act impulsively, lowered her brows as she considered her options. "You don't need to bother with me. I'll find my jacket."

"No doubt, but you're on your way to getting sunburnt. I'll get you there quicker."

She studied him with eyes that matched the Sierra sky. Eyes that'd sucked him in right off. "Okay."

He reached down a gloved hand. "Put your foot in the stirrup and give me your hand."

She let him help her up behind him. She grabbed onto his belt, her fingers sliding under his waistband for balance as she'd done before, and he nudged Birdie through the brush.

After riding in silence for a bit, he spoke. "How'd you end up on my ranch?"

He heard the gusty sigh behind him. "Just confirming, but you are the owner of Lone Pine Ranch, correct?"

"Lone Pine's mine."

She mumbled something that sounded like *figures*. "You know Vance Norris?"

"Yeah." People tended to know local assholes. Especially if they wanted your land and bought property next to yours they planned to ruin by building McMansions all over it.

If Shane had known the land had been for sale, he'd have made an offer and bought it in a hot minute and would've avoided the current thorn in his side. But Norris must have contacted the owner and made an offer well over what it's worth, and now the thorn was cutting deep.

They arrived at the bank of the creek. He dismounted, grabbed her jacket, and handed it to her. Once back in the saddle, he guided Birdie along the path.

"Um, just to be up front, Northwood Development, the company I work for, was bought by the Norris Group several months ago. I've, ah, recently been assigned to work with Vance Norris."

The night before, when she'd landed on top of him, he'd gazed into depthless blue eyes and felt something inside him shift. Something that had to do with more than instant sexual attraction.

Not that he wanted to be interested in anything more than casual. But her working for Vance Norris stopped any ideas he'd had in that direction dead in their tracks.

Norris was an entitled bastard whose top goals were to make as much money as possible, cheating and screwing over anyone in his path while amassing power for himself. The people who worked for him couldn't be trusted any more than their boss.

Shane shoved aside the disappointment. "Norris told you to come out here?"

"No. I mean, yes, he did. He wants me to talk to you, but that's not why I'm out here now."

He gave a dry laugh. "Of course he wants you to talk to me. I told him and his lawyer to fuck off when they approached me to buy my land. Their pitch is I'm somehow obligated to grant an easement after Norris was stupid enough to buy a landlocked property. He thought he could bully his way into me letting him cross my land to get to his. Money didn't work to change my mind. Threatening to sue me over the easement didn't work. Now he's sending a pretty woman."

She cleared her throat before speaking. "That's not how it is."

"That's exactly how it is. Norris is used to getting his way. He'll use whatever means at his disposal to accomplish that. You're only one more tool to be exploited."

"I told you that's not why I'm here. I have some—" She hesitated, then continued. "I have some concerns and wanted to see the property for myself."

"Right." They rode in silence for a few minutes, the sound broken by the creaking of leather, calling birds, and the quieter gurgling of water from the creek.

"Did Norris also tell you I sometimes spend an evening at Easy Money? That how you ended up there last night?"

She laughed, and it sounded caustic. "Give me a break. Do you really believe I went to that bar and somehow got in the middle of your fight, and was pulled down on top of you, all because I couldn't think of any other way to meet you?"

"I didn't notice you complaining about how you landed. Seems to me you didn't object, and now you're holding on to me while riding on the back of my horse. Could be getting close to me is part of the plan."

She immediately released his belt. "Wrong. That's what we call a *coincidence*. Besides, you told me to get up here and hold on."

He spotted a car and directed Birdie to take a fork in the path that led to the road. "Can't blame me for being suspicious. That's the way Norris works. Nothing's up front with the guy. Is it a *coincidence*," he emphasized the word the same as she had, "that you show up on my ranch after our supposed accidental meeting last night?"

He was surprised his back didn't immediately frost over her voice was so cold when she responded.

"There was no way I could've known the guy who crashed into my table was owner of Lone Pine Ranch. I met Vance for the first time this morning, and that's when I first heard about his project.

"On top of that, he referred to you by your last name so I didn't put it together. Regardless, I didn't come out here today to find you. Like I said, I wanted to check out the property before contacting you for an appointment."

"I'll save you some trouble. Tell Norris no. No to an easement, no to selling my land. No to the temptations of a pretty woman. The answer's always been no. That hasn't changed."

They reached her car. He couldn't miss her hesitation when he offered a hand to help her down.

He'd pissed her off.

Tough shit. He was pissed off himself because she'd let Vance Norris use her to try to get to him.

After another moment of hesitation, she put her hand in his and he helped her down. Then he swung his leg over the saddle and dropped down beside her.

She stood next to her car wearing the red jacket. He liked her look, which he pegged at stylish but comfortable, with a hint of goofiness with the green Chucks.

She pulled keys from her jeans pocket and stood fiddling with them in her hands, indecision evident on her face. Then she lifted her chin and looked him in the eye.

"I know you're not interested in what the Norris Group has to offer, and I get I'm the last person you'd want to meet with. But would you still consider it? I may have a different take on the project than what you're expecting.

"You don't owe me a damn thing, but if we could get together, I'd have something to report to Vance." She sighed. "Please?" She said the word with an eye roll, which unexpectedly made him want to laugh.

He never had a hard time saying no, and for some reason didn't like that saying no wasn't easy when it came to her.

On top of that, he wanted to see her again.

Which made him an idiot. But something about her pulled at him.

It had last night and still did today.

He could admit to the attraction, but Emery intrigued him on a deeper level, and that worried him. He didn't do personal relationships. Been there, done that, been burned, and was left with a pile of ashes to prove it.

He took off his hat and shoved his fingers through his hair, letting the breeze dry the sweat. "Norris tell you to have sex with me so I'll agree to whatever he's willing to offer?"

"No." Her cheeks bloomed pink. "I mean, he kind of hinted at something like that," she muttered "the asshole" under her breath, "but you're safe. I have no intention of sleeping with you."

Talk about waving a red flag in front of a bull. He shook his head. As much as he'd like to take up that challenge, he had a feeling Emery could suck him in a lot deeper than he wanted. Even if he was interested, unless she gave an indication that's where she'd like to go for herself and not the asshole Norris, it was a nonstarter.

"You're not reading him wrong. Trust your instincts with him." Norris was the worst type of bastard for putting women in that position. "Where do you live?"

"Sacramento."

"So you're only up here for this deal."

A look he couldn't interpret crossed her face. "Actually, I'm here for a personal matter as well."

When she didn't elaborate, he said, "Tomorrow, four in the afternoon, come to Lone Pine Ranch."

Refusing a meeting would've been smarter, but apparently he was still an idiot.

She looked surprised, then gave him a nod and a brief smile before getting into her car.

Back in the saddle, he watched her do a three-point turn, waiting until she was headed along the road.

He continued staring after her long after she'd disappeared around a curve.

Finally, he urged Birdie back the way he'd come.

CHAPTER SIX
Emery

Saturday morning Emery checked and double-checked the GPS to make sure she was in the right place. She pulled to the side of the road and stared at the tall sign painted with a smiling red apple welcoming her to Cider Mill Farm. The same farm Vance had said he'd wanted to buy before being forced to abandon the idea.

The farm was open to the public, and cars passed her to turn onto a gravel road. The dirt road she'd been on the day before was only a mile up Mill Creek Road toward Sisters, which meant Lone Pine Ranch was also close by. She dug out the letter she'd been carrying in her bag since receiving it a week ago. Postmarked New Zealand and signed by Clara Bryant, the contents had exploded like a bomb that blew up her world. She must've read it a dozen times, but once again she unfolded it.

She scanned through the contents, and the emotions that'd rocked her the first time she'd read it were still present: a combination of excitement and wariness. In the letter, Clara claimed to be Emery's grandmother. Her first instinct was to burn the letter, then had thought better of the impulse. She couldn't blame Clara for her son's failings as a father.

Emery had received the registered letter because Clara had hired a private investigator to search for her son's child and he'd found Emery.

When she'd been ten, her mom had told Emery her father was the famed nature photographer Gideon Bryant, with whom Delilah had a wild affair when she'd been studying in Europe. Delilah had been six months along when she'd contacted him through his publisher to let him know he was going to be a father. He'd replied and said he was happy if she was happy, but he was on his way to Mali and hoped Delilah and the child had a good life. Jerk.

At twelve Emery decided she'd been better off without a dad. He didn't want to know her? Well, she didn't want to know him. She and Delilah had gotten along fine without his help. Okay, maybe there'd been some lean times, but her grandma and grandpa had been there, a steady and supportive presence when Delilah returned to California from Europe, her two-year-old daughter in tow.

Dustin, Emery's stepdad, was a good guy, though like her mom, a dreamer. On the occasion he actually got paid for a gig, he was the guy who'd run to the store for milk, cereal, and bananas—Emery would make him a list—and return with Pop-Tarts and fruit punch, the kind with no fruit. The Pop Tarts were more fun, and his twin sons loved them.

As if her grandmother contacting her wasn't enough, Clara's second bombshell rocked Emery to her soul. She had a sister.

The very idea made her giddy, but meeting a sister when you were thirty meant a very different relationship than if they'd been raised together.

According to the letter, her sister, Delaney Bryant, had grown up with Clara at Cider Mill Farm, making Emery wonder what kind of relationship Gideon had had with his other daughter.

Delilah had been surprised Gideon's mother had contacted Emery, and felt she had nothing to lose by contacting the woman.

Clara had given Emery an email address and a street address in Sisters, California.

Emery was starting to think the name of the town was serendipitous.

When Gerald told Emery she was being sent to Sisters to meet with Vance Norris, she'd decided to take the opportunity and check out the address before responding to Clara's letter. There were so many scams out there, she thought it prudent to be cautious.

Putting her car in gear, she turned into the entrance of Cider Mill Farm, following an arrow to a field being used as a parking lot. Judging by the number of cars, the farm was a popular destination.

She parked her ten-year-old Jetta and stepped out, ready to start on her stealth mission. Clara's letter was securely in the small backpack Emery slung over her shoulder.

She followed a family making their way to the gravel road, the dad holding firmly to a sturdy toddler's hand, the little guy's other hand clutching a floppy purple dinosaur. The mom pushed a stroller with little feet clad in pink socks visible under a blanket.

The gravel road took her between apple orchards on one side and fields of what looked like berries on the other. Beyond was a grassy area ringed by tall pines and dotted with picnic tables. A stage built of wood stood at one end.

How fun would that be, bringing a picnic to the field and listening to music, surrounded by rolling hills and apple trees.

The gravel road forked, and signs directed visitors to the left where the road ended in a much smaller restricted parking area next to several old buildings. A tall structure like an oversize barn had "Cider Mill Farm" painted in block letters on the side.

The area in front was fenced off with construction materials stacked inside. Emery stopped to read a laminated sign explaining that construction to accommodate hard cider production at the farm was under way and Cider Mill Hard would be available in the coming months. Visitors should look for updates on social media. Icons for various platforms were displayed on the sign.

On the adjacent building, another sign identified it as originally a packing house, now used for the Cider Mill Farm Store and the Cider Mill Café and Bakery.

She loved how the rustic feel of the farm had been maintained and looked around in amazement. A quick internet search had revealed Clara Bryant was the owner of Cider Mill Farm. Emery had expected something small, maybe not even operational.

She sure hadn't expected all this.

A big man with longish dark hair, a beard, and the glint of dark green eyes strode from the construction area. Apparently, there was no limit to the hot guys in Payback Valley.

A woman clambered down the steps from an outside deck where guests sat at tables. When the guy spied her, he stopped, his lips spreading in a slow smile. He caught her hand, pulling her in for a kiss that went from zero to sizzling in a flash.

"Mmm, that's nice." When they finally broke apart, Emery interpreted the self-satisfied smile as that of a woman confident her lover adored her. "How'd it go? Will we get the tanks delivered?"

"Yeah. Tomorrow morning. We'll be ready to ferment our first batch of Cider Mill Hard by the end of the month."

"That's excellent, Walker." She beamed at him. "It's really happening."

The hot guy's name was Walker. It seemed to fit him.

"Yeah." He pulled her in for another kiss. "Missed you this morning."

"You did? I had to get to the bakery early to give Cam a hand. You could've gotten up at five too. Then you wouldn't've missed me."

"Wake me up next time and I'll help."

The woman caught sight of Emery. "Oh, sorry. We're blocking the entrance." She tugged Walker out of the way.

He glanced at Emery and his dark brows dropped as he studied her. He gave Emery one last look before following the woman around the corner of the building.

Shaking off the feeling something about her had given Walker pause, Emery stepped through the wide doors into the store, stopping to absorb the atmosphere.

Her immediate impression was the year could've been nineteen fifty and the merchandise wouldn't have been all that different.

Visitors wandered between wooden shelves stocked with jars and bottles of various sizes containing everything that could be made from boysenberries and apples: preserves, jams, jellies, and syrup, plus jars of apple blossom honey, all sparkling in jewel colors.

She thought the mason jars of apple and berry pie filling a smart marketing idea. A woman nudged a friend, pointing to cloth bags of mixes for biscuits, pancakes, and scones, and a spiral-bound cookbook contained recipes used in the farm bakery.

The friend flipped through the cookbook while the woman put a bag of scone mix in the basket she carried.

The rest of the store had seasonal items, and since they were heading into the end of September, fall-themed merchandise dominated the endcap displays with ceramic pumpkins, scarecrows made of straw, and beautiful orange and red wreaths made of fall leaves.

A middle-aged woman with salt-and-pepper hair sat at a cash register at one corner of the store, wooden pails stacked on shelves behind her. She waved at Emery.

"Welcome to Cider Mill Farm. I'm Franny. If you're interested in u-pick, the prices are posted." She pointed to the wall and a hand-lettered sign. "Let me know if you have questions."

"Thanks." Emery studied the sign. Seventeen dollars got customers a wooden pail to take into the orchard and fill with apples, and they got to keep the pail.

For twelve dollars, instead of a pail they got a cloth bag printed with the smiling apple and Cider Mill Farm logo. Prices for picking boysenberries were also listed, though a note taped over the board stated berry season was over for the year and folks should come back the following summer from June to August when there'd be berries aplenty.

What was it about picking your own produce that sounded so appealing?

The smell of cinnamon drew her through the wide connecting doorway to the bakery. On one side of the counter two teenagers operated a machine making mini apple cider donuts. Little donuts floated through hot oil until caught on rolling cylinders that deposited them onto a draining rack. The teens plucked up the hot donuts with tongs to dump into white paper bags where they doused them with cinnamon sugar.

Okay, there was no way she could resist all the deliciousness on display. She'd have to bend her Sunday-only indulgence rule to move it to Saturday.

Willpower was such a fickle thing, and she only had so much of it. To weigh the enticing options, she wandered to a case displaying baked goods. Mini cider donuts were tempting, but her mouth watered as she perused the assortment of apple and berry turnovers, pies, tarts, and more.

She had to remind herself she hadn't made the trip to Cider Mill Farm only for fun. Estimating ages for Clara and Delaney, she kept her eyes peeled for staff in that range.

"Can I get you something?"

A young woman approached the counter from the back of the bakery. Could this be Emery's sister? She wore a white apron with the strings circling around to tie in front of her slender waist. Her hair was a dull medium brown, though Emery spied lighter roots.

Why would someone with blonde hair take the trouble to dye it mousy brown?

One of the teens at the donut machine called, "Hey, Cam, the oil level's getting low."

"Excuse me for a sec."

Not Delaney. The woman, Cam, crossed to the donut area to take care of the chore.

When she returned, Emery gave her an easy smile. "This all looks so yummy. Is there anything in particular you recommend?"

"The apple-berry parcels are popular. They're a new item." The woman gestured to a square-shaped pastry baked with the corners turned up around the filling. "But there's really no wrong choice."

"The parcel sounds just right. And I'll take a cappuccino with it."

Since there were no other customers in the bakery, and because she was on her stealth mission, Emery asked, "This place is wonderful. Have you worked here long?"

The wary expression in the blue green eyes surprised her. "A few months."

"Are you the genius behind these creations?"

"I'm the baker."

Okay, Cam wasn't Miss Chatty. Emery pressed on. "I heard this is a family-run farm, are you a member of the family?"

"No." Cam arranged the pastry on a pretty blue-and-white plate then busied herself preparing the cappuccino.

"Do you know Clara or Delaney Bryant? Owning and operating a place like this must be rewarding, but I imagine it's a lot of work."

"Yes."

Which comment was she responding to?

Cam busied herself using the steamer to froth the milk, the noise making further conversation impossible. She set the cappuccino next to the plate and tallied the order on the cash register. While using her credit card to pay, Emery racked her brain to come up with a question about her grandmother Cam might actually answer, but before she could, the other woman nudged the plate and mug toward Emery.

With a quick "Enjoy" she disappeared into the back of the bakery once again.

Well, okay then.

Emery took her day-early indulgence out the door to the wood deck where she chose a corner table. Dappled sunlight filtered through the leafy green vine covering the overhead pergola. She forked up a bite of the apple-berry parcel, enjoying its deliciousness before taking a sip of the frothy cappuccino.

If she built her tiny cottage in the meadow with the little porch and its comfortable chairs, she could come to the farm for her weekly indulgence.

Living in her tiny cottage by herself might be lonely, but she was well aware you could live in a crowded apartment building in a big city and still feel lonely.

A couple at the table next to her bumped shoulders as they shared a wide wedge of apple pie. The man casually picked up the woman's hand and brought it to his lips, his eyes gleaming as he grinned at her.

Emery sighed. Breaking up with Derrick four months ago had been the right thing to do, but she missed being part of a couple. Having that intimate connection to someone.

Ignoring the pang of loneliness, she focused instead on the gorgeous view. Apple trees with their deep green leaves followed the hills rising steadily to the north. At higher elevations, pines dotted slopes that rose dramatically to the majestic mountain peak towering over the valley.

Two little girls in pigtails and matching sundresses skipped toward the u-pick orchard carrying wooden pails and followed by mom and dad.

She could still have that, the husband and children. She wanted her own little tribe. But when Derrick had suggested they move in together, she'd balked and their relationship hadn't survived.

Maybe being raised in an unconventional family made her yearn for what had always seemed like a bright and shiny dream. A dream she sabotaged because of her commitment issues.

Pushing away the unhappy thoughts, she nibbled on her pastry, wanting to make it last.

Walker, the bearded man she'd seen earlier, stepped onto the deck from the bakery, a steaming mug in his hand. He strode directly to her table and pulled out the chair across from her. Brow raised he asked, "You mind?"

Caught off guard, she said, "Um, no."

He sat, leaning forward, forearms resting on the table. "Walker McGrath."

"Okay. I'm Emery Marino."

"Cam says you were asking about Clara and Delaney. What's your interest?"

A uniformed sheriff's deputy coming up the steps to the deck caught her attention, particularly when Walker beckoned him with a chin lift. The deputy shot him a questioning look, but followed what was apparently an unspoken invitation and took the other seat across from her. He wore an El Dorado County Sheriff's Department ballcap, his nametag reading "Lt. McGrath."

She looked from one to the other. Walker's hair was a shade darker, their eyes were different colors, but there was no denying the similar facial structure and matching hotness.

"You're brothers."

"Yeah." The deputy extended his hand. "Sawyer McGrath."

She shook his hand. "Emery Marino."

Sawyer looked at his brother in obvious question, and Walker said, "Cam says Emery was asking about Clara and Delaney. I want to know why she's asking."

Emery felt her own brows lift. "She called the cops because I asked about someone?"

Sawyer shook his head. "I dropped by and happened to see my brother. No one called the cops."

"Clara and Delaney are our business." Walker's gaze was direct. "I want to know why you're asking questions."

She shifted in her seat. "Ah, I was curious?"

The hard green gaze didn't waver. "Not buying it. Try again, and this time be honest."

Sawyer spoke more easily. "We had some trouble a few months ago. My brother's not exactly subtle when he goes into protective mode."

"Okay, that's understandable." She wondered about the trouble while her mind circled back to what she'd seen earlier. "That woman you were with outside the store. Was that Delaney?"

Walker sipped his coffee, his gaze never straying from hers, obviously not planning to answer her question.

"You're asking about people we care about, Ms. Marino," Sawyer said. "You'll have to give us a reason to trust you."

The two men saw themselves as protectors of the Bryant women, and it was obvious meeting with Clara and Delaney would mean getting through them first.

Going with her gut, she rifled through her backpack and pulled out the registered letter. She flattened it on the table before handing it to Walker.

He took it from her, scanning the page before passing it to his brother. "I caught your resemblance to Laney. Clara, too, for that matter. That's the other reason I'm sitting across from you."

Emery felt her breath catch in her throat. Her brothers were a composite of Dustin and Delilah, and she'd always assumed she took after Gideon because she looked nothing like her mom. The idea she might share features with Clara or Delaney thrilled her.

While Sawyer read the letter, Emery recalled her initial impression of the woman Walker had kissed. Tallish, though not as tall as Emery, long black hair shades darker than hers, and where Emery was curvy, Delaney looked more athletic.

Emery was super curious about the resemblance Walker had seen.

"Are you her husband?" He wasn't wearing a ring, but some men didn't.

"Give me a couple months and I will be."

"Oh, that's lovely. Congratulations."

Sawyer handed Emery the letter. "Clara calls you and the other sister her lost grandchildren."

"Other sister? What other sister?" How could there be another sister?

"I'll let Laney explain since it's her story, and Clara's." Sawyer glanced at Walker, who nodded.

She had more than one sister? "You guys are killing me. Sisters, as in I have *two* sisters? I can't believe this. I want to meet them."

"We have only one of them here. The PI Clara hired thinks he found the other woman, but she hasn't responded to the letter Clara sent."

Emery let the information process. "Okay. I have another sister. Two sisters. That's awesome." She looked from one man to the other. "Did either of you know Gideon Bryant?"

"Not well. He made his way back to the farm every year or so when Laney was growing up. His visits would shatter her." Walker didn't bother keeping the derision out of his voice. "She'd do everything she could think of to get him to stay, but he never would. He'd take off and break her heart every time."

Emery shook her head. "That's awful. I don't know what's worse, never knowing him at all, or knowing you don't mean anything to him."

"Guess that's a conversation you'll have with Laney sometime."

She wanted to ask if they'd take her to Clara and Delaney right then, but knew she'd have to earn their trust first, and the only way to do that was to be honest.

"This is totally surreal. I knew my father was Gideon Bryant. My mom told me that much. I Googled him because who wouldn't? But other than his work, it seems he was private. There's not much information out there about him. I couldn't find anything about his family." She shrugged. "When I got this letter from Clara, I searched him again and learned he'd died a year and a half ago from dengue in Indonesia."

"That shook up Clara." Sawyer took off the ballcap, running a hand through dark brown hair that was longer on the top and short on the sides.

She caught the instant he froze, gaze riveted on something over her shoulder, before settling the hat on his head again.

She turned her head to see what had captured his interest. Carrying mugs and pastries on a tray, Cam followed a trio of elderly women across the deck. Once they were settled in their chairs, Cam set their orders in front of them. Tucking the tray under her arm, she used a cloth to wipe another table.

Emery glanced back at Sawyer who looked like he hadn't blinked the entire time his gaze had locked like a tracking beam on Cam.

Cam moved to another table, setting glasses and plates left by customers on the tray. She glanced up, cheeks flushing when she noticed their attention. She crossed the deck to their table. "Can I get you all anything?"

Her voice carried a slight twang.

"Since when do you wait tables?"

She cast a cool eye over Sawyer. "I'm not waiting tables. I'm waiting on one table, Lieutenant McGrath. That's singular. And I only asked because I know you and Walker. If that bothers you, consider the offer rescinded."

Walker leaned back in his seat, arms crossed over his chest, a resigned look on his face like he was used to the heated back and forth. "What my idiot brother should have said was 'Thanks, Cam, but we're good.'"

"I only meant she has enough to do in the bakery without adding waiting tables to her responsibilities."

"I'll decide when I have enough to do, Lieutenant. If we're a little short-staffed and I need to help outside, then that's what I'll do." Emery wasn't sure how Cam managed to smile warmly at her and Walker while blasting Sawyer with a cold front.

"If you two will excuse me, I'll get back to my responsibilities *inside* the bakery."

Cam went into the bakery and Walker slapped Sawyer on the back. "You think you can open your mouth just once without setting her off?"

"My mere existence sets her off."

"No, it's not that. It's your assumption she doesn't know jack shit about taking care of herself and needs you to constantly remind her of that fact."

"That's not how it is."

Walker shrugged. "Might think about it 'cause that's how she's seeing it."

Sawyer gave an exasperated sigh and glanced at Emery. "Sorry about that. We were talking about Bryant." He scrubbed his hand over his face. "Clara learned about the existence of her other two granddaughters after her son's death. I think hiring a private investigator to find you gave her something positive to do after Gideon died."

Emery switched gears from the fascinating sparks flying between Sawyer and Cam to the issue presented by the letter. "Since I was coming to Sisters for work, I did a search of the street address Clara gave and verified her as the property owner." At Sawyer's questioning look, she shrugged. "I was afraid the letter might be a scam so I was being cautious by checking out the place before making contact with her."

"That's reasonable," he commented.

"I only intended to drive by and see what I could see, but stopped when I discovered it was open to the public." She sipped the last of her cappuccino. "Do I pass muster? Can I meet Clara and Delaney?"

"Clara's not here and won't be for the near future." Walker's gaze remained riveted on her face as if he could detect any nefarious intentions on her part. "I'll talk with Laney and let her decide how she wants to move forward. I'll get back to you."

Walker's priority was obviously protecting his fiancée so he was acting as gatekeeper. Taking a notepad from her bag, she wrote her name and number and handed it to him.

"I'm staying at a hotel in Sisters until tomorrow afternoon. I could come back to the farm this evening or tomorrow before noon if Delaney wants to meet. I live in Sacramento, which isn't far if we can't arrange something before I leave."

Walker folded the paper and stuffed it in his shirt pocket. "We'll let you know."

She guessed that was as good as she was going to get.

CHAPTER SEVEN
Emery

"You're going out to a ranch to meet a cowboy?" Delilah's sigh carried over the phone. "How romantic."

Emery's phone was on speaker and she'd set it on the nightstand as she changed her top for the third time. Not that her suitcase held a lot of options. She was looking for something to match her navy cotton capris. Even if meeting with Shane was for business, she was going to a ranch and she seriously doubted Shane would be in business attire.

She gave a brief thought to running out and finding a shop with cute tops and maybe sandals to go with the capris, but she didn't have the extra hour shopping would entail before she was due at Lone Pine Ranch. And if Emery was going to help with the mortgage, she couldn't afford to splurge on new clothing. Besides, it wasn't like meeting at Lone Pine Ranch was a date or anything.

The v-necked top in deep magenta would work, and since heels were out, the green Chucks would have to do.

"This is a professional meeting, Mom. The new overlords of Northwood Development want to buy his property for development."

As Emery knew she would, Delilah went in hot. "Ranching is bad enough for the environment, but don't get me started on cattle." *Don't get me started* was usually the launching point for one of Delilah's rants. "They inject those poor animals with hormones and antibiotics, and cattle are the *worst* for methane production. But destroying the land for development? That's unconscionable." Then came the familiar refrain. "Really, Em, I don't see how you can work for a development company."

In Delilah's world, everything was black or white, good or evil, positive or negative. Veganism was good, meat consumption bad. Preserving the land was good, development bad.

Emery agreed leaving the land undisturbed and pristine when possible was the best option, but people needed to live somewhere, so her goal was to make development of that somewhere have as little negative impact on the environment as possible.

Trying to explain mitigation strategies with Delilah was like trying to convince teenagers they didn't need a cell phone. You could lay out all the reasons against it, but their minds weren't going to be changed.

Long discussions with Delilah on the topic hadn't convinced her of anything and gave Emery a headache every time.

But remembering her meeting that morning with Vance Norris, she said, "This time, you might be right."

"Ha, I told you. Okay, back to the date with the cowboy. Maybe he'll be cute."

"It's not a date and he's not cute. Not at all." Gorgeous, sexy, bitable, yes. But definitely not cute.

"You already met him?"

"Oh yeah." She related the story of the bar fight and landing on top of Shane, topping it off with him rescuing her from the bull.

"Oh my *god,* Emery. He made sure you landed on him instead of the floor. That's gallant. And rescuing you from a charging bull is even more dreamy." Delilah sighed. "Take a picture of him, *please.* I have to know if he looks anything like the fantasy I've got going."

It never ceased to amaze Emery that as badly as Gideon Bryant had burned Delilah, she was still a romantic.

"Time and place, Mom. This is a business meeting. I'm not taking a picture of him."

"He doesn't have to know. Pretend to be scrolling on your phone and take his picture. I'm dying to know what he looks like. Is he tall? Does he have good shoulders?"

"Yes, he's tall, and it's a definite yes on the shoulders." Emery couldn't suppress her sigh. "He's gorgeous, Mom. Is that enough to go on?" Emery knew she shouldn't encourage Delilah's propensity to see every man her daughter ran into as some kind of romantic hero and potential life partner, but she couldn't seem to help herself with Shane.

"I guess it'll have to be. I'll be dreaming of a gorgeous cowboy for you."

"I knew I said too much. I need to finish getting ready. I'll call you tomorrow when I'm driving home."

"Sounds good, baby, but hang on. Rowan wants to tell you about today's adventure."

Her mother handed the phone to Twin One, so referred to because Rowan and Griffin were so alike when they were infants Dustin had written T1 and T2 on their feet to keep them straight.

The twins spent every spare minute at the beach, swimming and surfing. Both were tanned with long blond hair bleached by the sun, as sleek and agile in the water as young dolphins.

Her brother said, "Guess what, Em, Griff got stung by a jellyfish. He's got red lines down his leg. It looks dope. I peed on him, just to help him out, you know?"

"Rowan, you know that's a myth. Urine doesn't help a jellyfish sting."

"But what if it does and I didn't try? What kind of brother would I be?"

"The kind who doesn't pee on his sibling?"

"That kind of brother is a loser. Here, Griff wants to talk to you."

"Hey, Em. I got stung by a jellyfish on my leg."

"I heard. How are you feeling?"

"It's red and there's blisters and still hurts, but not too bad. Dad gave me some Tylenol even though Mom says drug companies are destroying the world. Dad says sometimes you just need Tylenol."

"Sometimes you do. Listen, if there's a next time, don't let Rowan pee on you, okay?"

"Okay. I miss you." Griffin was her sensitive brother, more empathetic and perceptive than the headstrong Rowan.

"I miss you too, Griff. I'll be home for your birthdays."

The twins had been born twenty-three minutes apart, Rowan at ten minutes before midnight and Griffin thirteen minutes after, so they each had their own birthday. A fact they loved.

"But that's not for weeks and weeks."

"I know. How about we video chat tonight? You can show me the jellyfish sting and I can tell you about my visit to a ranch this afternoon."

"A ranch? That's cool. I'll take pictures of my leg and send them to you, but I still want to video chat."

She disconnected, and as happened every time she talked with them, she wished she was home surrounded by the love that was her family.

And now she had sisters, but she couldn't imagine her relationship with them ever being as close as what she had with the wild boys she'd helped raise.

***

Shane

Shane caught sight of the approaching car and straightened, then shoved the bale he was gripping by the wires into the trailer behind the Gator. They were at the hayshed loading the Gator with hay to be taken out to hungry cattle. Gage stood at the top of bales stacked eight high to the rafters. Having tossed down all they needed, he jumped down, bale by bale, while Shane and Harding heaved them into the trailer.

Shane kept an eye on Harding. The old guy wouldn't admit it, but the afternoon had gotten warm and the heat got to him more than it used to.

Shane had Bruno, the part lab, part pit, part whatever else mutt, in the Gator so he'd be out of the way of the bales Gage dropped.

Bruno spied the car coming up the dirt road and leapt out of the UTV, barking like they were under attack by a marauding army. Shane grabbed him by his collar before he could charge across the yard. He pointed to the dog and let go of his collar. "Sit. Stay."

Bruno sat, and he mostly stayed, but he quivered with the struggle, a low rumbling coming from his throat.

Harding squinted into the afternoon glare. "That Emery?"

"Yeah." How'd he guess that? Shane hadn't told anyone she was coming, mostly because he didn't want to get hassled about it.

"Figured we'd be seeing something of her considerin' how you been jumpy ever since you showed up with her ridin' behind you on Birdie yesterday."

"I'm not jumpy."

On the ground again, Gage butted in, "You had her up behind you on Birdie? That's sweet. Harding's right, you've been jumpy."

Shane flipped him off.

"See," Harding said. "Confirmation from the FBI agent. And for the past half hour, you been lookin' out to the road like you were expecting someone 'stead of focusing on the job."

"I noticed that too. You're hooked." Gage smirked. The man might be his brother in every way but blood, but Shane still wanted to punch him.

"Fuck off, both of you," he growled. Then said pointedly, "Harding, don't slip up and mention to our guest Gage is a fed. Besides Sawyer and Walker, we're the only ones who know and it needs to stay that way."

"I won't slip up." Harding grinned as he added, "Still think you're nervous 'bout invitin' your lady friend to the ranch."

There was nothing between him and Emery. Couldn't be. He might as well tell them so they wouldn't make a big deal out of her arrival. "She works for Norris. He's changing tactics and using her to make his pitch for the ranch. He figures I'll like the offer better coming from a woman."

Harding spat onto the dirt. "That nice lady is working for that worthless piece of shit?"

"Yeah."

"She'll see his worthlessness and quit workin' for him. She's too good a person not to."

Shane shook his head. "You talked to her for all of a few minutes yesterday and you figure you know her?"

"They were a good few minutes."

"Everyone's not sunshine and light, Harding."

"I'm a good judge of character, and I'm not wrong. Plus, I notice you're not meetin' her in town like you would if it was strictly business. You invited her to your home."

"You're busted, Shane."

Harding was nothing if not consistent, and Gage rarely missed an opportunity to give Shane shit.

Shane gave his friend a long look. In the last couple weeks, the grief and rage Gage had worn like a cloak since arriving at Lone Pine seemed to have lifted a fraction. It wasn't much, but it was something.

They watched as Emery stopped her car under the spreading oak in front of the ranch house. She stepped out and used the fob in her hand to lock the door. Bruno was quivering with excitement, his eyes pleading, but Shane didn't release him.

"She think someone's gonna break into that car?" Harding asked.

"Likely a habit."

Gage was probably right.

Shane figured living in Sacramento it was smart to be in the habit of locking your car. Emery did a slow turn to take in her surroundings.

He wondered how she'd see his place: the house with its log-cabin construction, the corrals where horses swished their tails against the flies, and the barn that needed a fresh coat of paint.

Could be she was considering how many houses could be crammed into the land between the mountain and Mill Creek Road.

She continued her perusal until her gaze landed on him. Hard for him to miss when that happened because it gave him a jolt he felt down to his bones. Bad reaction. He didn't want a jolt or whatever the hell it was when he saw her.

He didn't want to see the answering interest as her face lit up.

"Aww, she's got it just as bad as you," Harding said gleefully. "You want me and Gage to haul this feed out so you can talk to your lady?"

Shane didn't bite at the "your lady" reference. "No, I'll take it."

Harding ran his hand down his beard as he did when he was thinking. "Good. Take her with you. Show her what'd be paved over if Norris has his way."

Not a bad idea. He whistled for Bruno to come and crossed the dusty yard. The dog charged ahead, barking like a maniac. "Quiet, boy."

The dog quieted, but with a look at Shane like he was nuts for not recognizing the stranger danger.

Emery had caught her mass of curling hair back in a ponytail that somehow made her blue eyes look even bigger. When Bruno got close, she bent down with her hand held out.

The barking and growls were all for show because within seconds the traitor was on his back, looking like he was ready for dissection while Emery stroked his belly.

"Oh, aren't you beautiful. What's your name, sweet boy?"

"That's Bruno. He'll be your slave for life if you keep that up."

She turned her face up to Shane, a smile lighting her expression.

There it was again, that clutch around his heart he didn't know what to do with.

She gave Bruno a last pet and rose to her feet.

"Hi. I love your house. I always thought log cabin houses look so cozy. I bet it's wonderful inside with a fire in the fireplace when it's cold and snowy out."

"It is."

"The mountains are gorgeous. I don't see how you get any work done. I'd always be distracted because I'd be admiring the mountains and sky." Bruno was staring at her like a lovesick dope.

"I manage."

She pointed to the north. "What peak is that? I noticed it before. It's very dramatic." Hearing her voice, having her at his home, made him feel like the day had suddenly grown brighter.

He rubbed at his chest where an ache was settling in. He was fucked. Plain fucked. He shook his head to clear it and answered her question. "Payback Mountain. We're in Payback Valley." When she looked at him expectantly, he found himself adding, "The name comes from gold rush days. The three sisters the town is named for had a mine on that mountain."

"Why'd they call the mountain Payback?"

Before she'd arrived, he'd planned on not saying much. Best not to give away anything that could be used against him. But she looked so appealing and interested, he couldn't stop the words. "They called the mine Mother Lode. The mountain the ore comes from is Payback because the gold the women got out of it allowed them to pay back a loan they'd taken out to open the mine. The loan wasn't quite legal because women weren't allowed to borrow money in their own names in those days, but the sisters were persuasive and got the money, though at a higher interest rate."

"Yay, girl power."

"They were smart and prepared. They saved the town during a bad winter. Ask Harding. He knows more about the history of the area than anyone else."

"I will." She smiled again and he tried to push back on the attraction. He needed to practice a little self-preservation.

Emery might sound interested in his ranch, in the area. In fact, she acted like destroying his land so Norris could get rich building houses and golf courses was the farthest thing from her mind. But he couldn't let her appeal blind him to her true motives.

Remembering those motives should help him fight the desire to kiss her to see if her lips tasted as good as he thought they would.

He'd be smart to let her say her piece and get her off the ranch as soon as possible.

He took off his hat to run his fingers through his hair before setting it on his head again. He had work to do, but he'd listen to her spiel and move her along.

He gestured to the porch. "We can sit in the shade and you can make the pitch for Norris. I already told you I'm not changing my mind, but it's your time to waste."

Her face fell. "Could I see the ranch first? I don't want to get in your way, and I know I can't see all of it, but I've never been on a ranch before. I'm curious to know how things are done."

Saying no should've been easy. Instead, he found himself muttering, "Sure."

He tugged a strap on the little pack slung over her shoulder. "You want to put this in the house? I need to get feed out to the cattle. You can come with me."

"Really? That sounds fun. I'll leave it in my car."

He didn't know if feeding cattle was fun, but maybe it was to a city girl. She unlocked her car, tossing her bag on the passenger seat. When she had her keys ready to lock the car again, he took them from her and tossed them next to the bag before shutting the door. "You don't need to lock your car out here."

She glanced around. "I guess not. It feels weird not to lock it. Another thing to like about this area. Less crime."

"The valley has some, small stuff mostly, but not here on the ranch." If you didn't count Bobby stealing and slaughtering his calf.

But the mastermind, who'd been after his neighbor Delaney, had been caught, and like Bobby, was awaiting trial.

He led her across the yard to the hayshed.

"Hey Harding, Gage, it's nice to see you both." They'd given him shit, but neither Gage or Harding appeared any more immune to her bright eyes and her sweet smile than he'd been. Hell, she'd succeeded in suckering Harding in yesterday.

"Emery, glad you recovered from Shane tackling you." Gage nodded to her, then lifted his chin to Shane. "I'll get back to mowing. Want to get it done before sundown."

Gage strode off, and Harding stopped what he was doing to lean on his rake and give her a half smile. "Miss, you stayin' to dinner? I've got chops marinatin' and there's plenty." He frowned and tugged at his beard. "But I can find somethin' else if you're a vegetarian."

"No, I'm not vegetarian, but I—"

"Good." Harding could be smooth when he wanted, and Shane knew damn well he had an agenda. "I'm makin' pasta salad to go with the chops, and there's a good size watermelon from my garden chillin' in the fridge. How's that sound for a nice meal?"

Harding was talking in his slow, deliberate manner some people got impatient with. They'd cut him off or finish his sentences for him. Not Emery. She listened like she had all the time in the world, her gaze riveted on his face.

"Oh, that sounds delicious, but I'm sorry, I'm not staying."

"Why not?" He gestured to Shane. "This boy forget his manners and not invite you to eat with us?"

"Harding." Shane didn't have a hope in hell the old guy'd heed the warning tone.

"Ah, no." Emery cast Shane a desperate look but he figured if she wanted to decline, she would. Besides, sharing a meal with her wouldn't be the worst thing in the world.

"Thank you, Harding. I appreciate the offer but Shane asked me here to discuss business." She sounded truly regretful.

Harding sent him a look that said he was a dumbass and stupid with it before turning his attention back to Emery.

"We eat early around here. You go with Shane afore the cattle start chewing on the trees. I'll put a meal together, and if when you get back it don't tempt you, I won't bug you anymore."

"You might as well give up now," Shane told her. "Harding always gets his way."

CHAPTER EIGHT
Emery

Emery's heart skipped a beat. It'd literally skipped a beat when she first spotted Shane and it baffled her. She'd spent some time with him two days in a row. She should be getting used to his rugged sexy hotness, at least enough so seeing him didn't give her heart palpitations. But there he was, with his black cowboy hat slanted over his eyes, the silver belt buckle riding low on lean hips, and his hands. Why hadn't she noticed his hands before? Wide palmed, calloused, and long fingered. She bet he could do all sorts of wonderful things with those hands. A shiver raced down her spine.

He acted like he wasn't affected by her presence when all she wanted to do was climb him like a tree and see if he smelled as good as she remembered. Or felt as good, because he'd felt mighty fine when she'd been spread out on top of him at Easy Money.

She needed to calm herself down before she did something stupid like acting on her over-the-top reaction to him.

Delilah's instant infatuation with Gideon Bryant had always served as a cautionary tale, keeping Emery from losing her head. She also needed to remind herself of the purpose of the visit, and that she was an employee of the Norris Group with a proposal that would make her an unpopular person on the ranch.

Shane gestured to the passenger seat of an ATV-type vehicle. "Have a seat in the Gator. I'll be back in a minute." She determinedly did *not* watch his butt as he walked away.

Emery sat, and Bruno climbed up behind the seats and settled himself with a doggy grin like he was ready to go.

A minute later Shane returned, a tan cowboy hat in his hand. He stopped beside her and when she looked up, he settled the hat on her head. "This was my sister's." He adjusted the hat, warm fingers brushing her cheek. "It looks good on you."

She took a careful breath as her heart did that palpitation thing again. Shane Keller was a potent force, more so up close. She needed to be careful or she'd get burned. "Thanks."

Shane slid behind the wheel.

Determined to be a good guest, she asked, "You have a sister?"

He nodded.

"And?"

"And what?"

"C'mon, cowboy. Can we forget for a few minutes why I'm here and have a simple conversation?"

"Not sure that's possible. You want to destroy my livelihood, and being friendly might be your way of luring me in."

"Is it working?"

"Something's working." He gave her an inscrutable look that had her breath catching. "Won't matter, though. Norris isn't getting my land to turn into his latest development."

Did that mean if she wasn't working for the Norris Group Shane might be interested in acting on the attraction she hoped wasn't entirely one-sided?

Probably nothing more than wishful thinking.

"Thanks for the warning, but to set the record straight, I don't want your ranch turned into town houses." The truth was if the Norris Group got what they wanted, the ranch buildings would be razed and, if not town houses, something else would be built in their wake. But if the presence of endangered frogs was verified, their habitat would be protected from both town houses *and* the ranch. She sighed. While she usually tackled matters head on, this afternoon she'd like to enjoy a couple hours with Shane before having to face those other issues.

Before he could argue, she rushed to say, "Let's give being friendly a try. I have no hidden agenda, I promise." He didn't say anything, and since that wasn't a rejection, she continued on. "Tell me about your sister. Where does she live? Are you close? Is she older or younger? Is she married? Does she have kids?" A thought occurred that gave her pause. "I don't even know if you're married. Are you?"

"Christ, that's a lot of questions. No, I'm not married. You wouldn't be here if I were."

She didn't say "good," but wanted to. And what did he mean by that last comment? She cleared her throat. "Feel free to answer any or all of the rest."

He scrubbed a hand over his face, the whisker stubble on his jaw making a raspy sound. "Fine." He took a minute, then said, "Janey's thirty-five, a year and a half older than me. She's married and lives in Hangman's Loss on the other side of the Sierras. Brian's a cop and was hired by their police chief, a guy named Gallagher. Janey and I were close growing up and work to keep that closeness. She and Brian have two girls. They're a couple of firecrackers."

She could hear the affection in his voice. "Aw, you're an uncle. That's nice. And your parents?"

He gave her a narrowed-eyed look. "Is this a date? These feel like date questions."

She rolled her eyes. "I'm sitting in this ATV with you, and I'll probably have dinner with you later because I don't think I can say no to Harding. Of course it's not a date, but we don't need to be enemies. I can't help the questions. People are a constant fascination to me. Even you."

"God help me."

"It's not that bad."

"Wanna bet?" His sigh didn't have much weight behind it.

Bruno rested his muzzle on her shoulder, and she reached back to scratch behind his ears, finally turning to give him a good rub. He licked her cheek as she crooned, "Oh, who's a good boy? Bruno is, that's who." She looked up in time to catch an unreadable expression on Shane's face. She gave Bruno a last pat and straightened in her seat.

"Did the ranch belong to your parents?"

"Yeah."

She waited, and when he didn't add anything, growled, "Don't make me hurt you, cowboy."

The corner of his mouth twitched. "My parents are complicated."

"Believe me, I know complicated when it comes to parents."

He hesitated, but finally said, "Mom's driven, ambitious, had goals that kids, husband, and a ranch kept her from achieving. She and Dad split when I was in college. Dad goes along to get along. He was happy enough ranching because it was what he knew until he met someone on a dating site and wanted out. He's living with his girlfriend and her two sons in the Bay area."

"Okay. Where's your mom?"

"She went back to college and got certified as a CPA. She's living in Las Vegas, also with a girlfriend."

"As in girlfriend girlfriend, or friend girlfriend?"

"The first one."

"How do you feel about that?"

He didn't say anything and her stomach sank. Her questions had probably crossed the line from being friendly to nosy.

Then he said, "Good, actually. Mom seems happy for the first time ever."

"Watching your family come apart has to hurt, but it's good she's found her happy."

Harding appeared beside the Gator. "You two gonna feed them cattle or sit here and yap all day?"

Emery gave a start. She'd been so wrapped up in their conversation it hadn't registered they'd yet to move.

"Don't cattle eat grass out in the pastures?"

"Cattle forage on the range, but there's not enough to sustain them. We've had a dry summer, which only makes it worse. We supplement with hay." Shane pushed the start button and pressed the accelerator pedal. They started moving forward with hardly any sound.

"Oh wow, your ATV's electric. That's awesome. And it has enough power to pull a trailer loaded with hay."

Shane steered to a dirt road cutting between the barn and corrals before crossing a wide-open area between fences. "It's a Gator, and this model is a UTV. A utility task vehicle rather than an ATV. And yeah, all electric. Over at Cider Mill Farm they're converting to electric UTVs and have put up solar panels to charge them. I'll be doing the same. Delaney runs the place. She convinced me to go electric, and so far it's working well."

Emery froze. "Delaney?"

"Yeah, have you met her? The farm's not far from here."

"Um, no, I haven't." She realized her phone was in her bag in the car so even if Walker contacted her about meeting with Delaney, she wouldn't get the message until later. "I visited Cider Mill Farm this morning. They have a lot going on." It felt odd talking about Delaney with someone who knew her sister when Emery had only laid eyes on her for a short minute.

"They do." She felt his gaze on her. She must have projected her inner turmoil because he asked, "You good?"

"Yeah." She forced herself to stop twirling a lock of hair around her finger. Besides Delilah, she hadn't told anyone but Walker and Sawyer about the letter from Clara, but suddenly she wanted to tell Shane, someone who wasn't involved.

He wasn't her friend, and he'd probably known the Bryants for years, but maybe he'd be an objective ear who could offer a different perspective. More than that, for some reason she felt she could trust him.

She cleared her throat. "So, there's this thing."

"A thing."

They bounced down the uneven road, barbed wire fence on either side. "Yeah." She cleared her throat. What she was about to say suddenly seemed very important. "You see, Delaney Bryant is my sister."

He turned his head to stare at her. "You're shittin' me." Surprise resonated in his voice.

"I'm absolutely not."

Shane stopped the Gator in the middle of the road and turned in his seat so his attention was focused solely on her, dark gaze sharp. "Explain."

"Delaney's dad was Gideon Bryant. He was my father too. He and my mom had a thing in France. I was the result."

"Another thing."

"Right. Delilah was an art student and studying in Paris on scholarship. During a school break, she traveled to Provence where everything was gorgeous, including, apparently, an American photographer, Gideon Bryant. They had a wild, passionate affair during which they also had wild, passionate, unprotected sex."

"Delilah is your mom."

"She is. According to her, she was helpless against falling in love with a dashing and exciting older man. Gideon swept her off her feet. She told me about the walks along the cliffs over the shining Mediterranean, running together through the rain to take shelter in a little café, riding behind him on a Vespa through winding cobblestone alleys in ancient towns. Mom's a sucker for romance."

Having Shane's undivided attention was a heady feeling, and the thought flashed that maybe that's what her mom had experienced. That exhilarating rush of emotion at being the sole focus of a gorgeous man.

Her mother's story had instilled in Emery a healthy dose of skepticism for romance. She was all too aware such intense feelings rarely lasted. They burned bright until flaming out and fading to ash.

She brought down the brim of her hat to block the lowering sun. "Their wild, passionate romance only lasted a few weeks. Gideon had another assignment in the Caribbean, and he wasn't inclined to put it off or ask Mom to accompany him.

"Mom returned to her classes. I think for him, the affair was over and it was time to move on. When she finally tracked him down, she was six months pregnant. By then he was in Africa and was markedly uninterested in her news.

"She sent him a couple photos of me early on through his publisher, but never knew if they'd gotten to him because he never responded. They must have because I received a letter from Gideon's mother, my grandmother Clara, last week. She introduced herself and told me about Delaney. Clara would like to meet but didn't say whether Delaney shared that sentiment. The odd thing was the letter was postmarked New Zealand."

"Clara's on a world cruise with a friend. She's supposed to return in the next month or so. Delaney and Walker are planning their wedding for a date after she's back." He rubbed Bruno's head as he gave her an assessing look. "You never tried contacting Bryant?"

Clara was on a cruise. That was more information than she'd gotten from the McGrath brothers. She shook her head at Shane's question.

"When I was little, I'd make up stories about him, how he'd been searching for me and when he found me, he and my mom would realize they belonged together, they'd get married, and we'd be a happy family."

"And when you were older?"

"I went through a time when I was angry with him. I had these fantasies where he'd find me and I could tell him to fuck off and he'd suffer with the realization of how awesome I was and how much he'd missed." She laughed. "That never happened. Now I'm more curious about my grandmother and sister than Gideon. He sounds like he was a self-centered jerk."

"I'd agree with that."

"You met him?"

"Yeah. He'd come back to Cider Mill Farm every couple years. Those visits were tough on Delaney."

"How so?" Walker mentioned something similar, but hadn't let loose with any details.

"You'd have to ask Delaney."

What was it about the men in Payback Valley? First Walker, and now Shane, being so careful with Delaney's privacy. As much as she wanted to know more, she had to respect he wouldn't engage in something he considered private.

"I met Walker and Sawyer today. They're very protective."

"They have reason to be."

She was getting to know him well enough to know he wasn't going to explain something he figured was Delaney's business. "I want to meet Delaney, but they're the gatekeepers. Walker has my number and will set it up if she's willing. I get the feeling looking for me and our other sister was Clara's interest, not Delaney's."

"Other sister?"

"Yeah. Apparently wild, passionate affairs were a pattern for Gideon."

"The man had no sense of responsibility. The women involved should've sued his ass for child support." He shook his head. "The McGraths are protective, and so is Delaney concerning her grandmother. Add what's gone on this year, and there's an instinct to close ranks and keep those close to you even closer."

"What happened, or is that too personal?"

Shane stared into the distance with his hat pulled low over his forehead, an arm resting on the steering wheel.

"Couple things. One, James McGrath died. He raised his grandsons. He and Clara were together and Delaney adored him so it was a blow, though it did bring Walker home."

He drummed his fingers on the steering wheel.

"The other thing, a rogue cop fixated on Delaney back when she was a teenager. He also had it in for Walker. Then the fucker disappeared. Walker returns to the valley and the guy shows up again and kidnaps Delaney. She came out of it all right, but it could've been much worse."

"Was she hurt?"

"Some. You'll have to get the details from her if she wants to tell you."

No surprise there. "Did they catch the guy who kidnapped her?"

He gave her a considering look. "Yeah. Added detail, the guy at the bar the other night, Finley? He's out on bail pending trial for his involvement, including butchering one of my calves and leaving it for Delaney to find."

"I heard what you said to him at Easy Money. No wonder you confronted him."

"Yeah. He also shot up Walker's truck."

Shane started the Gator again. They drove on a road steadily climbing in elevation. They passed a wide field where Gage sat at the wheel of a big machine and the breeze brought the sweet smell of freshly mown hay.

"We've got to get this feed to the cattle. My point in telling you what happened is to give you some perspective on Delaney, and why Walker and Sawyer are careful. You'll have to earn their trust. Working for Vance Norris will be a strike against you."

Emery slumped in her seat. Her sister was going to hate her before they even met. She pulled her entire ponytail over her shoulder to twirl around her finger.

The Gator crested a rise and Emery's breath caught. "Oh, that's beautiful." A small lake shimmered like a bright jewel reflecting the late afternoon sky, the pines ringing it standing like tall sentries.

"That's our reservoir. It's fed by Rock Creek and supplies water to the ranch."

"Oh wow. That's really back to nature. Do you treat the water before using it?"

"Water going into the house goes through a five-stage filter, but the stock are all watered straight from the reservoir."

His voice went flat. "If Norris tries building on the bench, he'll need to pump water to a tank to supply the houses. That water will have to come from the facility in Sisters because I own the rights to water from Rock Creek. That'll be damn expensive for him. He'll also have to do a full environmental impact report."

He glanced at her as if gauging her response. "Norris has been accused of bribing officials to get zoning changed for his projects. I wouldn't put it past him to try something similar for this one."

"That's not right."

"People don't change much, and I don't see Norris suddenly becoming a stand-up guy. You should know the kind of person you're working for."

She couldn't say she was surprised. The more she learned about Vance Norris, the more she disliked him. "Thanks for telling me." Continuing to work for the Norris Group was becoming even more untenable.

Past the reservoir they came to a gate. Bastard stood on the other side and let out a loud bellow when Shane stopped the Gator.

"He's feeling ornery because he got that ball banded. It's irritating him some."

"How do you get through the gate without him escaping?"

"That's where you come in. I'll open the gate. As soon as it's wide enough, you're driving the Gator through. He'll follow you because you'll have the hay. Bruno will help convince him of the direction he's to go. Keep on about fifteen yards and stop. I'll catch up to you."

"You want me to drive?"

He cocked a brow. "Unless you want to open the gate?"

"Ah, no. But don't say I didn't warn you. I've never driven something like this."

"You'll be fine."

Shane hopped out, Bruno following him, and Emery took the driver's seat. Shane shooed Bastard back, then opened the gate.

He yelled, "Go, go, go," when Bastard made a beeline for the opening. She didn't exactly floor it, but the Gator zipped forward.

She thought her jolting start might topple the bales of hay but they stayed put. She glanced over her shoulder to see Shane already closing the gate and Bastard trotting after her, Bruno behind him.

She stopped and more cows came through the trees, ambling toward her and the hay she was pulling. Shane pulled bales from the back, using a tool to cut the wire to open them for the hungry cattle, then he called Bruno to jump in before hopping back in the Gator, this time in the passenger seat.

"Keep on the road. Quarter mile and we'll drop these last two bales."

She kind of liked driving the Gator. Eyeing the cattle busily munching hay, she said, "You know cattle are particularly bad for the environment."

"So are golf courses."

"True, but that doesn't have anything to do with the contributions cattle make to global warming."

"You're talking about methane emissions."

She couldn't keep the surprise out of her voice. "You know about that?"

"It's the industry I'm in. Why wouldn't I educate myself about its issues?"

"I guess I thought cattle ranchers would be in denial. Acknowledging the issue means having to do something about it."

"Maybe."

"So are you?"

"Yeah."

"Really?"

He gave a dry laugh. "Yeah, really. Have some faith. There are a number of ranchers who are trying to make the industry sustainable."

"*Good.*" Her response was heartfelt. "Will you tell me what you're doing?"

"You ask a lot of questions."

"I like learning." She cast a quick glance his way. "Please?"

His look made her think he was sizing up her sincerity. "There's a type of seaweed that can be added to the cattle's diet. It's been proven to reduce their methane production by over eighty percent. Getting the additive to dairy cattle in a barn is simple. The open range is a different matter. I'm working with a researcher at UC Davis to figure out how to do that."

"Wow, that's awesome. I mean, really, really wonderful."

He pointed ahead of them. "You gonna avoid that tree?"

"Yikes." She steered around the tree.

"You shouldn't be so surprised. Cattle ranchers don't want to contribute to climate change any more than you do."

She didn't like that she'd made assumptions about the industry without knowing anything about it.

They came to another fence and repeated the process to leave fodder for more hungry cattle.

Shane took the wheel to drive them back to the ranch house.

She enjoyed talking with him. *Really* enjoyed talking with him.

The constant zings of awareness didn't hurt either.

They'd skimmed over the real purpose of her visit, the Norris Group's plans to develop this side of Payback Valley with Lone Pine Ranch square in its sights.

Emery was grateful for the time to simply get to know Shane, but it was with the realization that ultimately he'd see her as an adversary and a threat to his way of life.

She leaned back in her seat with a sigh, scratching Bruno's head when he rested his chin on her shoulder.

If her plan worked development would be stopped, but so would raising cattle, at least in the area of Lone Pine Ranch that was frog habitat.

But until she heard back from the professor, she'd keep the presence of the little savior to herself.

CHAPTER NINE
Emery

Emery stepped out the front door of Shane's house, Bruno following at her heels. She wished the situation could be different. Shane could be a bit gruff at times, but his manliness gave her tingles in all the right places. Boy howdy did they ever.

Behind that gruff exterior she was beginning to suspect was a seriously decent person. And god knew he was pretty to look at. She'd yet to make her pitch, and the knowledge had hung over her throughout dinner. She had the mental image of a brooding murder of crows circling ominously overhead.

Standing at the top step of the porch she gazed out over Lone Pine Ranch where long shadows stretched as the sun dipped in the west.

The view was picturesque. Not breathtakingly beautiful like the meadow where she wanted to build her tiny cottage, but it held its own beauty.

Cattle grazed in a fenced pasture, and she was confident they were cows because of their babies nearby, plus they had udders.

See, she'd learned something.

Chickens clucking brought her attention to a coop on one side of the barn. It had a fenced area where chickens busily scratched at the dirt. She wondered if chickens ate bugs or only seeds. If she ever came back, maybe she'd be able to check them out and she'd learn about them too.

Dinner had been amazing. Harding was apparently the self-appointed house chef. According to him, if Shane or Gage cooked they'd eat burgers or tacos every day.

Harding's pork chops had been tangy and barbecued to perfection, the watermelon perfectly crisp and sweet, and the pasta salad was so good she'd gotten Harding's recipe for the homemade dressing he'd used.

She guessed the hardboiled eggs in the pasta salad had come from the ranch's chickens.

For most of the meal, she and Harding had chatted.

One question about local history and he was off and running, telling her stories about his great grandparents who'd settled in Sisters after the original gold rush had played out.

Despite being part of a small Black community and facing discrimination, they'd managed to successfully operate a small general store.

Gage had been quiet, his distant expression making her think his mind was on something far removed from their conversation.

Shane hadn't participated much either. She got the feeling he was holding back, probably because he didn't trust her.

That, she thought glumly, was hardly surprising given she worked for someone who would destroy his world, given the chance.

Shane appeared to have a successful ranch and a good life. It made her wonder why he hadn't found someone to share it with. Knowing he was around thirty-four, she wondered didn't a guy that age want a wife and a couple kids?

For all she knew, he could have a girlfriend. He hadn't mentioned anyone special, and when she'd asked if he was married, it would've been the perfect opening for him to mention one.

He didn't give off a *I have a girlfriend* vibe, but that could be because he simply saw her as Vance Norris's employee and vibes were unnecessary.

Then she remembered his comment that she wouldn't be there if he'd been married. Those words spoken in that gruff voice had sent a shiver down her spine.

She thought he could read the dictionary and she'd have the same reaction to his voice. But had he been suggesting he'd invited her to his house for personal reasons?

Shane had seemed resigned to Harding trying his hand at matchmaking. He'd made sure she sat next to Shane at the dinner table. After the meal, he'd yawned, stretched and told everyone he was tired, said Gage had helped with the dinner prep and was excused, so Shane and Emery were on cleanup duty.

Not that she minded, but the exasperated look Shane had sent Harding made her think he wasn't on board with his friend's machinations.

Now with the meal over and cleanup done, she needed to get out of Shane's hair and let him enjoy his evening without an unplanned dinner guest hanging around.

Her phone chimed and she noticed a voicemail from an unknown number. She ground her teeth together in frustration as she listened to the message.

Vance Norris didn't ask. No, that would be beneath him. Instead, he told her he wanted them to have dinner together that evening at a restaurant near her hotel. She wasn't calling him back.

While she was silently fuming over his imperiousness, her phone chimed again.

This time she smiled when she saw the caller ID.

Glad for the distraction, she put the phone to her ear.

"Hey, baby brother." Her smile widened when Griffin launched into a staunch objection to the baby brother reference. If she didn't mess with her brothers, who would? She lowered herself to sit on the top step of the wide veranda, pleased when Bruno lay next to her. She scratched the dog's belly as she listened.

"Mom said I might be able to get tutoring for math. Plus, both me and Row need running shoes for cross country." Griffin's voice lowered. "I'm sorry, Em. I know Mom and Dad are broke and you already give us money, so if you can't do it, I'll figure something out."

By math, Griffin meant AP Calculus. Both Emery's brothers were smart, but in different ways. Griff was all about math and science, while Rowan excelled in working with his hands and loved his woodshop class. Running cross country was good for them. They'd both made varsity the year before as sophomores and she had hopes if they did well they might get college scholarships.

"It's good you're willing to get help when you need it. I'll talk to Mom about tutoring and the shoes." She grimaced. The five hundred she was going to send Delilah had just ballooned to probably a thousand dollars. "But Griff, before we look for outside tutoring, find out what the school offers. That's usually a good option."

"Okay, I will."

"Let me know, okay?" He made a sound of agreement. "How's the jellyfish sting?"

"It got me from below my knee all the way to my ankle. I'll send updated pictures. I looked up pee as a treatment and you're right, it's bogus. I'm gonna have to beat up Row for peeing on me."

She suppressed the desire to laugh and swiftly headed him off to save her mother that headache. The wooden screen door slapped shut behind her.

"Griff, I need to go. Tell Rowan I'll call him tomorrow evening. I want to know what he thinks of the novel he's reading for English. Love you."

She clicked off her phone as Shane came to stand beside her.

"Got a boyfriend who's missing you?" There was an edge to his voice that made her wonder if Shane disliked the idea she might have a boyfriend. No way. There was reality and then there was wishful thinking.

"Ha, no. Griffin is my brother. Rowan is my other brother. They're twins."

Shane sat on the step next to Bruno who laid his head on Shane's thigh and closed his eyes with a doggie groan as Shane rubbed his head.

"How old are they?"

"Sixteen, and getting into all the things teenage boys can get into." She told him about Griffin's jellyfish sting. "Rowan was being *helpful*," she used her fingers as air quotes, "by peeing on it. They keep Mom busy."

"Sounds about right for teenage boys." She could hear the humor in his voice. "Their dad in the picture?"

"Yeah. Dustin and Delilah are married, I think officially, though I can't swear to them actually having a marriage license. They said their vows at the beach under a full moon, then had a big bonfire and vegetarian barbecue.

"Dustin's a good guy except for the part of being a provider. Sometimes he has money, sometimes he doesn't. I'll say this for him, though, he's always been there for us. He'd give you the shirt off his back plus the last dime in his pocket if you asked for it. He and Mom believe strongly in helping anyone in need."

"They sound like good people."

"They are. A little quirky, but good."

Her phone buzzed. The lock screen showed a message from Walker. She swiped it open with a finger not quite steady. Her breath escaped in a whoosh as she read the message.

"Walker texted. He's asking if I'll come to Cider Mill Farm tomorrow morning." She gave Shane a small smile. "I'm meeting Delaney."

"You're nervous."

She shrugged but didn't think she managed the nonchalance she was aiming for. When he continued staring at her, gold gleaming in his brown eyes, she felt exposed, like he could see into her very soul.

She sighed. "Okay, yeah. I'm nervous. Delaney's my sister and I don't want her to hate me because I work for the Norris Group."

"Want me to go with you?"

Her heart skipped a beat. "You'd go with me?"

"Sure, if you think it'd help."

"Oh my gosh. Yes, please. We barely know each other, but if you were there, I'd feel like someone was on my side. Which is crazy because you're friends with Delaney and have known her a long time and have known me maybe a minute."

The words came out in a rush as the ball of anxiety that'd been tangled in her belly since her conversation with the McGrath brothers that morning was now unravelling a little. "And I know you have work to do, but I'd feel a thousand times less nervous if you were with me."

He waited her out with a steadiness that felt as reliable as the solid presence of Payback Mountain. "Anyone ever have your back, Emery?"

She felt her eyebrows go up. "Sure, my family."

He cocked his head. "Seems you have their back. Not sure if it goes the other way."

"That's not true. My family loves me."

"Not disputing that. I'll go with you."

She opened her mouth, then paused, not sure why she wanted to argue. Instead, she said, "I'd like that. Thank you."

Having Shane with her would make her feel less alone. Maybe he was right. She was used to supporting her family and taking care of herself. It'd been years since she'd needed someone to support her.

Shane's suggestion wasn't personal, at least she didn't think so. But the promise of his solid presence at her side made the idea of meeting her sister for the first time seem a little less fraught.

Like she'd been doing minutes before, he gazed out over the wide spread of the ranch, squinting into the setting sun with fine lines around his eyes. She wondered what crossed his mind when he surveyed his land.

To her everything was fascinating and new, while his mind was probably on things like beef prices and the cost of feed. Emery wondered what it would be like to live and work the same land your family had ranched for generations.

According to Harding, the Keller family had first settled in the area in the late nineteenth century. There was a permanence to the ranch that felt important.

They sat in silence broken by the lowing of cattle in the distance. Maybe Shane didn't want to break the peace between them by bringing up the offer from the Norris Group. She squelched the desire to share with him the recording of the endangered frog.

She needed confirmation from her professor identifying the sound as belonging to the yellow-legged frog before she did anything.

Shane leaned back with his elbows on the step behind him. He looked all long and lean with his legs stretched in front of him. "Explain what's going on with you and Norris."

Her breath came out on a sigh. "Right. I guess I need to do that." So much for keeping the peace. "I want to give you some context first." He nodded for her to go on. "My degree is in environmental sustainability. Northwood Development hired me to find ways to mitigate the environmental effects of residential development. There's no zero impact, but a lot can be done to lessen the effect of building the houses we need to live in."

He gestured to the land before them, the gently rising hills dotted by oaks at the lower levels and pines on the upper ridges. "Look at this. There's no way to make the impact of what Norris is proposing acceptable. The result would be utter destruction."

"Not all of it. You must realize, though, that cattle ranching has serious environmental impacts, even beyond methane emissions. If the development goes forward, houses can be built in a way that respects the land."

"Do you really believe that?" He shook his head. "Whatever you believe, that's not what Norris is interested in. He'll want to get the zoning changed so he can cram in houses as close together as possible to maximize his profit. That's the way he works, Emery."

Her shoulders drooped. "Okay. Honestly, I'm afraid of that too. But I'm trying to figure out a way to make it work."

He shook his head. "Norris Group isn't interested in adopting sustainable development models. They may put a gloss on their proposals to sell them to the public as somehow ecofriendly, but that's all it is. If Northwood was the kind of company you describe, then my guess is Norris bought it to improve their own reputation."

Since she'd suspected something similar, she couldn't argue with him. "I'm going to try to make them better, and the only way I can do that is by working from inside the company. To be honest, and I know I shouldn't be telling you this, but I've already told Vance his plans for this area are problematic and the project might not get built."

He rubbed his jaw, his whiskers making a rasping sound. "He's not a guy who likes to be told no."

"It may not matter what he likes." Despite her bravado, Emery worried about Vance's displeasure being focused on her. She needed to be prepared if he decided the easiest way to deal with her was to fire her.

Her conversation with Griffin replayed in her head. She wished she could wave a magic wand and make her family's money problems disappear. If she only had herself to worry about, she could quit her job if it became untenable. But staying employed meant her parents and the twins kept a roof over their heads.

She rose to her feet. Bruno trotted down the steps to lift a leg on a large pine tree at the corner of the house. "I won't take up any more of your day. Thank you for letting me stay for dinner. It was nice of Harding to invite me. I didn't want to turn him down."

He stood. "Harding already liked you, but ask him about area history and you're his best friend."

She'd intended to walk to her car, but Shane's expression held her captive.

Why did one look from this man make her heart swell and have her thinking all kinds of naughty thoughts?

The moment turned awkward, at least for her.

She stuck out her hand to shake, cringing even as she did so. Before she could locate a hole in the ground to crawl into, he took her hand.

Instead of shaking it, he held it in his larger one. "Come by in the morning. We'll go to the farm together so you can meet your sister."

Her heart thudded as he rubbed his thumb over the back of her hand. She was so distracted by the feel of his skin against hers his words didn't register.

"That sound good?"

"Sure." She paused. "What?"

The upward twitch of the corner of his mouth made her think he didn't mind confusing her. He repeated what he'd said and she nodded.

He kept her hand in his until she couldn't stop herself from asking, "What are we doing here, Shane?"

He turned his hand so their fingers intertwined. "You mean this?"

"Yeah, this."

"Just checking if the chemistry I was feeling had anything behind it."

Her heart felt ready to burst. Nerves jumped and tingles exploded across her body.

"And does it?"

"Oh yeah. You feel it?"

She nodded.

"That's why I'm going with you tomorrow morning."

CHAPTER TEN
Emery

Emery pulled into a space in the hotel parking lot. She hadn't felt this light in years. Why could attention from a handsome cowboy so completely sidetrack her brain? She hadn't been able to think of anything except Shane since he'd walked her to her car. He'd held the door while she got in, and stood in the gathering shadows, staring after her as she drove away.

And, yeah, she'd checked the rearview mirror.

It wasn't simply him being handsome or a cowboy, though those attributes didn't hurt one bit.

Shane possessed some undefinable quality that made her want to be with him.

He pulled at her with the gravitational force of the sun. That he might feel something similar for her kept a grin on her face the entire drive back to her hotel.

While she felt she could talk with him for hours, at the same time she wanted to spend hours exploring his rugged body.

She had a pretty good idea she wouldn't be disappointed.

Humming the words to Taylor Swift's "Lover," she stepped out of her car.

The patio dining area of the restaurant across the parking lot glowed warmly from pretty lights strung through the trees. The sound of clinking silverware and a sudden burst of laughter carried in the breeze.

The sun had dropped behind the low hills to the west and turned the sky a deep blue with thin clouds glowing peachy orange as they reflected the last rays of the setting sun. She wondered if she looked in the mirror she'd find herself glowing as brightly because maybe, possibly, there might be a chance of a relationship with Shane.

Trying to keep the smile off her face so she didn't look like a lunatic smiling at her own thoughts, she strolled across the parking lot toward the hotel lobby. She was almost at the walkway to the door when she heard her name called.

The light cast from a lamppost showed Vance Norris striding purposefully toward her from the restaurant. An icy bucket of water dumped over her head couldn't have more effectively quashed her mood.

He was a walking, talking reminder of the obstacles to a relationship between her and Shane. Chemistry wouldn't hold up against any effort to bulldoze his land.

Vance wore a navy blazer over a light blue dress shirt open at the collar. He looked even more elite and privileged than he had that morning.

"Emery, I'm glad I caught you." He took her hand and brought it to his lips to brush a kiss on her knuckles, then released her.

Okay, maybe he thought the gesture was charming. At least his gaze was staying level with hers. "I guess you didn't get my message earlier. No worries. Let me buy you a drink."

He gestured to the restaurant. "The bar is as good a place as any. I've been thinking all day about the environmental issues you raised concerning the North Bench Project. I'd like to hear more."

She didn't move and he lifted a brow. "That okay? I wanted to catch you before you left town tomorrow. We can meet in the morning if you'd prefer."

He threw her off balance. Contrary to his previous behavior, he was being polite and not assuming she'd simply fall in line with his plans.

She stifled a sigh. It wasn't even nine in the evening, but she'd hoped for an hour or so to unwind, maybe read a little, and then turn in at a reasonable time. But her family needed help with the mortgage payment, and the twins would only have more school expenses as the year progressed, so she'd go to the bar with Vance and see if she could remain employed.

Plus, maybe he truly wanted to know more about her concerns. Though she doubted it.

She gave a slow nod. "Okay, sure."

"Well, let's go then." He held out his arm and flashed a grin, white teeth gleaming.

Since he seemed to be making an effort to be pleasant and the alarm bells in her head weren't ringing, she let him lead her across to the restaurant. They stepped into the bar with its mirrored walls and postage stamp-size glass-topped tables. Though nice enough, it lacked the welcoming ambience of Easy Money.

They took two stools at the end of the bar next to a large man wearing a navy ballcap and sitting hunched over his drink.

"What can I get you, darlin'?"

"Just ice water, thanks."

Vance raised a brow but hailed the bartender. "Ice water for the lady. I'll take three fingers of Johnnie Walker Blue."

Vance turned to her. "How'd you spend your day? Are you getting the feel of the area?"

"I think so. I drove through more of Sisters and liked what I saw. There are some beautiful Victorian homes in the older areas of town."

He nodded sagely. "People fall in love with the architecture. For some reason they think it's quaint. They buy a big Victorian, then realize those old places are money pits. They require lead abatement, rewiring, they're a bear to retrofit for air conditioning." He gave a mock shiver. "I'll take a home built in this century any day of the week."

"I imagine they—"

She broke off when his phone buzzed. "I gotta take this. Sorry, be back in a minute." Vance pushed through the patio door, phone to his ear.

The bartender placed a glass of ice water with a wedge of lime in front of her and Vance's whiskey at his place.

The big guy sitting next to her glanced her way as he sipped what looked like a soft drink. The visor of his ballcap worn low over his forehead shaded his eyes, but she could see his nose had a definite bump where it had likely been broken at some point.

She looked away and pulled her phone from her bag. The last thing she wanted was to make conversation with some guy at the bar. She'd give Vance ten minutes and if he wasn't back, she was leaving.

She scrolled through photos she'd taken of the meadow. She particularly liked the close-up of a bumblebee hanging upside down on a bright pink blossom.

She swiped to the recording of the frog and tapped play, hastily adjusting the volume down when the creaky groan of the frog sounded loud among the muted conversations.

"What you got there?" Big Guy eyed her phone.

"Nothing."

She glanced at him again. Her first impression had been he was fat. Now she realized his size came from muscles, maybe some fat, but lots of muscles too. Paired with his crooked nose, he had the look of a street fighter.

People likely left him alone as he tipped the scales toward scary.

She glanced toward the door. Through a window she spied Vance outside, phone to his ear.

She was more than a little relieved when the big guy turned back to stare at a muted TV set to ESPN where cars raced round and round a track with captions giving the narrative. She watched for a couple minutes, wondering how anyone could find entertainment in watching cars speeding around an oval track.

"Sorry to abandon you like that." Vance slid onto the stool next to her and picked up his drink.

Emery stifled a sigh. She'd been only one minute away from her ten-minute limit. One more measly minute and she'd have been on her way to her room.

"Okay, Emery, give me what you got."

Forty minutes later, feeling drained, she pushed open her hotel room door.

Throwing the plastic keycard on the nightstand, she fell back onto the bed and pressed her fingers to her eyes.

That was forty minutes of her life she would never get back since she hadn't persuaded Vance of anything. He'd listened, asked all the right questions, and then told her he still planned to push ahead with the project, and if she worked with him on this, he would be sure to bring her in on the kind of design she wanted to pursue, but that would be down the road, in the future, maybe in a year or so.

Which was total bullshit. She knew when someone was blowing smoke, and that's exactly what Vance was doing. For some reason he wanted to keep her working for him. He'd toned down the blatantly sexualized behavior and let her say her piece, but in the end he hadn't shifted his position one bit from where he'd been the day before when they'd talked.

In comfy pajamas and leaning against the headboard, she spent the next hour scrolling through job boards for companies and government entities with postings in her area of expertise. She didn't want to move to southern California or the expensive Bay area, so that limited her. Ideally, she'd like to move out of Sacramento to a smaller town. Someplace like Sisters. If she connected with Delaney, the opportunity to get to know her sister was an incentive to look for work in the area. A seductive voice in her head whispered that living and working in Sisters made a relationship with Shane possible.

She continued scrolling, then backed up to click on a posting. She studied the information, chewing her bottom lip. The job looked intriguing. The local county had a position open with their planning department.

She read the educational requirements, thrilled her background would qualify her for the job. The salary wasn't amazing, but it was better than what she earned currently, and the benefits package was generous. Excitement hummed as she reread the job description. The position closed in a matter of days so she'd need to update her resumé. She was going for it.

***

After checking out of the hotel, Emery stashed her suitcase in the trunk and, tossing her little backpack onto the passenger seat, got behind the wheel of her car. She'd slept past her alarm and now she was running late. Turning the key to start the engine, she told herself not to be nervous. She'd stop at Lone Pine Ranch to pick up Shane, then they'd drive to Cider Mill Farm where she would properly meet Delaney. Her sister. The sister she'd never met before. Delaney was likely nervous too. Unless Delaney was only meeting her to tell her she wanted nothing to do with a long-lost sister.

Pulling herself out of that rabbit hole, Emery pulled onto Main Street, appreciating the vibrant oranges and yellows of the flowers planted in window boxes and sidewalk planters. It made her wonder if the townsfolk purposefully planted in seasonal color schemes.

To give herself something to do besides being nervous, she mulled over the job listing she'd found. The county offices were located in Sisters. It seemed appropriate that she'd find her sister in the town of Sisters. Which made her wonder if Clara had located Gideon Bryant's third daughter.

If Emery got the job, she could move to town and be near Delaney and Clara, and maybe the third sister would want to live here too. And, of course, Sisters was where Shane lived, so getting a job here meant the possibility of something with him would be feasible.

Emery was optimistic by nature, but even she realized all that was a lot to hope for.

The extra income that came with the job wouldn't hurt, either. She'd help her family, sure, but maybe she could also swing buying an electric car. It'd have to be used, but she was okay with that.

According to Shane, Delaney had put in solar panels and had electric vehicles at Cider Mill Farm, so she must be interested in limiting her business's impact on the climate. See? Something in common.

A traffic signal on Main Street glowed red. Emery applied the brakes. Frowning, she pressed the brake pedal again. They felt different, maybe a little squishy.

Great, she'd need to get her brakes looked at. That would cost at least a hundred dollars and was another thing to add to her to-do list.

The light changed and she continued out of town, slowing to make the turn onto Mill Creek Road. Having traveled it before, she knew the road twisted and turned downhill for the first couple miles as it followed the creek before straightening for a long stretch. The long stretch was where Lone Pine Ranch bordered the road with Cider Mill Farm immediately past it.

Payback Mountain was silhouetted against the bright blue sky. Her weather app said thunderstorms were likely later in the afternoon, but she couldn't tell it from the cloudless sky.

She'd need to head home to Sacramento immediately after her visit if she didn't want to get caught in a downpour while driving out of the mountains.

With the first tight curve approaching, she tapped the brakes to slow the car. The brake pedal went nearly to the floor, farther than it should have. The car slowed, but not as much as it usually did, and it felt like it pulled to the right. Crap.

A glance in the rearview mirror showed an older model truck or SUV with faded red paint following close behind her. She'd seen it behind her at the stoplight in town, and now it was way closer than necessary. Tailgaters were the worst.

With the worry over her brakes and the guy riding her tail, she slowed, edging to the right and hoping the other driver would pass her. He didn't.

A horn blaring had her jumping in her seat. A quick look in the mirror showed he'd closed the gap between them even more. With her hands white knuckled on the steering wheel, she continued driving carefully, looking for a turnout. She'd pull over and let the jerk tailgater continue on his way. As long as her brakes worked.

A turnout appeared up ahead, thankfully before the next curve in the road. She stepped on the brakes again, this time the brake pedal went all the way to the floor. She was still going too fast.

Shit, shit, shit.

Heart pounding, she pumped the brakes. They still worked. Kind of. Enough at least she thought she'd be able to stop. She steered toward the turnout. "Slow down, slow down, slow down." The words were a mantra with no effect.

She grabbed the emergency brake and pulled up. That helped.

With one hand gripping the steering wheel and the other on the emergency brake, the car slowed. She prayed she'd be able to come to a stop before hitting the guardrail that circled the turnout.

All she could see beyond the guardrail was open sky. Maybe there was a gentle slope and if she broke through the car would roll to a stop. Or there could be a cliff with a killer drop.

She was so focused on gauging the distance and whether her car would stop she hadn't looked in her rearview mirror. The car jolted, snapping back her head.

Panic grabbed her by the throat. A lightning-fast glance in the rearview mirror showed the red SUV right there. There was a split second when she wondered why he'd followed her into the turnout. Then the SUV rammed her car again, sending her jerking forward into the guardrail. Rending metal made a screeching sound. Maybe it would hold. Then another jolt from behind and she was through the collapsed guardrail.

Grinding metal followed by a hard crash, an explosion of airbags. The sickening feeling of the car rolling. Then…nothing.

***

Emery blinked, trying to orient herself. She must've blacked out. She was on her side. Actually, the car was on its side. The airbags had deployed all over the place and were rapidly deflating. Throbbing around her temple told her she must've hit her head on something. She shifted her position and winced as pain stabbed up her arm. Blood smeared vivid scarlet on the white material of the front airbag. She swallowed convulsively against rising nausea.

Screeching metal had her turning her head, the pain making her wish she hadn't. She blinked against the darkness at the periphery of her vision. The passenger door was pulled open to reveal the outline of a man silhouetted against the sky. Thank god, someone to help.

She didn't know what she expected. Maybe to be asked if she was hurt. Perhaps if she knew what had happened. Certainly not for him to drop heavily into the car, making it rock ominously. "Where the fuck's your phone?" His voice sounded like his throat was coated in acid.

Her brain must've been operating on conserve battery mode because she was still processing his question when he reached for her with a gloved hand. She cringed back. If she could get her brain synapses firing again, she could figure out what he was doing.

No crisp shirt, no identifying patch or badge. Scraggly beard, longish dark hair streaked with gray under a grimy ballcap. Unless he was off duty, he wasn't with a rescue department.

He shoved aside the deflated airbag, his movement again making the car shift. Reaching past her knees, he grabbed her backpack.

Her vision started to narrow like she was looking through the wrong end of a telescope. She blinked again, clearing her sight enough to see him loosening the drawstring. He upended the pack and dumped the contents.

Debris scattered over her. Lipstick, loose change, and paper clips all dropped like confetti.

Her wallet fell neatly in her hand and tampons landed on her neck. Her phone plopped against her arm. With a grunt he swooped down and grabbed it. He threw down her pack and in a swift movement, shoved her phone in his front pocket. It took him some effort, but he boosted himself through the open door, the car rocking sickeningly.

Then he was gone.

She stared at the square of sky where he'd been.

It looked awfully dark.

She blinked and it went completely black.

CHAPTER ELEVEN
Shane

"Wake up for me, Emery." The cut on the left side of her forehead looked shallow but oozed blood onto the side air bag. The crushed bumper on the rear of her car told Shane this was no accident. The car had gone through the guardrail, and someone had helped it along. Keeping the seething anger belted down to be dealt with later, he lightly tapped her cheek. "Come on, darlin', wake up."

She moved, a groan coming from her throat. "Don't want to."

Some of his tension eased and he felt like he could breathe again. "Yeah, you do. We're not in a safe spot here. Can you open your eyes?" He brushed a thumb along her cheekbone as she lifted her lids a fraction. It looked like the effort cost her. "That's it, all the way now. I need your help to get you out of here."

Her mouth moved like she was trying to speak. The second try was more successful. "Okay," she agreed even as her eyes drifted shut again.

"Damn it." A finger on her carotid told him her pulse was steady. Despite the airbags, she must have hit her head on something hard enough to knock her out. Getting her out of the overturned car by himself would be difficult. It would be easier if she were awake and able to help.

She shifted, then winced, and he brushed her cheek again. "Eyes, Emery. Open your eyes."

She did, revealing irises as blue as the night sky before the stars appeared. Eyes that'd hooked him first thing. "There you are. Stay with me now."

Sirens wailed in the distance. About damn time.

"Shane."

"Yeah?"

"Want to tell you something."

"What?"

"Love your name. Coolest name ever. Hero cowboy name."

They were in her car balanced precariously on the edge of a two-hundred-foot drop and she was probably concussed, yet she still made him want to laugh. Or kiss her. Which told him exactly how screwed he was.

The car shifted, making a crunching sound, and he prayed to whatever gods were out there the cable he'd attached to the winch on his truck would hold. "Emery's a good name too. When we get you out of here, you can tell me how your mom came up with it."

"Okay." The siren grew closer then abruptly cut off.

He released her seatbelt and moved his hands carefully over her. He felt the swelling at her wrist at the same time as she sucked in a breath.

"Looks like your wrist might be broken. We'll be careful. Can you put your right arm around my neck?"

Voices carried, along with the sound of equipment being mobilized.

She did as he asked, wrapping her arm around his neck and holding on when he pulled her to standing. Their heads were through the opening of the passenger door. He held her firm against him, her head secure in the curve of his neck. He spotted the rescue crew from the fire department making their way down the slope in their safety gear.

A firefighter called out. Shane turned his head and recognized Mateo Reynoso.

"Thought that was your truck up there, Shane. We're stabilizing the vehicle. How's the driver?"

"Shallow laceration on her forehead, fractured or broken wrist. Unconscious when I got to her, but alert now."

There was the clunk of metal on metal as the cable attached to the winch on the firetruck joined his. He let out a careful sigh of relief knowing there was another length of steel keeping them from tumbling over the cliff.

Nose against his neck, Emery breathed him in.

"Did you sniff me?"

"Yeah. You smell good."

"You kill me, Emery."

"I want to bite you, right there."

Blood drained from his head to arrow straight south. Shit. "Maybe we can do that when you're not concussed and we're in a safer place."

"'Kay."

"And Emery? Later when your brain's not addled you're going to remember this. Don't be embarrassed. In fact, we'll schedule neck biting as soon as you're up for it."

"Good." Being concussed made her agreeable in a way he didn't think she would be normally. She tipped her head to look up at him and gave him the sweetest smile.

He was surprised his heart didn't make a splatting sound as it hit the ground at her feet.

Which might have something to do with why she triggered every protective instinct he possessed. He wanted to get her to safety then track down the motherfucker responsible for her nearly ending up dead.

Mateo scrambled onto the car, safety ropes trailing behind him. "Got yourself a girl, Shane?"

"Seems like."

Mateo dropped down a harness. "We'll get her up first, then you."

Shane nodded and secured the straps around Emery.

The rescue team did what they were good at and fifteen long minutes later, Emery was safely on a gurney. He followed her up, glad when he was no longer at the edge of the cliff and could shed the safety gear Mateo'd insisted he wear.

The EMTs weren't any more immune to Emery than Shane was. Maybe she'd told them they smelled good, too. Whatever she said had them chuckling as they immobilized her arm.

Face pale, her gaze latched on to his as he approached.

"I need to talk to the cops, then I'll catch up with you at the urgent care."

She grimaced, all trace of her earlier goofiness gone. "I'm fine, Shane. I'm sure the clinic in Sisters will fix me up fine. I'd feel bad if I continued pulling you away from the ranch."

He shook his head. "I'll be there soon."

After a quick conversation with the EMTs, Emery was loaded into the back of the ambulance, the white bandage on her forehead a stark contrast to her dark hair.

Once the ambulance was on the highway heading back toward Sisters, lights flashing and siren wailing, he pulled his phone from his pocket and slid behind the wheel of his truck.

Sawyer picked up on the first ring. Shane put the phone on speaker and his friend's voice filled the cab.

"Shane, what's up?"

"Listen, Emery was in a wreck on Mill Creek Road. Her car went through the guardrail before the second curve."

"She hurt?"

"Yeah. Banged up. Wrist is messed up. She was unconscious when I first arrived on the scene, so maybe a concussion. Ambulance has her and she's on her way to the clinic in town."

"Shit. Okay. She was coming to meet Delaney this morning. I'll let her know." There was a pause. "How do you know Emery?"

"She was on her way to pick me up for the meeting at the farm. I'll explain more later, but I want to get on the road and follow her into town. Need to tell you something first."

"Shoot."

"The back of her car was hit, multiple times by the look of it. Emery was forced off the road." Shane raised his voice to be heard over the roar of a tow truck backing into the pullout. They'd use the tow truck to pull Emery's mangled car up the slope and away from the drop-off to oblivion. "Whoever did it left behind red paint."

A Sisters police cruiser came to a stop next to his truck. He recognized the deputy who exited her SUV cruiser. "Beth's here."

"Good. Tell her what you told me. She'll document everything. You going to the clinic?"

"Yeah. One more thing. Emery works for Vance Norris. I don't know if that fact has anything to do with her car being forced through a guardrail, but I don't trust the bastard."

"Got it. Keep in touch."

"Will do." Shane ended the call.

He talked to Beth, then, tires spinning in the dirt, got himself back on the road, speeding as fast as he dared in the direction the ambulance had taken.

**

Emery

Emery screwed her eyes shut against the dull ache in her head. It was better when she was drifting.

"I think she's regaining consciousness. Should we call the nurse?"

"The doctor said she wasn't unconscious, just asleep. We'll wait on the nurse."

Emery didn't recognize the first voice, the woman's voice, but Shane's low rumble soothed her.

He'd arrived minutes after the ambulance had brought her to the emergency clinic and the medics were rolling her into the building.

She was used to taking care of herself, but his presence while the doctor was assessing her had been reassuring.

Her fractured wrist had been splinted and the doctor had asked all sorts of questions, which had led to the determination Emery likely had a mild concussion.

A CT scan, luckily available at the facility, had been ordered. Shane had been with her when the results had shown no brain bleed, and she'd seen some of the tension in his body ease.

After that, she'd been moved to a bed in a dimly lit room to rest for a couple hours before the doctor was supposed to see her again. Hopefully, she'd be released.

The clinic didn't do overnight and she didn't want to have to go to a hospital in Sacramento. She'd drifted off to the low rumble of Shane's voice carrying from the hall as he talked on his phone.

She didn't need pliers to pry open her eyes, but it was a near thing. She gave it another try and blinked open her eyes. Shane stood beside the bed, arms crossed over his chest, a frown on his face as he watched her.

"Hey."

He leaned down so his face was near hers. His eyes looked dreamy in the shadowy light. She felt like she could stare into them forever. Except those eyes looked worried. Worried, and if the gold sparks were an indication, more than a little angry.

"Hey yourself. How do you feel?"

"Head hurts."

"Concussion will do that." He brushed hair back from her face.

"I'll let the nurse know she's in pain." Emery shifted in time to catch the dark-haired woman exiting the room.

She pushed herself up against the pillow and found the button to raise the head of the bed as awareness and memories returned. "Was that Delaney?"

"Yeah."

Great. Meeting her sister while looking weak and frail was not how she'd wanted their introduction to go down.

Her plan was to present herself as competent and capable, and someone worth knowing.

More memories returned and Emery closed her eyes.

Had she really sniffed Shane? *And told him she wanted to bite his neck?*

Maybe she'd only thought about biting his neck rather than actually saying what she wanted out loud. Hopefully, he'd attribute her lack of inhibition to the concussion. A quick peek showed him studying her, expression grim. She plucked at the wrapping around the splint on her left arm. That was going to be fun to live with as it went from just below her elbow to the tips of her fingers. It could probably be worse.

"I, uh …" She cleared her throat. "I wasn't hitting on you. In the car when you were helping me? I wasn't hitting on you."

"Weren't you?" The corner of his mouth turned up, lightening his expression.

"No. I was really out of it. I'm sorry I was all over you like that."

He leaned closer. Despite that hint of a smile, his low voice was dead serious when he said, "Emery, you can be all over me like that any time you like." He pressed his lips, warm and firm, to her forehead.

"There's a lot going on right now. But this thing between you and me? It's real and I'm not letting go of it." His lips widened to almost a full grin. "Figured since you think I smell good and want to bite my neck, we have a good start."

"I have a *concussion*. You can't blame me for losing the filter on my mouth."

"I like unfiltered Emery." He straightened. The edge of anger was back, all signs of humor erased from his face. "How's the head? I want to hear what happened, but the doc said if your head hurts to take it slow."

"The headache's not too bad."

"Then let's start with what you remember about the crash."

Images flashed: the brakes failing, fear the guardrail wouldn't hold, the hard jolt as her vehicle was rammed from behind. She'd seen the condition of her car when the firefighters had pulled her from the wreck. The secondhand Volkswagen she'd saved for with her first job out of college, the car she'd put a good-size down payment on so she could afford the monthly loan payments, was a crumpled heap. "My car's ruined."

He took her hand, held it firm in his as his thumb brushed over the back. "I'd say so. How'd it get that way?"

"A guy in a big SUV, like a Suburban or Expedition. Older model, I think. Red. He rammed me from behind. Stole my phone."

"Stole your phone?"

"Yeah. My brakes weren't working properly so I was pulling over in the turnout. He was right behind me, aggressively tailgating. I thought he'd pass when I pulled over. I was scared I wouldn't be able to stop, then he was right there and rammed my car. He pushed me through the rail."

Gold sparked and any doubt he was full-on pissed off disappeared. "What about the phone?"

"The car was on its side and this guy must have climbed on the car. He came down through the door." She went to raise her left hand to rub her forehead, then remembered the splint and lowered her arm with a grimace. "He found my bag, shook everything out, and took my phone. I think it must've been the guy who rammed me. I don't think he called for help."

Shane swore. "Fucker wasn't about to call for help if he'd pushed you through the guardrail."

"How did you find me?"

"I called the hotel when you didn't show like we'd arranged. They said you'd checked out. I went looking for you, saw where the guardrail had been punched through and called it in."

"You found me before the fire department got there."

"Damn right I did."

She didn't know why tears threatened at the back of her eyes. She blinked several times and took a careful breath. "Why would a random guy want to hurt me, total my car, and steal my phone? It doesn't make sense."

"Maybe it's not random. There's got to be a reason he targeted you. Can you describe him?"

She frowned. "He wore a dark blue baseball hat backwards. It had the Dodgers logo. He looked rough around the edges, you know? He had a beard and was wearing a black sweatshirt."

Voices sounded as the door swung open. Delaney entered, followed by a uniformed Sawyer. Emery stared at her sister. A long fall of black hair framed a heart-shaped face dominated by striking blue eyes. Emery had looked in the mirror often enough to realize the shape of those eyes and the arch of the brow over them mirrored her own.

Shane stepped back when Delaney came to stand beside the bed. "You're awake."

"Yeah. Hi." Emery didn't know what to say.

What were the rules for meeting your sister for the first time?

She lifted her hand to shake. Delaney stared at the offered hand, then took it in her own. A connection surged between them, binding them together.

At least that's how it felt to Emery.

"Hi." Delaney dropped her hand and stepped back, and the connection was broken. "How are you feeling?"

"Like I'm ready to get out of here." She glanced at Shane. "Can I borrow a phone so I can call my mom and stepdad?"

Sawyer set a bag he'd walked in with on the bed beside Emery. "I asked the deputy at the scene to clear the contents out of your car before it was towed. Your suitcase and the box from your trunk are in my cruiser. Did you have a cell phone? She didn't find one."

"Oh no. My glass bowls from the mid-century store in town. Did they break? They were in the box."

"The recovered box is in my cruiser. It was taped shut. I can't tell you if anything's broken." When the shopkeeper had learned Emery was driving home, she'd packed them tightly with padding. Maybe they'd survived the crash intact.

"The phone?" He obviously didn't understand the nostalgic value of glass Pyrex bowls from the fifties.

Emery glanced at Shane, who nodded. She was grateful when he conveyed what she'd told him about the man stealing her phone. She caught Delaney's speculative look as her gaze tracked from Shane to Emery.

"From the damage to your car, it's obvious you were hit from behind." Sawyer cocked his head at Shane. "I get why you did it, but that was quite a risk you took."

"What do you mean? What risk?" Emery looked from one man to the other.

Delaney spoke. "He means your car was teetering on the edge of a sheer drop, and our hero here climbed in to rescue you."

"Hold on now, you're overstating what happened. I secured the car with a cable before doing anything else. No way could I leave her there." Shane rubbed the back of his neck.

Smiling slightly, Delaney spoke. "According to Mateo, Shane did what he could to secure the car, but climbing in to get you was dangerous."

Learning Shane had risked his life to save hers had her emotions all over the place. Emery didn't bother keeping her heart out of her eyes when she mouthed, "Thank you."

Delaney went up on tiptoes to kiss Shane on the cheek. "Thanks for saving my sister's life, hero."

Sister. With that simple word, Delaney had acknowledged Emery. She felt a knot of uncertainty and worry unwind.

"I'm not a damn hero," Shane muttered, clearly not realizing the importance of the moment.

Despite the car crash, Emery didn't think her heart could be fuller. Not so much because Shane risked his life to save hers, but unless she was reading the signals totally wrong, he was as interested in her as she was in him.

On top of that, she had a relationship with her sister to explore. Emery hadn't known until that moment how worried she'd been Delaney would refuse to acknowledge their connection, or worse, not care about it.

The door opened again and the doctor who'd treated Emery, a woman with gray hair and kind eyes, swept into the room. "Okay, folks, my patient needs an eval before she can be released. Plus, her brain needs a rest. Y'all need to vamoose."

Sawyer scowled. "When can I talk to her?"

"She needs to rest, Lieutenant. That means no reading or screentime or scrolling on a phone. Tomorrow's soon enough if you have interrogation in mind, and even then, only as long as Emery has no headaches and continues to feel better."

As the others exited through the door, Shane took Emery's hand, his grip firm. When it looked like he'd protest being kicked out, she said, "Go on, I'm fine."

Despite worry over insurance, both medical and auto, and trying to figure out how she would get around with no car, Shane's presence made her feel like everything would be okay.

He let go of her hand. "I'll be in the waiting room."

An hour later, Emery was belted into the passenger seat of Shane's truck. He turned left out of the clinic parking lot. "My hotel's that way." She pointed to the right.

"Doc said you need someone with you overnight to keep an eye on you."

She gave him a side-eye. "My mom was ready to drive out here and you said she didn't need to."

"That's right, she doesn't need to. I'm taking care of you."

"Oh, really."

"Yeah, really. Delaney said you could stay with her at the big house at the farm, but I thought you might want to ease into that relationship."

She let out a gusty breath.

"That a problem?"

"No. You're right. I'm nervous about my relationship with Delaney and don't think I'm ready to be an overnight guest in possible need of care." She eyed him again. "But I don't know if I want you hovering over me, either. I'd be fine at the hotel."

"Not a chance. You'll stay at the ranch with me. I'll put you in the guest room."

"How about we try this: 'Emery, would you like to stay at the ranch with me? I have a guest room and promise not to hover.'" She smiled sweetly.

"Yeah, what you said. Except I never hover, so it's not an issue."

"Okay."

"You'll do it? Great. Harding will be ecstatic."

"Glad someone will be happy."

The look he shot her held banked heat. "He's not the only one."

CHAPTER TWELVE
Emery

"You let me know if I can get you anythin' more." Harding set the mug of hot tea next to the couch where Emery rested with her feet tucked under her. Bruno was sprawled on the rug before the wide stone hearth of the fireplace, every now and then giving a twitch as he dreamed his doggy dreams.

"The tea is all I need, Harding. Thank you." She didn't like being waited on, but Harding was so determined to take care of her, she hadn't wanted to hurt his feelings by declining his offer to make tea.

"We don't get many women here at the ranch. Shane prefers to entertain his lady friends in town." He waggled his brows. "Means you're special to him, if you ask me."

"Shane was kind enough to offer me the guest room because it would be an almost four-hour drive for my mom to get here. I wouldn't read more into it than that."

Emery was certainly grateful for the offer. Sure, she had friends in Sacramento she could've called, but she didn't feel up to explaining about the crash for the umpteenth time.

"Nah, there's more goin' on than the boss man bein' kind." Harding ran a hand down the length of his beard. "Regardless, I'm in the first-floor bedroom down at the end of the hall." He pointed in case she didn't know where the hall was. "Gage is in the foreman's cabin t'other side of the barn. Shane's bedroom is upstairs and you'll have the guest room right next to it. It has its own bathroom. Won't be anyone to bother you up there as it'll be you two all alone."

She gave him a sharp look, and he put his hands up in a sign of surrender. "Just sayin'. I'm turning in now. G'night."

Just sayin' indeed.

As he'd been at dinner, Harding wasn't exactly subtle in his matchmaking efforts. She sipped the herbal tea, letting its warmth calm her. The doctor had said Emery would be sore from the accident, and she was right. The pain pills were starting to kick in, easing the aches some. Emery would've liked to go outside with Shane to help with the ranch work, but he'd insisted she rest and now she was glad he had.

The tea was soothing, and so was Shane's home.

The furnishings were a classic rustic style giving an overall impression of practical comfort. The warm wood tones from the exposed beams and the hardwood floor were complemented by the deep reds of the cushions that picked up the red and gray of the Southwest-style Native American rug stretched in front of the hearth.

She closed her eyes, letting her mind drift.

The accident, the trip in the ambulance, the hours she'd spent in the clinic, all had left her exhausted.

She'd borrowed Shane's phone to talk to her mom. It had taken some convincing before Delilah had given up on her determination to drive across the state so she could take care of her daughter.

Emery still found it hard to believe the guy who'd rammed her car had stolen her phone. They'd tried tracking it, but according to Shane, the jerk thief must have put it on airplane mode because they couldn't locate it.

Emery's eyes snapped open when a sound from outside had Bruno charging to the door, barking furiously. She pushed to her feet as Shane, freshly showered, came down the stairs, and then opened the door. He gave Bruno a command that had him quieting, his gaze finding hers as he held the door open wide.

Delaney and Walker came in, Delaney stooping to give Bruno a quick rub.

She carried a bakery box and handed it to Shane. "It's pie. Cam baked it for you and Emery," she told him.

Emery couldn't help wanting to soak up details of her sister's appearance. Where Delaney was long and lean compared to Emery's curves, and Emery's hair was dark brown with red highlights to her sister's black, they shared a similar facial structure and eye color.

When Emery had searched the internet, she'd found a few images of Gideon Bryant and knew both she and Delaney had gotten their blue eyes from their father.

Sisters shouldn't be strangers. Emery wanted to connect with Delaney in a meaningful way. She wanted what Gideon had essentially robbed her and her sisters of: family.

She wondered how different their lives would've been if they'd known each other as children. It made her all the more curious about their still-missing sister.

Delaney crossed the living room. "Hey, how are you feeling?"

"I've been better, but glad to be alive, all things considered." The cut on her forehead hadn't been bad and had required only a small bandage. She gestured with her splinted arm. "This will take some getting used to, but since I'll have it for six weeks, I'll have to figure out how to live with it. I'm glad I'm not left-handed."

Delaney gestured to the couch. "Sit before you fall down. You look exhausted. You need to rest so we won't stay long." Walker dropped onto the loveseat across from the couch, tugging on Delaney's hand so she'd join him.

Shane returned from the kitchen, where he'd taken the pie, and sat next to Emery, his arm stretching along the back cushion behind her, his fingers tangled in her hair.

"We got an update from Sawyer," Walker said. "Deputies found an early nineties red Ford Bronco with front end damage abandoned on a dirt road up by Lost Lake. That's about eighteen miles from where the crash occurred. The vehicle had been reported stolen three days ago and the plates had been swapped with another vehicle."

"They find any evidence in the Bronco?" Shane asked.

Walker shook his head. "Sawyer said they're dusting it for prints. If there are any and if the guy's in the system, that'll help, but it'll take a couple days before we hear anything."

Delaney glanced at Emery. "Do you recall if the driver was wearing gloves?"

She tilted her head as she sifted through the mental images. "He was. I remember seeing him wearing black gloves when he was shaking out my bag."

"Can you describe him again?" Walker asked.

She furrowed her brow. "White male, not young so maybe in his late forties or fifties, and average build." She sighed. "I'm sorry it's not very specific."

"You know if they're checking the brake lines for tampering?"

Shane's question was directed at Walker and had Emery sitting straighter.

"Wait a minute. You think this wasn't some random road rage incident? I thought the guy was mad because I was going too slow for him. If someone messed with my brakes, which given how they were acting I wouldn't be surprised, then it means I was targeted." She didn't know why it hadn't occurred to her before, but now the idea had her stomach clutching.

Shane's thumb stroking the back of her neck helped center her.

"There's no way it was random," he said. "Add this to your calculation. If the guy dumped the Bronco up by Lost Lake, unless he had another vehicle stashed up there, someone must've picked him up."

"So there's more than one person involved." Emery chewed on her bottom lip. The very idea someone wanted to cause her harm was so ludicrous she wanted to dismiss it out of hand. But being out of the realm of her experience didn't make it any less probable.

Delaney spoke, her brows drawn over her eyes. "I don't think whoever did this necessarily wanted Emery hurt. What they wanted was her phone."

"There are easier and less risky ways of stealing a phone," Walker pointed out.

"Yeah, but there's no guarantee we're dealing with a smart guy, and if Emery is like me and always has her phone on her, then forcing her to crash in an isolated area might've seemed like a reasonable option."

Emery studied her sister. "Delaney's right. If the guy wanted me dead, he could've pushed the car over the cliff after stealing my phone. He didn't. He steals my phone and hops out of my wrecked car, but without causing me any more injury." She hated the idea she'd been so vulnerable.

Walker leaned forward, resting his arms on his knees. "Question is, what's on your phone someone would want so badly?"

Emery rubbed her forehead, which started aching again and made it hard to think. "I don't know. Maybe nothing if he just wanted to sell it."

"Emery needs rest," Shane pronounced. He rose to his feet, and Walker and Delaney followed suit. "You're welcome back tomorrow if she's up to it, but that's it for tonight."

"Wait, I'm fine. I'm going back to Sacramento tomorrow so I won't be able to talk then."

"What the hell? You can't leave tomorrow." Shane glowered at her.

"Until I get a settlement from the insurance company for the crash, I'll need a rental car. Luckily my insurance covers that. But unless Sisters has a place to get a rental, I'll need to take care of that in Sacramento. And while I'm taking tomorrow off, I plan to return to work Tuesday." Which reminded her she needed to call Gerald and let him know she wouldn't be in. Better yet, she'd email him.

She might not have her phone, but thankfully she'd stashed her tablet in her suitcase before leaving the hotel, which seemed like days ago.

"The doctor said your brain needs rest. You can stay here until you're better." Hands on his hips, and a scowl on his face, Shane's demeanor had irritated male written all over it.

She raised a brow, then wished she hadn't when it pulled at the cut on her forehead. "Um, thank you. But I have things to take care of. Besides, the doctor said my concussion is mild."

The scowl deepened. "Which is still a concussion. I'll take you in the afternoon if you need to go."

"Actually, I'll take her. Sorry, Shane, but it'll give us a chance to talk." Delaney cut in, grinning as her gaze slid from Shane to Emery. "Will eight in the morning work for you, or do you want to leave earlier?"

She beamed at her sister. "Eight is perfect, thanks. I'll be ready."

She walked with the group to the door. Walker stepped onto the veranda, but at the last minute, Delaney turned and wrapped an arm around Emery's shoulders in a hug. "I'm glad you weren't hurt more than you were," Delaney murmured. "I never thought I needed a sister, but I might need you."

Eyes squeezed tight, Emery responded, "I'm glad you're my sister."

They released each other and moments later the door closed behind Walker and Delaney. Emery swallowed against the sudden tightness in her throat.

"C'mon, I'll walk you to your room."

Feeling suddenly awkward, she said, "Listen, I appreciate you bringing me back here. If I'd returned to the hotel, nothing would've stopped my mom from coming to take care of me and she has enough to deal with. But I'm not fragile. I can walk myself to my room. Harding showed me the guest room when you were outside. You've been very kind to a stranger, and I don't want to be any more trouble to you than I've already been."

Totally wrong thing to say.

"What the hell? I'm not kind, and you're not a stranger." He bit off the words. "You want to know the picture I've got in my head?

It's you unconscious and bleeding in your car. Had it slid eight more feet it would've gone over the side of the mountain with you in it. You looked damn fragile to me."

"I'm *not* fragile and I've been taking care of myself for as long as I can remember." She evened her tone. "I get you're upset with me, though I don't really understand why."

He shoved a hand through his hair before bracing both hands on his hips. "Okay, maybe I was upset with you. Some. I was with you when the nurse went over your release orders. You're more active than recommended for someone with a concussion."

"The nurse said to back off if symptoms return."

"And will you?"

"Yes. You're doing a lot for someone you've known only days. Thank you."

"We're past that." The expression on his face intensified. "Any other woman in the same situation? She'd be at the hotel. This is about you and me, and whatever the hell this thing is between us."

"You don't seem too happy about it."

"Damn right. I didn't need this complication in my life right now, but it's here so I'll deal with it."

Incredulity had her sputtering. "Deal with it? Like you deal with Bastard when he knocks down a fence? There's something between us, but you're not happy because it's complicating your life? What am I supposed to do with that? I should get a hotel room so you don't have to *deal* with anything."

"Not happening." He reached out and gripped the open front of her sweater and tugged her closer.

Gulp. She'd had such a visceral reaction when she'd first seen him. Now that reaction was amplified because his looks were only the frosting on a scrumptious cake.

The appeal of the man she was coming to know was adding layers to the initial feeling of connection, making him irresistible.

She stifled a giggle at the image. Maybe he could be her once-a-week indulgence.

Up close his deliciousness made her yearn with hunger.

The overhead light burnished the tawny highlights in his hair to match the gleam in his eyes. His beard stubble was dark brown on his cheeks and golden over his chin.

With his knuckles brushing against her breasts and his gaze blazing a path over her face, she thought she might combust on the spot. Simply ignite and go up in a whoosh of flames.

That he might have anywhere close to the same feelings about her was too fantastic to believe.

She wheezed in a breath to try to regain a degree of coherent thought, but this close to him, where she could smell him, her thoughts were scattered like confetti after the ball dropped on New Year's.

But first and foremost? The desire to know what he tasted like was a deep-seated craving. She went up on her tiptoes to find out.

Eyes open, their gazes locked, she touched her lips to his. The burning in his eyes matched hers. She ran the tip of her tongue over his lower lip and all she could think was *oh my*. He tasted dark and smoky and she wanted *more*.

Her heart beat so frantically she thought it might erupt right out of her chest.

He froze, but he didn't release his grip on her sweater.

She could've sworn there was a war going on inside him. The *this is awesome* side must've gained the advantage because he let out a groan and pulled her closer, his mouth parting, his tongue sliding along hers and sending shivers of need racing along her nerve endings.

Lips, tongue, teeth—his were a perfect match to hers.

As a first kiss, it was perfect.

The kiss spun out and made her crave having his lips and tongue doing their magic work somewhere else on her body.

His lips left hers and he delivered soft bites along her jaw until he reached the sensitive skin below her ear. "I knew you were trouble the first moment I saw you," he murmured the soft words and kissed her neck.

They were still standing in front of the door and he braced her against it, hitching her up with her legs around his pelvis to ride his impressive erection through their clothing.

With her left wrist splinted, she slipped her other hand under his shirt to stroke the wide planes of his chest, her fingers threading through his soft chest hair.

His mouth back on hers, he put his wonderfully calloused long-fingered hands to good use. One wide palm swept under her shirt to cup her right breast, his thumb sliding under her bra to brush over her nipple, while the other gripped her bottom to hold her steady.

She was completely lost in him until he froze, his hands went still, and he broke the kiss. His head came to rest next to hers against the door at her back.

"Stop. Fuck." He was breathing heavy. "We can't do this. What the hell was I thinking?"

"I know what I was thinking and it wasn't stop."

"You've got a fucking concussion, Emery. That's serious."

His words brought reality crashing back. "Do you have to be the responsible one?"

"Apparently." Gently, he lowered her until her feet touched the floor. He may have stopped the fun, but rubbing against him, she proved his self-control wasn't absolute.

He sucked in a deep breath and held it like he needed that minute to gather himself. Then he took her hand. "C'mon."

"Where are we going?"

"You're going to your room where you can sleep and not be a temptation. Me? I'm taking a cold shower."

She'd expected hot, she'd expected sexy, but lord, she hadn't expected sweet.

"Can we have pie first?"

CHAPTER THIRTEEN
Emery

Emery leaned against the counter and closed her eyes, willing the coffee to do its job. Once the caffeine kicked in, she'd need to get something in her stomach so she could take the pain meds. She'd woken to find she had aches and pains in places she hadn't even known it was possible to have aches and pains in. Her neck was sore, her hips ached, even her ankles hurt. Why was that? The seatbelt had kept her from flying around as her car had rolled, but she hadn't come out of the adventure unscathed.

This morning, she'd come down the stairs to find a light on over the kitchen sink and coffee already made. It was only six and still mostly dark, but already Shane was out the door.

A scrawled note said for her to help herself to whatever food she could find.

He'd also written his phone number and email address with the note for her to take the paper they were written on so she could contact him when she got a replacement phone.

The enormity of what she'd lost with her phone was still sinking in.

Luckily, because of work, she'd made sure all her contacts were backed up to the cloud and she could access everything from her tablet or her computers at her apartment and her office.

Mindful of her rest orders, she'd done only the minimum the day before: cutting service to her phone and putting a hold on any accounts accessible from the device.

She'd have to tackle those details again once she got a new phone.

She glanced around the kitchen. A side table was cluttered with papers and receipts held down with a small paint can. A spindly houseplant sat in the corner, looking forlorn. She took the plant to the sink to give it water then moved it to a windowsill where it would get more sun.

She peeled a banana and slowly chewed as she perused the contents of the refrigerator.

It was tempting to make a breakfast out of the amazing apple pie Cam had sent with Delaney, but as Emery had already twice broken her once-a-week-indulgence rule, she needed to be sensible this morning.

Peanut butter toast would work. She pulled out the peanut butter and a jar of boysenberry jam with a Cider Mill Farm label, plunked two pieces of whole grain bread from a loaf on the counter into the toaster, and figured it'd do.

Hampered by her splinted arm, making breakfast took twice as long as it should, but she was loading her dirty dishes into the dishwasher and working on her second cup of coffee when she heard the outside door of what she thought must be a mudroom or service porch open, followed a minute later by Shane coming through the kitchen door. Bruno trotted after him, his nails clicking on the tile floor.

Emery didn't bother pretending not to stare. She'd absorb him through her pores if she could. Head bare, his broad shoulders encased in a heavy flannel shirt, his long legs clad in denim worn white at the seams, Shane made her mouth water.

He'd taken off his boots and wore black socks with red and white Santa hats.

"Cute socks."

"They were a Christmas present from my nieces. I need to do laundry." He'd carried in a travel mug and metal basket of blue and brown eggs. After setting the eggs on the counter, he crossed to the coffee machine to pour the last of it into his mug.

"Shall I make more?"

He shook his head and leaned a hip against the counter. He studied her over the rim of his mug as he sipped.

"How are you feeling?"

"Good."

When he drew out that long look and added a lifted brow, she sighed. "Okay. Maybe I woke up feeling like I'd been tossed around in a car as it was rolling down a mountainside, but coffee and peanut butter toast helped."

"Good. You take the pain meds?"

"Not yet. I didn't want to on an empty stomach." Bruno leaned against her leg and she bent down to rub a hand over his head. "And I don't need the heavy-duty stuff. I have Tylenol in my purse. I'll take that."

He opened a cupboard, uncapped a bottle, and shook out two tablets. He extended his hand until she held out hers. He dropped them in her palm, then filled a glass with water.

"You're such a mom."

He shook his head. "Nah. I'm afraid of Harding. He'd kick my ass if I didn't take care of you. Can't risk it."

She swallowed the pills and put the glass in the dishwasher. "You're not afraid of Harding. Where is he, by the way?

"Having breakfast with his lady friend."

"Harding has a lady friend?" She couldn't help the broad smile. The idea of Harding having a romance delighted her.

"Yeah, Martha Watkins. She's retired from civilian work for the sheriff's department. Her husband died a few years back and Harding's decided he's not getting any younger and should make his move. He's taking her to Three Sisters Bakery, then said he'd be going to her place to help clean out her pipes."

"Oh my god. Is that a euphemism for sex?"

"If it is, I don't want to know." His eyes glittered with humor. "He said to tell you don't be a stranger and come by when you're in town again."

"I will." The clock on the microwave said it was nearly seven. Delaney would be by in a little over an hour. "I should shower."

"Gage'll need help moving cattle to the lower pasture. I need to go too."

Neither of them moved.

Then, slowly, his gaze on hers, he fisted a hand in the loose material of her pajama top—the one adorned with a moose wearing sunglasses and a caption reading *Born to be Wild*—and tugged her to him. "Promise me something."

He leaned against the counter, legs spread, and continued reeling her in until she bumped against his body. The heater must have come on. Or maybe there was a giant solar flare, and the planet was burning to a crisp.

All she knew was suddenly she was hot.

As in off the charts, redlining, ready to combust *hot*.

"Okay."

He looked all cowboy gorgeous, and her brain synapses were going haywire. He smelled of the outdoors.

No one would blame her for giving in.

What promise did he want?

It didn't matter, it was his as long as he kept holding her firm against his, ahem, hardness, and looking at her with warm gold glinting his eyes.

The corner of his mouth turned up and she thought he'd guessed the effect he had on her.

"You aren't going to ask what the promise is before agreeing?"

"Nope."

She leaned forward and sniffed his neck.

"You get this close to me and smelling as good as you do, I'll promise you just about anything." She might've touched her tongue to the skin beneath his ear.

How else could she verify if he tasted as good as he smelled?

He inhaled sharply. "God, you're killing me, Emery." His voice was a perfect growly grumble.

With another deep breath like he needed to steady himself, he tugged her up to her tiptoes. The delicious hardness nearly made her swoon.

He ducked his head so they were lined up mouth to mouth. "I want you to promise to be careful."

"I'm always careful."

"You don't always have someone forcing you off the road and stealing your phone. I want you to be extra careful." All humor had vanished. "Pay attention to who's around you. Lock your doors when you're home."

"And don't talk to strangers?"

"And don't talk to strangers."

His mouth was right there.

"You going to kiss me now?"

"Oh yeah."

The kiss was everything it had been the night before, but more.

He bit her bottom lip, and when she parted for him, his tongue, flavored by coffee, slid against hers.

It felt like she was being immersed in liquid chocolate: warm, delicious, and seductive.

Sensation flooded the already present heat to form a swirling pool of need low in her belly.

Frustrated with her splinted left hand, she used her right to tug up his shirt so she could run her fingers over his rippled abs and into the hair covering his chest. It was becoming her favorite thing to do.

She loved the outline of heavy muscles revealed by his clothing, but she *really* wanted to see him without his shirt.

She had incredible fantasies of him without his shirt.

He cupped her rear and pulled her into him.

The firmness she'd felt before had become more substantial.

Gloriously substantial.

She wanted to see that part of him naked too.

She rubbed against him and they both were breathing heavily.

She didn't do hookups, didn't have sex on the first date, or even the second or third.

If she was going to share that part of herself with someone, it was going to mean something, which meant she'd had a small number of partners.

But with Shane, all those barriers melted away. If he'd suggested going upstairs to help her with her shower—she did have a splinted wrist after all—she'd have accepted without hesitation.

When he broke the kiss, he slowly set her away from him. "You're a menace."

"I'm a menace? You're the one who kisses like warm chocolate."

"Warm chocolate?"

"Yeah," she said firmly. "And I'm not explaining that."

He shot out a short bark of laughter. "Oh yes, you are. Maybe not right this minute, but I'll get it out of you." He sobered. "But you are a menace. I can't be within a dozen feet of you and not want you."

"Back at you, mister."

"Good. I don't want this to be a one-sided attraction."

He gripped her shoulders and laid his lips on her forehead.

"Go take your shower so you're ready when Delaney gets here."

***

Sitting in Delaney's smallish SUV, Emery glanced at her sister. "I appreciate you taking me to Sacramento. You must have a mountain of work to do at your farm."

"There's always work at the farm. But like I said last night, we need to talk, and as much as I love Walker and Shane, we need time together without them." Delaney steered along the dirt road. "Meeting a sister after nearly thirty years is a big deal."

Emery looked down at her fingers clutched in her lap. "It is. I was afraid you wouldn't want anything to do with me. You have your grandmother and your life with Walker. Not everyone wants a sister dropped in their laps."

Delaney hitched a shoulder in a half shrug as she took the turn onto Mill Creek Road. "I had concerns when Clara told me she planned to contact Dad's other daughters. Gran's not without resources, and I don't want her taken advantage of."

"That's honest. Here's honesty back at you. I don't want money or anything material from you or Clara. What I would like is to get to know you. I'm assuming she's on board with that because she contacted me. You, I'm not so sure of."

"I guess I'm not sure myself. I like the idea of having a sister and when I heard you'd been in a car crash, I'll admit to feeling protective of you. I guess Shane and I have that in common."

Which made her feel like a child who needed looking after. "Terrific, my sister and the hot cowboy think I'm incompetent and need looking after. I wonder how I made it this far in life without either of you."

Delaney grinned. "Not sure, but you've got us now."

"It's not only me the men of Sisters are protective of, by the way. I had to get through Walker and Sawyer before I could even talk to you. And Shane's like a vault. He'll tell me next to nothing about you or the trouble you had earlier in the summer. All he'll say is to ask you because it's your story to tell."

They passed the sign for Cider Mill Farm as the road followed the tumbling Mill Creek.

"Do you want to hear what happened?"

"Of course, I do. I'll admit I searched for newspaper articles. Your kidnapping even made the TV news in Sacramento, but I'd like to hear about it from you."

Delaney nodded. "Okay." They drove down the mountain, and she shared what had been a tumultuous several weeks earlier in the summer.

She ended by saying, "James's death hit me hard. Then Walker came home, and that brought a whole raft of feelings I didn't want to deal with.

"Being kidnapped and taken into that mine…" She shivered. "Do you know there are rats in mines?

"Suffice to say, I'm glad I survived and, except for bringing Walker home, I'll be glad when the trial is over and I can put that all behind me."

"Wow." Emery hoped she'd have the same fortitude to protect herself and escape if she was being held captive by a man who threatened to rape and kill her.

"You had to be strong to get yourself out of that situation. I'm glad Walker was there for you."

"He was my rock through it all." Delaney glanced at Emery, her gaze thoughtful. "You end up with Shane and you'll have that too. That man's got a backbone of solid steel."

"I don't have Shane." Except for those hot kisses, because she was thinking maybe those meant something. She qualified, "There are sparks between us, but currently that's about all there is."

"It's early days. Shane's a cautious guy by nature, and was made more so by a bad relationship some time ago." She grinned at Emery's questioning look. "To stick with the theme, you'll have to get the details from him because it's his story to tell."

"You people are the worst."

Delaney laughed, then her expression sobered. "Dad was a shit who never lived up to his responsibilities with his children. If he'd been any kind of father, we would've grown up knowing each other. We weren't given that chance, but that doesn't mean we can't make it for ourselves. If it's where we decide we want to go, we can make a family out of what he left behind."

Building a relationship with Delaney would take time, but if they were both willing, it could work.

"I'd like that. I have my mom, stepdad, and my brothers, but I always felt something was missing. I thought it was Gideon, but I realize now it wasn't. It was you and our other sister." She paused. "Have you or Clara heard anything from her?"

Delaney shook her head. "Gran called last night and we talked. She hasn't gotten any response to the letter she sent. I told her about the car crash and meeting you. She's glad you weren't hurt worse than you were."

"Me too."

"She's due back from her cruise in December. Walker and I have our wedding scheduled for New Year's Day. It'll be at Cider Mill Farm."

"Oh, that'll be romantic. Do you get snow up here?"

"We do. Not as much as at higher elevations, but I'm hoping there will be some for the wedding. The farm is gorgeous when it snows.

"Our season will be done and we'll be closed to the public by then. Even though we're keeping it small, there's still a lot of planning involved." She glanced across the car. "Will you come? I'd like you to be there."

"I'd love to come to your wedding."

"Good. I'll send you an invitation." She shot Emery a grin. "Shane's already invited, but hasn't responded yet. You can be each other's plus one."

CHAPTER FOURTEEN
Emery

Emery fought her way through rush hour traffic. She wanted to get home, make herself a cup of tea, then burrow into her bed to sleep for the next ten hours.

The day had started exceptionally well. She'd had good morning kisses from Shane, and Delaney driving her to Sacramento had felt like a particularly sisterly thing to do.

But the day had been on a steady downhill slide since then.

She'd gotten a rental car. Always fun. Then suffered through the misery of purchasing a new phone.

Gah, phones were stupid expensive. She'd gotten her accounts— all with new passwords—switched over. She'd rather stab herself in the eye with a fork than do that again anytime soon, but at least she'd been able to keep the same phone number.

Her family and friends, including Shane and Delaney, had all gotten texts to let them know she was back in the modern world of instant contact.

Her mistake had been notifying Gerald, because he'd immediately demanded she stop by the Northwood office building and check in with him.

She'd then had the dubious pleasure of sitting in that awful chair in front of his desk and seething while he muttered and fretted over whether she'd been properly deferential to Vance Norris.

The nerve. She had a bandaged forehead and splinted wrist, but Gerald was more worried she'd offended the big boss.

Gerald tapped his fingers noisily on his desk. "He's vice president of the Norris Group who now oversees our division," he stated the obvious. "And in case it's news to you, his father is president of the firm." *President of the firm* had been spoken with a reverence that put Leon Norris on the level with royalty. The tapping continued.

Emery felt her head nodding up and down. Nodding when speaking to Gerald was her go-to. What else could she do with someone who always acted like he needed to teach her something she already knew?

He must've realized he'd lost her attention because he cleared his throat noisily. "You want to keep your job? Don't overreact to every little thing Mr. Norris says."

She barely stopped an eye roll. A male supervisor telling her not to overreact to sexual harassment from another male supervisor. Perfect.

Fed up, she said, "Don't gaslight me, Gerald. He stared at my cleavage, and he said to do whatever I needed to get Shane Keller to come to terms. He stated clearly he'd tried, the lawyers had tried, and now they were sending in a woman to do what needed to be done. I was there, I know what he was saying. I'm not overreacting."

"I recommended you for this job and working with Vance is part of it. Next time don't wear clothing that shows cleavage. This is a big opportunity for both of us. Don't let me down." He gave a final hard tap on the desk to punctuate his statement.

"I was professionally dressed," she ground the words through clenched teeth. "He needs to treat his employees with respect, and he needs to take a course on avoiding sexual harassment of those employees."

Twenty minutes later she'd stalked out of the building rubbing her temple, then wincing when the movement pulled at the healing cut on her forehead. This headache was worse than the concussion.

One bright spot in her day had been the email from her college professor confirming the sound she'd recorded was indeed the critically endangered yellow-legged frog. Good for the frog, but its presence along Rock Creek made everything more complicated.

It was after seven in the evening and dark by the time she made it back to her apartment in suburban Sacramento. She liked the area, and though the distance meant more of a commute, being outside town, the rent was low enough she'd been able to swing the payments without a roommate.

Climbing out of the rental, her splinted wrist had her fumbling with the key fob to lock a car she wished she hadn't needed.

She crossed the parking area toward her unit.

A nice perk of her apartment complex being older was fifty years ago builders hadn't felt compelled to fill every square foot of the property to maximize the number of rentable units. Case in point, her U-shaped building formed a spacious courtyard with a pool area and a grass lawn in the middle where children often played.

Emery liked that the people who lived in the apartments facing the courtyard were neighborly and came from so many backgrounds they resembled attendees at a United Nations conference.

Rolling her suitcase behind her, she spied Barb, the retired woman who lived in the unit two doors from Emery's. Armed with her dark green poo bag, Barb had Georgie, named for Prince George of Wales as they'd been born about the same time, on his sparkly leash while he did his business in a pool of light cast by fixtures lining the walkway. It was a good thing she kept Georgie on a leash because his tiny Pomeranian self was so fluffy Emery often worried he'd be swept away by a stray breeze.

"Hey there, sweetie," Barb called, then did a classic double take. "Oh my gosh, what happened?" Emery sighed. Usually, she enjoyed talking with Barb, but she'd been oh so close to locking herself inside her apartment and shutting out the world. She didn't want to explain about the car crash yet again.

But because Barb was a friend, Emery crossed the grass, stooping to pay homage to the royal prince. "Hey there, Georgie. Have you been a good boy?" Georgie gave his cute little yip that meant indeed he had. Some of his white fluff was gathered in a cute little ponytail on top of his head and dyed purple.

Emery straightened. "Hi, Barb." She raised her splinted wrist. "I was in a car accident. I fractured my wrist, but it's nothing serious. My car was totaled, though. I'm more upset about that than anything." Which was a lie. As she'd gone through her day, she couldn't shake the feeling she was missing something about why someone would run her off the road.

"A fractured wrist seems serious to me. And I'm sorry about the car. That's awful." Barb's hair shimmered from a new purply-silver dye job. Yep, it matched Georgie's.

"Nice hair color for you and Georgie."

"We both needed a little pick-me-up last night and we indulged in some pampering. But tell me about the accident, dear."

Emery gave a few highlights, glossing over the fact there'd been nothing accidental about what had happened to her. Barb would only worry if she learned how Emery had been pushed through the guardrail by a big SUV.

"You spent an extra day in Sisters? I could've sworn I saw you last night. Georgie had to use the potty so I brought him out. He's like an old man having to pee all the time. You'd left on that hall light and I swear I saw you moving around behind the shades."

Emery always left a light on when she was gone. She glanced at her window still lit by the dim glow from inside. Barb could be ditzy at times, but Emery didn't doubt she saw what she saw. Which made Emery feel nauseous.

"No, this is the first I've been home. I came down from Sisters this morning and spent the day dealing with the rental car company and then popped in at the office." Not wanting to explain what had happened to the old one, she didn't mention having to get a new phone.

Her headache was low-level, but she wanted to lie down and close her eyes more than she wanted world peace.

Well, maybe world peace should win that contest, but it was a close call.

The capper was she was hungry and wished she'd thought to pick up takeout for dinner because she didn't want to cook, and knew she wouldn't find much in her refrigerator.

"I must be mistaken then." Georgie, who understood his role as the cutest puffball ever, did a little dance as he chased a moth to the end of his leash.

Barb frowned. "Right about that time, Georgie started yapping like he had news all our neighbors should wake up to hear. I don't know what set him off, carrying on like that. When I finally got him quiet and looked back at your place, I didn't see what I thought I'd seen. You're not usually up at two in the morning so I figured it'd been my imagination."

Georgie tugged on his leash and Barb, never one to deny Georgie his every wish, said, "His royal highness wants his evening treat. I'll talk with you later, Emery. Sorry about your bumps and bruises."

Emery waved her friend off and fished her keys from her purse. She didn't think Barb had been imagining someone in her apartment. And Georgie wouldn't go off for no reason. Especially at two in the morning.

Could the guy who'd pushed her through the guardrail and stolen her phone have figured out her address? Using the flashlight from her new phone, she examined the doorknob, and nearly jumped out of her skin when the phone rang in her hand.

Caller ID read Hot Cowboy. An entire avalanche of feeling whooshed through her that she didn't know how to deal with. She turned off the flashlight and swiped to answer the call.

"Hello?"

"Emery."

The mere sound of his rumbly voice in her ear had the tension in her shoulders easing. "Shane, it's you."

Some of that tension must have transmitted through the connection because his immediate response was, "What's wrong? You okay?"

"I'm fine. Mostly. It's been a long day."

"Where are you?"

"Outside the door of my apartment." She was a strong woman. She took care of her own business, but she found herself telling Shane the rest. "My neighbor said she thought she saw someone inside my apartment last night."

"She call the cops?"

"No, she wasn't sure, and she thought it could've been me. It's probably nothing."

"What's your address?"

"Why?"

"Give me your address, Emery."

"Fine." She rattled it off. "Now tell me why."

"Because I don't want you opening that door until I can check it out."

"What? How will you check it out?"

He ignored her question. "Find someplace to hang out until I get there."

"You can't drop everything to drive here. I'm a big girl. I can check it out myself. If someone was in my apartment last night, they'd be long gone by now. I would call the police if I thought there was real danger. You don't need to drive down the mountain."

"I'm coming. Can you stay with your neighbor?"

New side of Shane: he could be more than a little domineering.

She blew out a gusty sigh, then pulled her suitcase over to the pool area and opened the gate. She was glad she'd worn slacks instead of a skirt because the daytime warmth was fading fast.

She didn't need a white knight charging in. She wasn't a damsel in distress. But she was too damn tired and dispirited to argue, and she *really* didn't want to go into her apartment alone. She set her purse on a little table, then sat on the chaise lounge, leaning back against the cushion, the phone still to her ear. It felt so good to stretch out she wasn't sure she'd entirely suppressed her groan of pleasure. "I'll wait by the pool."

"I'll be there as soon as I can." She wondered at the dip in his voice that made it sound more growly than usual.

She suppressed a shiver. "Okay."

With her phone back in her purse, she opened her suitcase to dig out a sweater before fighting with the zipper to close it again. If she could wish away the cumbersome splint on her wrist, she would.

Driving from Lone Pine Ranch would take Shane the good part of an hour. Then there'd be the return trip. It was too much, and he shouldn't do it, but him being willing to make that sacrifice amped up the warmth encircling her heart.

He made her feel cared for.

Like she meant something to him.

Something special.

She sighed and relaxed further into the cushion of the chaise. Other than being invited to a neighbor's barbecue, she hadn't spent much time at the pool. But sitting there in the cool evening had her thinking she might make a habit of it.

It wasn't Lone Pine Ranch, but still peaceful in its own way.

Eyes closed and under the sweater she'd arranged over her upper body like a blanket, she let the quiet hum of the water pump and the swish of traffic on nearby streets soothe her.

She wanted to drift, but all she could think about was Shane.

The strength of their attraction was a bit overwhelming. She was afraid she could too easily tumble into deep like. And deep like was only one level from the big L.

She needed to stomp hard on the brakes to stop any such nonsense. If Shane were inclined, she had no doubt a hot lusty affair would be mutually satisfying. But big L?

Her mother had fallen fast and hard in love. But in a matter of weeks that blaze had burnt itself out and she'd found herself pregnant and alone in Europe.

Not that Delilah had ever expressed regret for her affair with Gideon Bryant. As she said, how could she when she'd gotten Emery out of the affair?

While she appreciated the sentiment, she didn't understand how the experience hadn't tempered Delilah's enthusiasm for passionate affairs, of which there'd been several before she'd settled down with Dustin.

It was Emery who'd taken to heart the lesson that calm rationality and caution were best when considering matters of the heart.

Her relationship with her last boyfriend was proof enough. She hadn't lost her head with him, and they'd had some good times. Calm good times, but good times all the same. So if that was what she wanted, why had she broken up with him when after months of seeing each other he'd started hinting about moving in together?

She'd known Shane four days. And it wasn't as if she'd spent ten hours a day with him each of those days. They barely knew each other. But the emotions he pulled from her scared her. It shouldn't be possible to feel so much for someone she didn't know.

Emery had the uneasy feeling Shane could all too easily breach every defense she put up. Not that she'd been able to erect much in the way of defenses.

With him, her walls had been more like those of a sandcastle than a fortress.

CHAPTER FIFTEEN
Emery

The pool gate clanking had her eyes springing open. Shane, looking impossibly tall and broad shouldered, strode toward her silhouetted against the rippling blue light of the pool. The gold in his hair glinted under the light.

She moved her legs and he sat next to her on the chaise. Gazes caught, yet neither spoke for a long minute.

She cleared her throat. "How did you get here so quickly?"

"Hydraulic seal for my disc mower is leaking. I drove down late this afternoon to a farm supplier to get the part. It's not far from here." Why did she feel let down because he hadn't made a special trip when she'd called?

Because she was a crazy person, that's why.

"Oh good. You were already in town."

"Something like that. Give me your key and I'll check out your apartment."

She nudged him and when he stood, she shifted to rise to her feet. "*We'll* take a look."

"Emery, I'm here to make sure you're safe. Stay here while I check it out."

"You're no more bulletproof than I am." Shaking her head, she said, "I admit I was nervous about going in by myself after what Barb told me. I'm probably overreacting, but I'll be fine if you're with me."

"I'm not bulletproof, but I can deal with a problem a lot easier if I'm not worrying about you."

Keys in hand, she grabbed the suitcase handle and pulled it through the pool gate to the door of her unit, Shane following a step behind. "We go in together. I'll even let you enter first, but I'm coming in with you."

He must've guessed she wasn't budging so he held out his hand for the key. He eyed the door, a frown furrowing his brow. "You don't even have a deadbolt."

"No. I asked for one when I moved in and the manager said he'd do it. That was months ago."

Shane tried the doorknob and, finding it secure, slid the key into the lock and pushed open the door.

"I always leave a light on," she whispered. "The dining table is to the left."

He paused. "Why do I need to know the location of the dining table?"

"You know, in case you need to dive for cover."

"And the dining table's going to provide cover?"

"I don't know. Maybe? It's better than thin air."

He grunted. "Leave the suitcase outside until we know what's what."

Peering around him, she let her gaze travel over the familiar furnishings.

Dim light cast shadows over the living room and the kitchen to the left. Shane flicked on the overhead light. The cream-colored couch she loved but had paid too much for was as she left it. Its throw pillows in jewel colors were still sitting at either end of the sofa. In front of the couch was the coffee table with its trio of pretty glass bottles. On the floor next to it was the basket holding balls of yarn, needles sticking out like alien antennae where her abysmal efforts at knitting sat. Everything looked undisturbed.

"It looks normal," she whispered.

He put a finger to his lips. "Wait here."

He crossed the room, flipping on another light as he entered the kitchen area. He peered in the broom closet, then slid open the pocket door to peek in her tiny laundry room. A moment later he disappeared down the hallway. She moved to the hall while he opened the closet in the second bedroom she used as an office, then followed him into her bedroom. After he'd checked her closet and behind the shower curtain in the master bathroom, he returned to stand in front of her. "No one's here. Anything seem off to you?"

"I'm not sure, I guess I need to look for anything missing. Nothing stands out right now."

"Okay. Let's do a more in-depth search. Think of things that are easily sold."

Since she used the tablet she'd had with her in Sisters for streaming, she didn't own much in the way of electronics, not even a TV. She returned to her office.

Her stomach dropped. "My computer's gone." She stood by her desk and stared at the empty space where her desktop was supposed to be as if it would magically reappear.

"Shit. Anything else?"

She looked around. "I don't have a whole lot that's valuable. My printer is still here, my—"

She broke off and ran into her bedroom, holding her breath as she yanked open a narrow drawer in her armoire. She pulled out a small carved jewelry box and lifted the lid. "It's still there," she breathed. Most of her jewelry wasn't worth much, a few necklaces and earrings. A couple of beaded bracelets. But she had one item she cherished above all others.

She picked up the small, square-cut garnet ring in an antique gold setting. Feeling Shane behind her, she murmured, "This was my grandmother's. She wore it every day and left it to me when she passed away." She pressed it briefly to her lips before slipping it on her right ring finger and closed her hand in a fist.

"I don't care about the computer, but I'd be heartbroken if this ring was stolen. It's not worth much, but it was my grandmother's." She didn't know why her voice was suddenly wobbly. The ring hadn't been stolen, but she found herself fighting tears.

Shane's arm settled on her shoulder and turned her into him. As if drawn by a magnet, she rested her head against his chest and gave a quiet sigh when he wrapped his arms around her.

His embrace provided quiet, unshakable support.

For the first time she understood how being in a real relationship with someone as strong and steady as Shane Keller would make her feel less alone. He was that person who'd act as a bulwark against whatever life threw at her.

She wasn't a crier, but tears were soaking into Shane's shirt.

He tightened his hold, resting his cheek on top of her head.

"I don't cry," she sniffed. "Unless it's a video of a dog being rescued, I never cry." He lifted his head and she tilted hers back so she could see his face. "You know the ones where the dog is so pitiful. He's been neglected and his fur is all overgrown and his eyes are so sad. Then they clip off all that hair and it's like his personality is set free and he gets adopted by his forever family. At the end of the video, he's running through grass and playing with other dogs and you just know he's so happy to be alive."

"You cry over dog videos." His lips quirked in a ghost of a smile.

"Yeah. Not because my apartment's been broken into. I'm tougher than that. Except today, apparently."

He stroked a hand up and down her back in a soothing motion while his other hand remained firm at the back of her neck. "A lot's happened in the past couple days. You're entitled."

The caliber of comfort he offered helped even her out. He loosened his hold but didn't let go.

"You're really good at taking care of people, even when they don't think they need it."

"I take care of the people I care about."

Her heart tripped.

She cared about him too.

A lot.

They'd spent no more than a total of twelve hours together, but the feelings he pulled from her were more intense than anything she'd experienced with any other man.

It was like being swept into a swift-moving stream with nothing to hold on to, and no idea where she'd end up. The feeling was scary as much as exhilarating.

Sure, she'd always thought one day she'd get married and have a family, but she'd assumed she and her imaginary partner would ease into a quiet caring that came from shared experiences.

Love might happen but it would be a comfortable kind of love built on mutual respect, not the blow-your-socks-off kind that exploded in intensity before fizzling out to nothing.

He tilted his head. "What's going on in that brain of yours?"

"Overthinking things, as usual."

"Overthinking us?" His gaze dipped to her mouth.

She nodded.

He lowered his head until his lips were a breath from hers. "I like that you're thinking about us. I think about us."

She closed the last fraction of an inch between them so her lips were on his, and there it was again, the heat. The raw intensity. The feeling she was on the edge of a cliff.

She'd literally been on the edge of a cliff when her car had been pushed through the guardrail, and he'd been the one to rescue her.

Their kiss had sparks igniting along her nerve endings and zinging all the way to her toes. His mouth moved, his tongue sliding against hers, his hands holding her firmly against him, close enough to feel the obvious sign he was all in.

He moved his mouth to her neck and she tipped her head to give him better access.

Maybe they should have sex.

A bout of Hot Cowboy Sex could provide a way to release these crazy feelings building inside her, like a pressure valve of sorts.

"Sure, but don't count on the feelings going away part."

Her eyes widened. "I said that out loud?"

"Oh yeah. I'm all for sex, but we've got to call the police to report the break-in and theft." He gave her chin another nip. "But maybe we could call them later."

She groaned, not only because of what he said, but because the evidence of his desire was becoming more firmly insistent.

"Hello, Emery?" The voice carried from the front door. "Are you okay, dear?"

Reality returned with a crash.

"I'm fine, Barb," she called, her gaze locked on Shane's. "That's my neighbor. I guess sex is off the table."

His grin turned wolfish. "Sex on the table sounds interesting," he murmured, even as he eased his hold on her hips. "But now is not the time."

He followed her to the front door where Barb stood, Georgie tucked under her arm. He gave a happy little yip when he saw her.

She took Shane's hand to pull him forward. "Barb, this is my friend Shane Keller. I was a little nervous after what you said so he came by to check out my apartment."

Barb's gaze went from their joined hands to her face. She beamed out a smile. "Oh my. I didn't know you had a boyfriend, and such a nice-looking one too."

"Oh, Shane's—"

He squeezed her hand and spoke over her. "I appreciate you keeping an eye on Emery's place while she was away. If you don't mind, I'd like to ask you more about what you saw last night."

"Of course." Barb's expression turned worried. "Georgie and I adore Emery. Do you think someone broke in? Was anything taken?"

"Yes. Emery's computer was stolen." He turned to Emery. "Call the police while I talk to Barb. Tell them you want an officer sent out to take a report."

Emery went to retrieve her phone, not sure how she felt that Shane didn't want her to correct Barb's assumption they were together.

She made the call to the non-emergency police number. The person who took the call directed her to take a careful look for anything else that might be missing and assured her an officer would be sent around soon.

She went back to the office, checking the drawers of her filing cabinet. The thief apparently hadn't been interested in her personal papers because her birth certificate and passport were still in the small filing cabinet where she'd left them. In her bedroom, she meticulously opened every drawer of her dresser, looking through the contents.

Nothing seemed to be missing.

She moved to the armoire. Nothing was missing. She couldn't see a thief being interested in her clothes.

She pulled open a drawer. Then, frowning, ruffled through the contents. She didn't own much in the way of sexy underwear, but the single pair she had was gone. She certainly hadn't taken them to Sisters. She pulled open the deeper drawer where she kept her bras and suppressed a groan. The sexy bra to match the sexy underwear was also missing.

She returned to the living room chewing her bottom lip. Her suitcase sat near the wall beside the closed front door.

Shane stood with his head bent as he tapped on the screen of his phone.

"Where'd Barb go?"

"She said it was the dog's bedtime and didn't want to get him off schedule."

"Georgie rules the roost there."

"I picked up on that. What do you like on your pizza?"

"You're ordering pizza?"

"I'm hungry. You hungry?"

She nodded.

"Then I'm ordering pizza." He held up his phone and she saw the logo of her favorite pizza place. "This place good?"

"Very."

"What do you want on it?"

"Veggie with no green peppers."

He gave her a look that struck her as funny. She was smiling when she said, "We can go half and half and you can get meat lovers on your side."

"I don't need meat lovers, but an all-vegetable pizza is just sad."

He finished putting in the order and was shoving his phone in his pocket about the same time a knock sounded.

She looked through the peephole, then opened the door to a policeman who introduced himself as Officer Mendez.

Emery started at the beginning, explaining about the car accident and her phone being stolen before getting to Barb thinking someone might have been in her apartment.

"And now my apartment's been broken into, and my desktop computer was stolen." She gave a dispirited shrug. "I don't know if this can be tied to the theft of my phone, but it seems suspicious."

Officer Mendez examined the door lock and checked the windows. He returned to the living room, scribbling notes in a little notebook. "Have you done a thorough search looking for anything else that might be missing?"

Telling herself not to be embarrassed, she said, "Underwear and a bra."

The officer scribbled. "Description?"

Emery huffed out a breath. "They're a set, blue satin with black lace. They were in my armoire."

A quick glance at Shane and she knew he was pissed off. His face was drawn in a scowl.

Officer Mendez tucked the notebook in a cargo pocket. "The computer's easy to hock. And while most B and E guys don't take trophies, that's what taking the underwear feels like to me. It happens." Which gave her the creeps. "There's no sign of forced entry. My guess is the person who broke in probably bumped the lock. It's not uncommon. There are even how-to videos online to teach you exactly how to do it." He nodded to her door. "A deadbolt is helpful and makes bumping more of a challenge, but not impossible. You can also get a keyless lock with a code. Not a chance that could be bumped."

"I'll take care of it in the morning," Shane stated.

Officer Mendez said, "I'll make a report and turn this over to a detective. There are surveillance cameras at the corners of the buildings, but it docsn't look like your apartment was in range. Regardless, the detective will likely ask for any footage. I'm guessing they'll also want more information if they think the break-in is tied to the crash and your phone being stolen." He handed her his card. "They'll be in touch, but until then, call me if you find anything more missing or anything else happens."

Emery closed the door and turned to Shane, her heart beating heavily as she studied him.

Strong, steady, reliable.

He hadn't left her side while dealing with the break-in and the police.

He'd rescued her and had taken care of her after the crash.

He made her brain go haywire and was so appealingly hot-cowboy sexy, she knew her heart was in big, big, trouble.

CHAPTER SIXTEEN

Shane

Shane closed the door and locked it. Not that the simple handset had been much of a deterrent. The pizza had been excellent. He wasn't much of a wine drinker, but the white zinfandel Emery had poured had gone down easy. He crossed to the tiny kitchen and picked up his wineglass, draining the last few drops.

Emery was washing up. She'd changed into some sort of loose flowy pants and a black tank top, her feet bare.

He'd bet money her goal had been comfort and she hadn't been trying for sexy, but that's how it hit him.

She fumbled a knife and it clattered in the sink. Her movements were jerky and he had a good idea where her nervousness stemmed from.

He moved beside her and when she reached for his glass, he nudged her aside.

"I got it."

He washed and rinsed the glass and set it on the drainer and when he turned around, he bumped against Emery holding the oversize pizza box.

"I, um, I'm going to take this out to the dumpster. It's behind the building."

"I'll take it out."

"I'm fine. I can take it."

He held her gaze until she sighed and rolled her eyes. "Fine. Okay. But you can't put it in the regular dumpster. It goes in the blue recycling dumpster."

"Got it. Blue dumpster."

He gripped the box, and when she didn't release it, he raised a brow. "You gonna let go?"

Her knuckles were white where she still held the box. "Yeah." She seemed to have to consciously will her fingers to loosen. "Right." She stepped back. "There you go."

He let himself out the front door and into the cooler evening air, but it lacked the bite of night at the ranch.

He couldn't stop his grin at Emery's nervousness. He didn't know how he'd come to read her so easily, but he knew exactly what was making her nervous. Sex. He was there, she was there. From the get-go there'd been a strong sexual pull between them, and now she was wondering if he was staying the night. And if he was staying the night, where he'd be sleeping.

He was staying, all right. No way would he leave her alone after her place had been burglarized. As soon as the hardware store opened in the morning, he was picking up an electronic lock and installing it. Then he'd be having a talk with the apartment manager about why that hadn't been done before.

As for where he'd be sleeping? That was up to her.

He tossed the pizza box in the blue dumpster, made a stop at his truck, then let himself back into her apartment. She was still standing in the kitchen.

He set the holstered gun he'd gotten from the lockbox in his truck on the counter. Her eyes went huge, then her gaze tracked him crossing the room until he stood in front of her. He reached for her hands, and lacing his fingers with hers, he pulled her to him.

He brought her hand to his lips where he pressed a kiss to her palm. "I'm staying here tonight. The gun's extra protection in case your visitor is stupid enough to return."

"Okay. I know you have a ranch to run, but I'll sleep better if you're here. I'll pay you back for your time. Maybe I can help feed cows again."

"Cattle. Not cows."

"Right."

"You're not paying me back."

"But—"

"You're not paying me back. That's not how this works."

"This? What is this?"

"Hell if I know. Guess we'll figure it out together." Her slow smile made his breath catch. Damn. She made him feel like a fucking hero.

The grip she had on his heart tightened.

Never before had he experienced such an all-consuming need for another human being. He'd been engaged once, and thought he'd been a hundred percent all in, but even that hadn't been close to what he was feeling with her.

Emery scared the hell out of him. He'd like to chalk it up to lust, because there was plenty of that. But his wariness came from understanding himself enough to know what he was feeling for her had grown way beyond physical attraction.

What was he going to do when she didn't need him anymore?

Experience told him leaving might not be easy, but eventually, that was what would happen.

Women walked away, at least from him. For reasons he didn't understand, the women who'd been most important in his life needed to be free of him to be truly happy. So they left. His mom had done it. Liz, his fiancée who'd said she loved him but couldn't *be* with him, whatever the hell that meant, had done it. Lesson learned.

Emery was a lot more complicated.

She needed him now, so he'd deal with what was in front of them while protecting himself from heartache the best he could.

Damn hard to do when she was staring at his mouth. Then she licked her lips and blood arrowed straight south.

Later. He'd figure out how to keep control later because right now he didn't have it in him to fight craving her.

A craving that went beyond sexual desire, as huge as that was.

He bent his head, put his lips on hers, and dove in.

Her urgency matched his. The taste of her mouth drove him to the brink of control.

He released her hands so his could skim over her breasts, the shape and weight of them an intoxicating delight. He released her lips to nuzzle her there as his hands moved to stroke over the arc of her hips to the roundness of her ass.

Her curves made him burn and he wanted to explore them slowly and thoroughly. To savor them.

He boosted her onto the counter and stood between her legs.

She moaned deep and the vibration carried all the way to where his growing erection pressed against her, heat to heat.

Her fingers latched on to his belt buckle, her splint brushing against him, an unwelcome reminder of how close he'd come to losing her.

He kissed his way to her ear and murmured, "How's your head?"

"Fine, good," she panted.

He put his hand over hers to stop her busy fingers while he could still think. Her tongue swept over the skin on his neck and he went rock-hard.

When he could manage the words, he muttered, "What about your arm? Arm okay?" He drew her earlobe into his mouth.

"Arm's good. I'm good. All of me is fantastic. Ready for whatever you're up for. Literally."

She rubbed against him and the desire to open his zipper and rip aside her clothing so he could mindlessly plunge in made him feel as randy as a wild bull.

Grasping for his last shred of sanity, he put his hands on her shoulders and drew in a shuddering breath. It didn't help his slippery hold on control when she took the opportunity to begin working his belt loose.

He ground his teeth. Grabbing her hands, he held them tight and leaned his forehead against hers. "Stop for one damn minute. I can't think with your hands on me."

"Good. Less thinking, more kissing." Her lips and teeth moved to the underside of his jaw.

"Jesus Christ, Emery. You were in a car crash. You have a concussion. This can't be good for you."

"You are so, so very wrong. This could be the best thing for me if you'd stop talking and let your warm chocolate mouth do its magic."

He let out a strangled laugh. "My mouth isn't warm chocolate."

"It's warm chocolate to me and I want it on other parts of my body."

"Holy shit."

He'd thought he'd been hard before, but now he was engorged to the point of pain.

She'd managed to loosen his belt and had her fingers on the top button of his jeans.

Pulling at the last strands of control, he tipped up her head to meet her eyes. "You sure you're okay?"

She'd worked open the button. "Yeah. But I won't be if you don't do something about this staggering need I have for you."

She didn't have to tell him again.

He scooped her off the counter and, with her legs wrapped around him, carried her to her bedroom. The lamplight from the corner gave her skin a warm glow and brought out the red in her hair. He laid her on the bedspread, propping himself over her. She reached for the zipper of his jeans, but he grabbed her arms, raising them over her head.

"Keep them there," he ordered. He edged up the hem of her tank top, grinning.

Using his teeth, he tugged it farther to reveal her gorgeous breasts cupped by a silky black bra.

"God, you're beautiful," he breathed the words against the warm skin in the valley between her breasts before turning his head to push aside her bra and take her nipple firmly into his mouth.

He felt her move and he released her long enough to give her a dark look of warning that had her keeping her hands over her head.

"Good girl."

He tugged down the other cup and moved to take that nipple into his mouth while he slid his hand under the elastic waistband of her pants.

He ran his fingers over smooth skin to the edge of her underwear.

Then slid under.

And in.

She arched against him, lifting off the bed, saying his name with a strangled moan. He kept at it, working her before pulling his hand free and shifting off her.

"Don't you dare stop," she warned. "Don't you dare stop what you were doing."

"Not stopping." He tugged off her tank top and bra, then bent forward to peel down her pants. He pulled his wallet from the back pocket of his jeans and pulled out a condom.

She was naked except for the scrap of black underwear. He stood over her, his gaze snared with hers. He moved back when she reached for his partially open fly.

"Not fair," she complained. "You still have your clothes on."

"Never said I was fair." He reached back and pulled his shirt over his head. Emery's reaction made all the long hours of working the ranch worth every minute.

Her gaze slid over him like liquid heat. She swallowed with a gulp like she wanted to keep from drooling.

"You're the one who's beautiful. I want to lick you all over."

"You're going to get yourself in trouble, woman."

"God, I hope so." Her comment ended on a whimper as he leaned over her, pulling her arms over her head once more before capturing her lips in a kiss that was as wild as it was intoxicating.

When she moved, he growled, "Keep your hands up."

She writhed under him, her hips undulating in a mind-blowing rhythm that had him clenching his jaw.

"But I want to *touch* you. *Please.*"

His gaze burned into hers. "I want this to be good for both of us so hands to yourself, for now."

But he didn't keep his hands to himself. Hell no. He slid her panties off and got busy. Stroking, licking, sucking, he did it all to the accompaniment of her increasingly frantic pants of "Shane, Shane, *Shane.*" The last said on a keening moan as he used his mouth and fingers to send her hurtling over the edge. She rode it long and hard, not holding back until she collapsed against the pillow.

She lay with her hair spread out like a bronze halo, a dazzled look on her face. "You're really good at that."

"Yeah?"

"Yeah. Stupendous. In fact, you are so good you should do it again. Often. As often as humanly possible."

"Good plan. I hope you have a fast recovery time."

He brought his lips back to hers because he couldn't get enough of her mouth.

He didn't stop her this time when she lowered her arms to close a hand around him, stroking from base to tip. A groan rumbled from deep in his throat.

"Let's take care of you, cowboy," she all but purred the words.

He allowed her to torment him until he couldn't take it anymore and moved to hold himself over her. They locked gazes as he eased into her warmth, not stopping until he'd filled her.

The air between them throbbed as they began to move, slowly at first, then faster as they built a rhythm.

Higher and harder, her burning blue eyes locked on his as the surge built.

The world was spinning out of control and they were hurdling through space, joined and breathless.

The spinning got tighter, hotter, and the tension built until he felt her let go again. He let go with her in a rush of sensation. They held each other for breathless moments, their hearts thudding against each other.

When he realized he could still breathe, he bracketed her face, his lips holding hers even as his body continued to pulse, hers quaking beneath his.

He took her with him as he rolled onto his back, and though she moved to his side, her arms stayed around him and his around her.

He tried to ignore whatever was between them, while knowing in his soul it went deeper and grew stronger with every breath he took.

***

Emery

Emery drifted awake, feeling better than she thought possible. Sure, she was still a little achy in places, and there was the splint on her arm, but her body felt well-used in all the best ways. The best sex in her life did that to a woman. But it was the ache around her heart that made her nervous.

Maybe she could ease out of bed, get some coffee, and give her brain a chance to fully engage before she had to face the man responsible for her morning-after glow.

There were all sorts of mental arguments she could make, but whether the gods had smiled on her, or it had been her lucky day, or just plain physics, she hadn't gone over the cliff in her car.

But now she feared she was in total free fall where her heart was concerned.

Once she hit bottom she'd no longer be able to deny she was in love with Shane Keller.

There, she'd admitted it to herself. She was falling in love and didn't think she could do a damn thing to keep her heart from hitting the ground and shattering in a million pieces when it got there.

She wondered if this was how her mother had felt when she'd fallen for Gideon Bryant.

But where Delilah seemed to embrace the rush, Emery felt out of control and unable to do anything to save herself.

It wasn't lost on her that the man who'd rescued her from a cliff edge was the very one who'd pushed her over this bigger and scarier precipice.

She didn't want to be falling alone.

With a sigh, she opened her eyes and found herself nose to nose with Shane.

His eyes were open and his gold-brown gaze looked depthless, making her wonder if he was having similar reservations about what was happening between them.

He reached out a long finger, and her heart gave a hard thump when he traced it down the side of her face. He shifted forward to press his warm lips briefly to hers.

"We'll figure it out."

Well, there was her answer.

"Okay."

He wasn't making promises, which was good because she wasn't sure she wanted promises. But she was relieved she wasn't the only one working her way through their emotional minefield of what appeared to be *their relationship*.

Her gaze traveled over his face. As he'd done with her, she brought her hand to his face, brushing his tousled hair from his forehead, her fingers gliding over his smooth skin until she reached the dark shadow of his beard.

Her fingers moved over his stubble, making a rasping sound. By the time she'd traced the line of his neck and pushed back the sheet to reveal the strong line of his shoulder, his breathing had quickened.

He reached under the covers and brought her body flush against his.

His mouth on hers caught her gasp of pleasure as he slid inside her.

Yum. Morning sex with Shane was an excellent start to the day.

CHAPTER SEVENTEEN
Emery

Emery tapped her fingers on her desk as she waited for her computer to back up her day's work. Following the directions she'd received to avoid bright lights due to her concussion, on this Thursday night she was working with the lights off in her office at Northwood. It seemed to help. The headaches had let up and she was feeling better all around. She'd even managed to work out a way to type despite the splint.

Most of the office was in shadows. Northwood's employees had headed home hours ago. She hadn't because Vance had ordered her back to Sisters for a mid-morning meeting tomorrow. She was working late to make sure she'd be ready to drive up the mountain first thing.

She could've done some of the work the night before, but instead she'd holed up in her apartment and added polish to her resumé before sending it in for the job with the El Dorado County planning department.

She'd keep looking for other positions, but hoped her background would appeal to the county hiring committee. The more she thought about it, the more she was convinced the job would be perfect for her. If she was selected for an interview, the tricky part would be she'd need a letter of recommendation from a current supervisor, and Gerald would get weird about it.

Luckily all her files were backed up to the cloud so even though her personal computer had been stolen, she'd been able to access her resumé and work from her tablet.

It made her nervous to think about a thief going through her computer. She'd deleted the device from all her shared networks, hoping if someone managed to get past her password, they wouldn't be able to gain access to any personal information.

No word from the police on finding her computer or whether they thought the break-in had anything to do with her being forced off the road, or the guy who'd put her there, who then went into a teetering car to steal her phone.

She rested her chin in her palm and let her mind wander.

The morning she'd woken to Shane in her bed seemed so long ago. He'd said they'd work it out. Which, granted, could mean anything, but then he'd reached for her and proved the heady experience of the night before wasn't a one-off.

Maybe his plan was to soften her up with the best sex of her life. Over breakfast of toast and eggs, he'd launched a campaign to get her to come back to Sisters with him. *She could stay at the ranch where she'd be safe. Harding would be thrilled to cook for her. Bruno missed her.*

Shane had been irresistible with his sexy bedroom eyes and fast grin. But beyond having work that kept her in Sacramento, she wouldn't let fear keep her from living her life or drive her out of her home. And, honestly, spending more time with him, especially in his fabulous log cabin nestled in the trees on his wonderful ranch… Too dangerous.

Since Tuesday morning, they seemed to be cautiously circling one another. Sure, he'd said they'd figure it out, but she didn't think either of them was sure of anything except their awesome chemistry.

Last night, she's been in her pjs and propped against the headboard of her bed, telling herself the sounds she was hearing were normal creaks and groans of an old building, and there was nothing to be nervous about.

She'd been rereading her application packet and had just hit send when Shane called. She hadn't told him about the job, mainly because she wasn't sure what message it would send if she was applying for a job in the town near where he lived.

She was probably overthinking it, but she couldn't help wondering if his protectiveness was because of the strange things happening to her, and whether their deepening attachment had more to do with proximity than the desire to build something lasting.

She figured that went both ways. She was as wary of a relationship as he seemed to be.

Curled up on her pillow, phone on speaker, they'd talked for well over an hour.

He'd given her some insight into his hesitation. His rumbly voice had been quiet as he shared how he'd been engaged to a woman he thought he was building a life with, only to realize it'd been an illusion. The woman had left him.

After hearing the outline of the story—he'd been skimpy on the details—she guessed they had something else in common: emotional apprehension.

After they'd said good night, she'd been ready for sleep because he'd talked her through her nerves about being alone. With his soothing words in his deep, soothing voice in her head, she'd slept soundly.

Slipping off her low heels, she leaned back in her office chair as she replayed their conversation. She'd been tempted to go to Lone Pine Ranch with him, but she didn't want him thinking of her as his responsibility.

Beyond that, she'd still have to get to work and the idea of commuting from Sisters to Sacramento held little appeal. More specifically, nowhere in their discussion had he suggested she should return to Lone Pine Ranch for him. For them. To see how their relationship might evolve.

The emotional explosion he stirred up was worrying and she simply wasn't ready to face being in love with him.

He'd installed an electronic handset on her apartment door, and she'd listened carefully as he'd explained how it worked. She felt more secure, though anyone who wanted to get in could still break a window to gain access. But with her computer already stolen, she had nothing left to steal.

Her grandmother's ring was staying on her finger.

A shelf of romance novels and balls of yarn were safe. She didn't have a TV, and really, she didn't have anything a robber would want. If theft was the intruder's goal, he had to've assessed there was nothing of value left to steal.

The elevator at the end of the hall pinged, bringing the spin of her thoughts to a sudden stop. The doors made their swishing sound as they opened, and she recognized Gerald's voice carrying down the hall. He was using the annoying, unctuous tone he reserved for those he was trying to impress.

"Come on back to my office. Staff's gone home for the day so we have the place to ourselves. In fact, I have a bottle of Jack hidden in my file cabinet and we can have a drink."

Emery frowned, not so much about the Jack, everyone knew he kept a bottle in his office, just like they knew he'd been imbibing when he came out of his office singing sappy country western songs.

He didn't know she'd be working late. She hadn't told him about her computer being stolen when he'd insisted she turn in her work on a team project before leaving in the morning. He must've figured she'd work from home and she hadn't bothered to correct his assumption.

So here she was, adding the finishing touches to get it done. She was more than irritated the rest of the team had until the end of the following week, but Gerald had insisted.

"No alcohol," came a deep voice.

"Righty-o," Gerald chortled. "I only keep the whiskey because some clients expect it. Tell me, do you have family in the area?" His overly loud and effusive voice carried in the space empty of its usual hum and chatter. His behavior was over the top even for him, which made Emery think he was nervous.

"No."

Was the man a client? While it wasn't unheard of to meet clients after hours, those meetings were usually conducted at a restaurant or bar, not in their closed offices.

Neither man glanced her way as they passed her partially open door. With the lights off and her computer screen set to dark mode, her office was in shadows. But she could see them. The lighting in the corridor showed Gerald with a man who stood a full head taller. Even in profile with his shaved head, the bump of his nose, and the hulking physique, he looked dangerous.

"Do you come to town often?" Gerald gave another shot at conversation and got another one-word response.

"No."

"Lucky you. Sacramento's great, mind you, but sometimes it's nice to get away. Hard to find time with work being so busy. They say idle hands are the devil's workshop, you know?" Emery rolled her eyes.

"You live in the Bay area, then?"

"No." Hulk wasn't biting despite Gerald's best conversation starters.

The sound of his voice muffled and Emery figured they must've gone into Gerald's office at the end of the hall. Telling herself whatever Gerald was up to wasn't her business, she returned to her work.

She clicked on an icon to open a document. Ten more minutes and she'd be done. Then she'd go home and get a good night's sleep before leaving for Sisters in the morning.

Even though she'd told Shane she was fine staying at her apartment alone, she'd been uneasy since he'd left. The car crash, the whole phone being stolen while the car was hanging on a cliff's edge, and then her computer being stolen, all added up to her having a target on her back, but she had no idea who had her in their sights.

Upside of going to Sisters? She'd be able to spend time with Shane and Delaney. Both of those relationships were fraught with complications.

Delaney had called when Emery was commuting to work this morning, asking for her address for the wedding invitation. They'd ended up in a conversation she thought had surprised them both.

They'd talked. Really talked, the conversation flowing easily. As Emery had traveled down the freeway, Delaney had shared what she knew about their father, and a little of how his irregular visits had impacted her childhood. Luckily, their grandmother and James McGrath, who'd been like a grandfather to Delaney, had supported her throughout her life.

She'd asked about Emery's family, and she told her sister about her brothers and parents, and how growing up she felt like she had to be the responsible person in the family, especially after the twins were born.

Delaney shared her and Walker's love story. They'd been together while Delaney was in high school up until he'd been imprisoned for a crime he hadn't committed. Given their history, and how Walker had cut her off, Delaney had every right to be wary when he'd returned to Sisters years later. When a predator had targeted Delaney, it'd been their resourcefulness that saved her and led to where they were today. Besotted.

Emery felt she and Delaney had moved past the cautiously friendly stage to a place where they were working to build a connection. Returning to Sisters would give them the chance to spend more time together. The dark cloud hanging over the upcoming visit was working with Vance.

She wished she could quit her job. But obligation to her always-broke family forced her to stay. Maybe something would come of the application she'd sent last night. In the meantime, she'd continue to search postings for similar positions.

Copying and pasting from one page to another, she reread her document for typos. Almost done. She needed a conclusion that said "our proposal is the best" with punch. She stopped typing as raised voices carried down the hall. Gerald was getting loud. She couldn't hear Hulk's voice.

Cautiously, she rose from her seat and moved to the doorway. Gerald's voice rose to a near screech. "You can't ask me to do that."

There was the low growl of the other man's reply. Then more distinctly, "You're doing it. Boss took care of your problem, now you're taking care of his. That's how it works."

What problem? What was he asking Gerald to do?

Icy fingers skittered down her spine and the fine hairs at the back of her neck stood on end; every instinct she possessed told her the big guy was a serious threat.

Peeking down the hall, she spied Gerald's door ajar. She chewed her bottom lip, considering her options, then made her decision. Quickly and quietly, she shut down her computer. The door to the stairs was just past the elevator. She'd carry her shoes and if she could get down the hall without being seen or heard, she could take the stairs and slip out of the building. No one would know she'd overheard any of the argument between Gerald and Hulk. *Who was he?* He looked like every fixer she'd ever seen in a gangster movie.

With her shoes stuffed in her purse hanging on her shoulder and phone on silent in her hand, she moved around her desk. She paused when she heard Gerald shouting, fear underlining his bluster. "You said you had an opportunity for me. What you're asking isn't an opportunity, and it's too risky. I'm not going to jail."

The other man's reply was terse with impatience. "The opportunity is you get to pay off your debt. You owe the boss and he expects you to pay. Do this and you're halfway there." He talked over Gerald's increasingly strident refusal. "I'm not asking. If the boss wants it done, it gets done."

"No, no, no. I can't do it, I'll get caught." Gerald's voice rose even higher. "If I get caught, I'll tell the cops you're the one who ordered me to do it. I may just call and tell them what you're up to anyway."

What an idiot. Hadn't Gerald watched any murder mysteries? Didn't he know not saying what you intended to do was better than threatening someone who looked like he could snap your neck without breaking a sweat?

"No, fuck you, fuck you." The sound of what she thought was a drawer being slammed shut was followed by more of Gerald's shrill bluster, "Get out of my office and don't come back. I'll pay back the boss, but on my terms, not his."

"Big mistake, asshole."

There was a sudden scrabbling sound and the thud of something hitting a wall. Emery's breath lodged in her throat. Gerald's voice carried, indistinct and frantic, until dropping away. Silence seemed to echo through the empty office space.

Straining to hear past her heartbeat thundering in her ears, her entire body instinctively tensed for flight. She eased forward to her office doorway and took a quick peek out. Gerald's door was maybe forty feet down the hall. A soft thud sounded, and she felt ice seep into her bones.

She tried to breathe normally. Maybe she was overreacting. Maybe the men were finally talking in reasonable tones she couldn't hear.

No, no, no. She wouldn't talk herself out of the reality of what she'd heard.

Hulk asked Gerald to do something illegal, and she had to believe if he discovered her in the office, she'd be in danger. Mortal danger.

As long as she remained in the building she was in danger.

Trying to control her breathing so she could remain calm, she scanned her office. She could hide under her desk. She'd be out of sight and could wait until the men were gone before leaving.

If she was under her desk and out of sight, she could call nine-one-one.

She chewed her bottom lip. But what would she tell the dispatcher? That she was scared because she heard two men arguing?

She heard movement from Gerald's office, and she froze on the spot.

Whatever instinct had stopped her from leaving her office earlier now told her not to make a sound.

She shifted into deeper shadows, hoping to remain hidden if one of the men glanced through her door's narrow opening.

She'd been full of bravado when she'd insisted on entering her apartment with Shane. But she'd doubted anyone would still be there and hadn't been truly scared.

She was scared now. Down to the marrow in her bones scared.

What she wouldn't give to have Shane at her side. He was so steady and solid, and he made her feel safe. There was something undeniably appealing about a strong man who didn't need to flex his muscles but was simply there when he was needed. Who had her back, no matter what.

Footsteps, firm and heavy, came closer to her office door. For a fraction of a second she thought there'd been a hesitation in his step, a pause in the rhythm of the footfall.

She bit her lip to the point of pain, holding her breath until the steps continued.

The hall light illuminated Hulk as he strode past, his profile revealing a heavy brow and the uneven slope of his nose.

She frowned. Something about him struck her as familiar.

He wasn't the man who'd dropped down into her overturned car to steal her phone. Of that she was sure.

But… She'd seen him somewhere.

The clank of the heavy exit doors told her Hulk had taken the stairs instead of the elevator.

Emery crossed her office, careful to stand to the side of the window so she wouldn't be seen. The blinds were slanted so the back parking lot was visible. Her rental car looked like a beacon announcing an employee still in the building.

She prayed Hulk had parked in the front near Gerald's designated spot. She couldn't leave until she was sure he was gone.

Needing to know which way Hulk had gone, she darted across the hall and down a short corridor to her friend Sahri's office. Once through the door, she eased it shut behind her and crossed to a window that looked out to the front guest parking lot where the administrative staff had designated spaces. Gerald's midlife crisis car, a Porsche Boxster, sat parked in his spot.

A relieved sigh shuddered out of her when the glow from the parking lot lights revealed Hulk making his way to a car parked near the driveway. He wasn't hurrying, but he wasn't wasting time either.

Within seconds he was in the car and heading along the driveway to the road.

Emery took a deep breath and felt her heartrate begin to settle.

She'd check on Gerald.

Unless the Hulk had convinced him, he'd refused to do something illegal so he was probably feeling good about himself.

Even as she imagined him reclining in his big chair with his bottle of Jack Daniels, she knew that something had happened.

Something bad.

She should leave.

She hadn't finished the project, but she'd let him know she'd work on it over the weekend and have it to him by Monday. He'd have to accept that because she felt too unsettled to stay in the office any longer.

Not questioning the impulse to lighten her step, she walked with as little sound as possible to Gerald's door. It was slightly ajar.

She tapped lightly.

"Gerald?"

No response so she rapped again, the door swinging wide.

He wasn't seated at his desk, and his chair was pushed back against the wall.

She opened the door wider to reveal more of the office.

No Gerald.

Had he slipped out when she'd been watching the parking lot?

She stepped inside to look around the door, and it was as she turned back that she spied the tip of a shoe on the floor next to the desk.

She frowned and stepped forward for a closer look.

It was a slip-on loafer-type shoe Gerald favored.

Maybe he'd decided to get comfortable and was wandering around the office in his stocking feet.

Even as she had the thought, she rounded the desk and froze. Her mind struggled to process what she was seeing.

Gerald wasn't wandering around in his stocking feet. He was lying in a crumpled heap on the floor, his face turned up under the glare of fluorescent lights.

She gasped and clutched her stomach as it gave a queasy roll. She couldn't pull her gaze away from his eyes, bright red with blood and staring sightless toward the ceiling.

She nearly jumped out of her skin when her phone vibrated in her hand.

Hot Cowboy.

She fumbled the phone and dropping it on the floor. She scrambled to pick it up while backing out of Gerald's office. She rushed to her own, slamming the door shut and turning the lock.

"Emery, what's going on?"

"Shane, he's dead. Oh my god, he's dead."

"Are you safe? Who's dead?"

"What? He's dead."

"Emery. Are. You. Safe?"

"I think so. It's Gerald. He's dead. I found him in his office. His eyes are bleeding." She dropped her eyelids against the image of Gerald's sightless gaze and the huge, hulking man she was positive had murdered him.

She'd been right there.

Fear stabbed through her, making her voice quaver. "What if he comes back?"

She could hear Shane's voice muffled as he spoke to someone else, then said to her, "Who comes back?"

"I think that man must've killed Gerald. I didn't do anything to help him." Oh god, she'd been feet away while a man was being murdered and had done nothing to help.

On some level she knew her brain wasn't functioning properly. Her body was shaking so badly she could hardly hold the phone.

"If you'd tried to help him, you could be dead now too. Emery, listen to me. I want you to get to someplace safe."

"I think I'm safe. I'm in my office."

"The killer, where is he?"

"He left. I saw him get in his car and drive away."

She heard a whoosh like the biggest sigh of relief ever. "Good. Is your door locked?"

"Yes."

His low and rumbly voice soothed her. He knew what to do. She held on to his voice like a lifeline. "Okay. First thing, share your location with me. Can you do that?"

"I can do that." She shut out everything else to concentrate on pulling up her location on her phone and sending it to Shane. Her fingers were shaking so it took several tries. "I did it."

"Okay, got it." Again, his voice was muffled as he spoke to someone else. There was the sound of a car door closing and an engine starting. "Gage made the nine-one-one call. Cops should be there within minutes. Emery, stay in your office and don't open your door to anyone unless you're certain they're the police."

"Okay." She'd backed against the corner wall and slid down until she was sitting, her splinted arm wrapped around her knees. She clutched the phone to her ear, her connection with Shane was the only thing keeping her from totally freaking out.

"Darlin', Gage and I are on our way. Stay on the phone with me until the police get there."

She gave a shuddering sigh. "All right." She paused. "Shane?"

"Yeah?"

"Thank you."

CHAPTER EIGHTEEN
Frank

Frank flexed his fingers to loosen them. He was gripping the steering wheel too tightly. He hated any sign of tension, any evidence he didn't have total control. He looked through the windshield, searching for movement. The spot where he'd chosen to park wasn't perfect, but he couldn't risk being seen. He had a view of what was important: the front door of the Northwood Development office and the parking lot. Luckily there were no security cameras. He'd looked. He was hanging around because when he'd gotten in his car he'd decided to circle the parking lot looking for other parked vehicles to see if anyone else was in the building.

His surveillance had shown only one lit-up office window. Gerald's. There was no evidence of a cleaning crew or security, but there had been a lone sedan parked in the lot behind the building.

He contemplated going back to check out the car, see if there was anything to give him information on where the driver might live. It'd be simple to break a window to get the registration. He should have done that when he'd first spotted the car, but now he was antsy and it felt too risky. So he'd sit and watch.

Gerald Slater had assured him the building was empty and they could conduct their business without danger of being overheard. But it seemed the asshole had been wrong.

Maybe he shouldn't have killed the fucker. It wouldn't have happened if the asshole hadn't annoyed Frank beyond all reason.

Boss would be pissed, but too late to worry about that.

Self-discipline was key to his profession, and it ticked him off he'd lost control and grabbed the shit by the throat.

He should've given Gerald a little scare, made him think twice before refusing to follow an order. Even if the order from the boss had been beyond idiotic.

But Frank had watched as his hand squeezed and squeezed until the guy's eyes bugged out of his head.

When he'd finally decided to let go, it'd been too late.

He supposed he could've tried CPR or something, but it hadn't been worth the effort. If the fucker regained consciousness, he'd for sure raise a stink about Frank choking him and the situation would've gotten messy.

Not that the situation wasn't messy now. Nothing freaked out people more than discovering a dead body.

He drummed his fingers as he considered another possibility. He could go back in and retrieve the body.

If he'd taken the time to think, he'd never have left it in the first place.

He could throw dead Gerald in the trunk and dump him over a bridge into the American River.

Weight him down a bit and he'd never surface, leaving people to wonder what had become of the bastard.

He shifted in his seat to stretch his back as he contemplated the plan. As it was, no one was likely to discover the body until staff showed up for work on Monday morning.

He could recover the body, then take care of the other little chore Boss had assigned him.

He stared at the lone vehicle in the parking lot, weighing his options.

Going back in was beginning to make more sense. He'd do a search of the building to find anyone who might be working late.

It was possible the car belonged to someone who'd gone out to dinner or clubbing with a colleague. They could've driven together and planned to return for the vehicle at the end of the evening.

But if someone was in the building, he'd need to deal with them.

He was working out a plan when he heard the faint wail of a siren. He wasn't concerned. Big cities always had sirens blaring somewhere.

The Northwood Development building wasn't on a busy street but was located a short block away from a major thoroughfare. Add the half mile to the freeway on-ramp and emergency vehicles were common.

He drummed his fingers. He'd go back in. It was the only logical solution.

He'd figure out if the owner of the car was in the building. If they were, he'd deal with them.

With that person and dead Gerald safely in his trunk, he'd be on that freeway and gone in less than twenty minutes, thirty tops. It would take time for the cops to figure out a double murder had been committed.

Frank would need to lay low, maybe head to Costa Rica for a week or two. Boss could deal with his own shit while Frank let things cool down.

The siren had been joined by another, the shrill sound growing louder. He expected them to continue along the thoroughfare. Then he jerked to attention, sitting up straight in his seat.

Fuck. Revolving red and blue lights turned the corner and three police cars were racing up the street toward the Northwood building. He ducked down in his seat as they sped past his car, then lifted his head enough to see over the dash and watch in disbelief as the cops swarmed the front of the building.

The only way they could've been notified was if someone in the building had called them. Which meant Gerald had been found.

Fucking son of a bitch.

This was all Slater's fault. He wouldn't be dead if he'd done as he'd been told.

The cops were out of their vehicles, guns drawn, and entering the building, leaving one officer standing next to the cruisers. No chance now of dealing with a potential witness.

What a fucking shitshow.

Frank needed to get far, far away from whatever was going on, but starting up his car and driving away would be like a bright neon arrow spelling the out words "Here's your guy" pointing right at him.

But staying put wasn't much of an option, either. All they'd have to do was search the area and they'd find him.

He forced himself to wait and watch. The need to light up clawed at him, but cigarette smoke would alert a cop someone was around who shouldn't be.

He sat there for thirty fucking minutes until two officers exited the front of the building, a woman between them.

When Frank recognized her, he slammed his palm into the steering wheel.

Tall for a woman, lots of curling dark hair, and curves he wouldn't mind getting his hands on.

Goddamn Emery Marino.

He knew for a fact she worked on the same floor as dead Gerald. Which meant she could've seen Frank. Might even have recognized him.

Seeing no other option, he started the engine and put the car in drive. Keeping the headlights off, he eased the car into a slow U-turn. No brakes meant no brake lights to give him away. Keeping an eye on the rearview mirror, he was on the freeway before he allowed himself a sigh of relief.

Whatever Emery Marino was doing in that office this late, one thing was for sure: she'd signed her death warrant.

He'd take care of his other job, then figure out what to do with the woman who'd proven to be a huge fuckin' pain in his ass.

***

Shane

"You want to ease up on the gas pedal, pal? I'd like to make it there in one piece."

"We'll get there in one piece," Shane growled. The drive had never felt so long. When the exit finally appeared, he took it, only to have the signal at the end of the off-ramp take twice as long as it should to cycle through to a green light.

Finally, they were moving again.

Emery had managed to completely upend his life.

She was involved in a crime scene and all he could think was he had to get to her.

To know she was safe.

To protect her.

It hadn't been any different when she'd suspected her apartment had been broken into.

She certainly could take care of herself. Women had fought too long and hard for him not to respect they could do pretty much anything they set out to do.

But Emery was in physical danger and every instinct he possessed demanded he act as her shield.

Another red light had him biting off a curse as he stopped the truck. If he wasn't careful, his back molars would be ground to dust and useless because his jaw was so tightly clenched.

It was a damn rude awakening to realize his need to protect Emery wasn't about her being female, but because without him having a fucking clue how it'd happened, she'd become *his*.

Love at first sight was utter nonsense.

At least he'd always thought so.

Since meeting Emery, he could now say definitively he believed in lust at first sight.

He believed in earth-shattering attraction at first sight.

He believed he could crave another person like his next breath at first sight.

The result was an uneasy feeling he was in deeper than he wanted to be.

Liz had destroyed any faith he'd had in the happily-ever-after dream. His parents' divorce had confirmed it.

Didn't seem to matter, though. Emery had proven he didn't have an ounce of control over his heart.

He and Emery had known each other a short amount of time, but that's all it had taken for her to become seriously important to him.

Maybe not love, he assured himself, but something uncomfortably close.

"Take this turn and then Northwood Development will be at the end of the block," Gage said while looking at Shane's phone.

He took the turn and as they approached the four-story building, blue and red lights from the police cars reflected off glass windows.

He pulled into the parking lot and immediately spotted Emery flanked by a couple cops. He parked and was out the door heading straight to her.

Emery looked lost amongst the milling cops and his gaze latched on to her like she was his magnetic north.

He actually *felt* the moment she spotted him because it was like a physical locking in place, gears meshing that worked best when together.

Then she was sprinting across the short distance. He rushed forward, and then she was in his arms.

He didn't think he'd ever let her go.

He absorbed her trembling into his body, turning down his face so they were cheek to cheek.

"It's going to be okay, darlin'. I got you."

He breathed her in and the clutch of fear surrounding his heart eased for the first time since she'd picked up his call.

She burrowed into him and he felt her chest expanding with a deep breath, then shuddering as she slowly released it.

He rubbed a hand up and down her spine. "That's it, baby. Breathe. You're safe."

Her trembling subsided, and he brought up his hands to frame her face and tip back her head. He used his thumb to wipe dampness and smudged makeup from under her eyes.

"I'm not usually a mess. I don't fall apart."

"No, you don't. But there's nothing wrong with leaning on someone if it steadies you so you can be strong."

Eyes huge, she nodded. "You make me stronger," she whispered.

"Goes both ways, darlin'." He pressed his lips to hers, and that mere touch soothed his soul. He forced his attention to the matter at hand. "Have you given a statement?" She shook her head. "Okay, we'll deal with this one step at a time. The sooner you've given your statement, the sooner we can get home."

She nodded, then said, "Can we stay like this a minute longer?"

God, how could his heart withstand it?

He pulled her into him and stood with her head tucked under his chin. With his arms around her, he held on.

Over her head he watched Gage approach the cops. Once his friend figured out what the police wanted from Emery, they'd be ready to deal with it.

***

It was past midnight before Shane turned the car onto the ranch road. The taillights of his truck ahead of him glowed red as Gage parked it in front of the garage. Emery hadn't argued when he'd urged her to come home with him, or when he'd taken the wheel of her rental car. No way in hell was he leaving her alone tonight. They'd made a quick stop at her apartment to pick up the bags she'd already packed. Barb had promised to keep an eye out for anything suspicious around Emery's apartment, and he'd call the manager in the morning to give him a heads-up to be vigilant.

She'd given her statement at the police department. While Gage hadn't revealed his federal law enforcement background, his familiarity with the system had gained them key information. They'd learned evidence indicated Gerald Slater had been grabbed by the neck and choked to death.

The cops had questioned Emery at the scene before she'd been escorted to the police station to give an official statement. Because initial questioning had been informal, Shane had been present.

She'd given a solid description of the man who'd come into the office with Slater, despite only seeing him from the side. There were questions she couldn't answer. Like whether he'd been wearing gloves, the color of his eyes. If he had fucking tattoos. The cops dusted all surfaces he might've touched: in the office, the elevator, the outside doors. But Shane guessed they wouldn't find anything.

Learning the Northwood Development building had *no* security system infuriated him. What business didn't have at least surveillance cameras?

He glanced to where Emery sat in the passenger seat. He'd thought she might sleep on the drive up the mountain, but she'd been quiet, and stared out the side window and into the blackness beyond.

The anger he'd been fighting to control since she'd called kept threatening to break free. He may relish the idea of pummeling the murderer with his bare fists for putting Emery in yet more danger, but his priority had to be her protection.

It made him furious to know she'd been subjected to yet another trauma, and he hadn't been able to do a damn thing to protect her.

That wasn't going to happen again.

Given Gage's experience, Shane figured his friend's assessment was probably better than most. Based on Emery's description of the guy's behavior and the conversation she'd overheard, Gage's take was the murderer sounded like a professional, a hired gun, but not a very good one.

Emery thought he'd seemed cool and in command, exerting authority over Slater. But grabbing a guy by the throat and squeezing the life out of him was up close and personal, and showed his control had snapped.

Which all begged the question why a professional would be hired to deal with Gerald Slater. It sounded like Slater had owed the boss—and wouldn't Shane like to know who the hell that was—and from Emery's recounting of the conversation, Gage thought it likely Gerald had a hefty debt the boss had paid.

The boss expected Gerald to pay his debt by doing something illegal. Whoever had hired the suspected murderer, Shane continued to circle back to the fact that Gerald had been employed by Vance Norris, and if there was something shady going on, Norris was no doubt neck deep in it.

All that was a lot, but the capper for the evening? The detective who acted like he watched too many cop shows and thought he was hot shit, and had conducted Emery's interview, was an asshole.

The line of questioning made Shane think the detective considered Emery a possible suspect in Slater's murder. The guy was an idiot if he was going there, because no way in hell did she have the upper body strength to take down a grown man like that.

Shane didn't often feel moved to violence, but by the end of the interview Emery had looked pale and drawn, and he'd been ready to pound the fucking idiot with his fists.

Telling the detective to pull his head out of his ass probably hadn't been the best tactic, but it was better than slamming the guy against the wall and shaking some sense into him. The detective was wasting time taking the investigation in a direction that was total bullshit.

Shane cut the car engine. When Emery didn't move, he turned in his seat. The sound of Bruno barking his head off carried from inside the house. "Emery. Talk to me."

The hand that had been twirling a lock of hair stilled and she turned to him, the light over the garage revealing dark smudges under her eyes. "I'm exhausted. I can't believe Gerald's dead." She rubbed her temple. "I can't get that image out of my head. Him lying on the floor with his eyes blood red and open. I could tell he was dead."

He picked up her hand, her fingers ice cold despite the heater having been on full blast the whole way home. He clasped both her hands in his to warm them.

"Strangulation can cause blood vessels in the eyes to burst." Gage had passed on that detail.

Her fingers clutched around his. "Right. Okay."

She seemed to gather herself. She'd been through hell during the past few days and he thought she'd be scared or overwhelmed. But a spark in her gaze told him she was nowhere near defeated.

"We need to find who killed Gerald. He wasn't a good boss, but he didn't deserve for that man to murder him."

Her brows lowered like she was trying to remember something.

"Anything else?"

She spoke slowly. "I'm not sure, but when Gerald walked past my office with Hulk, I thought he looked familiar."

"Hulk?"

"He was a big guy. Really big." She shrugged. "Seems appropriate."

"Okay. What seemed familiar about him?"

"I'm not sure. His size and hard face make him a pretty intimidating figure, so I'd think I'd remember if I'd met him." She shook her head. "I don't know. It might come to me when I'm not exhausted."

He kissed her fingertips. "You're a hell of a strong woman, Emery Marino," he murmured.

Her smile was like the fireplace on a snowy winter day. It burned hot and warmed him to the core.

He was going down for the count with her, and gave in. He wasn't even going to bother to fight it.

As tempting as it was to stay cocooned in the car, the temperature would only get colder. Gage had already taken off for his house and it was time to get Emery settled.

He released her hand and exited the car. Holding open her door, he murmured, "C'mon, darlin'. Let's get inside."

Regardless of having spent the night together at her apartment, and knowing there was so much more to them than the mind-bending sex he couldn't get off his mind, he figured she needed space to get her head together.

Plus, he wasn't sure she'd caught up with him on their relationship status.

That deserved a conversation when he and Emery could talk without everything else that was going on being a distraction.

Upshot was for the time being, her bags were going into the bedroom next to his.

Emery disappeared into the room, shutting the door firmly behind her. Minutes later he heard the shower go on.

Bruno followed him into his bedroom, turning around three times before settling on the dog bed. In boxers and the old t-shirt he slept in, Shane lay on his back, an arm over his forehead.

At nearly one in the morning, he was damn tired, but he lay awake, listening to the water running as she showered.

He ignored the stirring of his blood when his mind conjured the image of her naked in a steamy bathroom.

Not what she needed right now.

He must've drifted off because the clock on his nightstand blinked two when he startled awake to find a dark shadow next to his bed. The freshly showered scent told him it was Emery.

"You okay?"

"No. I can't sleep. My brain keeps taking me back to what happened with Gerald." After another long pause, voice quieter, she asked, "Can I sleep with you?"

Without hesitation, he held up the bedding. She crawled in, lying down at the edge of the bed, her body rigid. That wasn't going to help her much.

"Come here, darlin'." He put an arm around her and pulled her against his chest until they were spooned together. Infinitesimally, seemingly one muscle at a time, she relaxed into him.

She breathed deep and released her breath in a shuddering sigh, turning her face into his shoulder. "You feel so good. You smell good too."

His chuckle shook them both. "Right back at you. Ignore the evidence of how good you feel. I know now is not the time, but my dick doesn't."

She turned her head and kissed him on the jaw. "You're a good man, Shane Keller."

With her secure in his arms, he lay awake thinking over all that had happened.

His suspicions centered around Norris Group.

Vance Norris presented a version of himself to the people of Sisters that ran contrary to how he conducted his business.

He portrayed himself as a community leader whose projects benefited the citizens in the area and would lead Sisters into prosperity.

In reality, he was transactional. People were in his good graces only as long as he personally benefited.

Shane thought he acted like a medieval overlord whose benevolence only lasted as long as the little people were on his side. Once crossed, he was ruthless, willing to destroy whatever and whoever was in his way to getting what he wanted.

Winning was everything. Losing was not an option.

While Norris had never faced criminal prosecution, he'd operated his business in shadowy areas of the law, always seeming to be able to stay on the legal side of the line.

Norris wanted the land Lone Pine Ranch was sitting on. Currently, he was using soft tactics, but Shane was under no illusions he wouldn't play dirty when that approach didn't get him the desired results.

And Emery was caught in the middle.

Shane breathed in deep, her scent reminding him of a mountain meadow under a summer sky. Using her had been a colossal miscalculation on Norris's part.

Nothing he could do would get Shane to sell, so his machinations were doomed to failure.

Beyond that, Emery had too much integrity to be used as a pawn.

The more he thought about it, the more Shane was convinced what was happening to and around Emery was all on Norris.

No way were the incidents isolated.

Norris had already crossed the line, but evidence tying him to everything that'd happened so far was tenuous.

Tonight the connection was clearer. And for putting Emery in danger again, Shane would take him down.

In the meantime, he had to keep her safe.

Recent events had proven keeping her close was the only way he could protect her, so that's what he intended to do.

He pulled her tighter against his chest, her steady breathing reassuring, and knowing she was where she belonged, he let himself drift to sleep.

CHAPTER NINETEEN
Emery

Emery stretched and opened her eyes, blinking at the unfamiliar surroundings. The chinked log walls, the four-poster bed, the sheer curtains over the windows. Not the room she'd slept in after being released from the hospital. While she hated feeling scared and weak, asking Shane if she could sleep with him didn't embarrass her as much as she would've thought. Right now, though, she didn't have the bandwidth to examine that.

Memories from last night came in a flood of images that set her heart pounding.

The hulking man, Gerald staring sightless with blood-red eyes, then the terror of waiting for the killer to find her.

She'd sat in a corner on the floor in her dark office, listening for any whisper of sound indicating Hulk had returned.

Then, finally, the sound of wailing sirens had broken the silence and she thought maybe she would be safe.

Only sheer determination had kept her from falling apart when the police rushed in.

They'd escorted her out of the building while it was searched, and the crime scene dealt with.

There'd been so many questions. What had she seen and heard? Why had she been working late? Could she give a description of the man she'd seen with Gerald? What was her relationship with her boss?

Then she'd seen Shane striding across the parking lot, so tall, solid, *stalwart.*

When he'd reached her, she could see and feel his relief.

Without hesitation, he'd wrapped her in his arms, holding her to him like she was something precious, the police radios and conversations around them muting as she absorbed his strength.

He'd held her close until framing her face with his big hands and tilting back her head, his gaze glittering with a storm of emotion.

"You okay?"

She'd nodded numbly. "You're here, so I am now."

The gold in his eyes blazed hot. He'd opened his mouth to speak but two officers had approached with more questions.

Shane had taken her hand in his and hadn't let go, refusing to leave her side through the rest of the ordeal.

She couldn't help but think of Sandra's Bullock's character's comment to Keanu Reeves's character at the end of *Speed*: "...relationships that start under intense circumstances, they never last."

Her relationship with Shane had moved quickly, surely because the dangers she'd faced had heightened emotions for both of them. But, because he was a good man down to his soul, she suspected they would've gotten to where they were anyway.

Last night, he hadn't hesitated when she'd asked to sleep with him. He'd pulled her against him, and like magic, the fears and anxieties of the night had faded and she'd been able to sleep, feeling warm and protected.

That had everything to do with who Shane was as a person, and even if they'd taken it slow, he still would've been who he was: a good guy.

She hoped like hell the line in *Speed* wasn't prophetic.

A glance at the clock on the nightstand had her doing a double take. She *never* slept until nine. Shane was likely out on the range throwing a lasso around cows, *steers* she mentally corrected, in all his hot cowboy glory.

A buzzing came from the nightstand on the other side of the bed. Shane must've brought her phone in while she slept. She picked it up and realized he'd also put it on silent so she could sleep undisturbed.

What kind of crazy did it make her when that simple kindness melted her heart?

Seeing the caller ID, she accepted the incoming call.

"Hi, Mom."

"Hi, my baby. How are you doing?" A rush of emotion brought the sting of tears to the back of Emery's eyes. Her relationship with Delilah had always been complicated, but she never once doubted her mother's love.

"I'm good now, but it's been rough."

"What's going on? Has something else happened?"

When she'd spoken to Delilah before, she'd skimmed over the details of the car crash, not wanting her to worry. The current situation called for honesty.

Emery told her mom about the events of the past few days from being forced through the guardrail, to her apartment being broken into and her laptop stolen, to Hulk and Gerald's murder. Delilah's instinctive desire to keep Emery safe came as no surprise.

"Gerald was murdered? Oh, that poor man. I feel bad for him, but that you were there terrifies me. You're a *witness*, Em. It sounds like the only witness. Once the killer figures that out, you'll be a target. Are you at your apartment now? Come home. You'll be safe with us."

"I'm safe, Mom."

"You're not safe if you're anywhere that killer can find you. Come home, baby."

"No, Mom, I'm fine. Really. Shane came to Sacramento last night. His friend Gage was with him and they drove from Sisters to the Northwood office.

"They went with me to the police station and stayed with me through everything. Shane's been a rock. I'll admit being there when Gerald was murdered freaked me out, and I'm still freaked out. I can't help thinking I should've done something to prevent it. Maybe if I'd shown myself, that man would've left."

"Or he would have attacked you too. That man killed Gerald, Emery, and it's not your fault. There's no way you could've known he intended murder."

"I know, but it's hard not to think I could've done something and the result might've been different." She rubbed a fist over her forehead as if she could physically erase the memory. "It was an awful night but, I don't know, I guess I feel like I can deal with anything as long as Shane is with me."

"Oh my," Delilah murmured. "He sounds wonderful. Emery, I'm so happy for you."

"Yeah, well, don't get ahead of yourself. It's the way he is. He's protective by nature."

"Can't help calling it as I see it." In a more serious tone, Delilah added, "I'm glad you found someone special, Em, even if he is a rancher. Maybe you can convince him to switch to organic farming?" she added.

Emery wiggled a finger under the splint on her wrist to scratch the itchy skin. "Actually, Shane's working with researchers at a university who are developing techniques to lessen the negative impacts cattle have on the environment. I was really impressed with the changes some ranchers are instituting to lessen methane emissions."

"That's something, I guess. But there's no getting around the fact that a plant-based diet will always have less negative impact on the environment than commercially produced animal protein." She paused and Emery could imagine her shoulder shrug. "I'd like to meet Shane to talk about that, but with everything that's going on, now is not the time. Are you at your apartment? Did he spend the night with you?"

"Mom."

"What?" Delilah used her innocent tone. "I think you know what to do with a hot cowboy if you catch one."

Emery put a hand to her suddenly warm cheeks. "Oh my god."

"I've always been up-front with you about sex. Don't tell me you've become repressed. And sex can be especially beautiful when you're falling in love."

"Now you're way, *way* ahead of yourself. I met him only a week ago."

"Does that make a difference? Sometimes attraction is instant and you're only wasting time by resisting. Let yourself go and enjoy the ride, Em." She laughed. "Literally."

Emery again rubbed her closed fist over her forehead. "I don't do insta-love, Mom. I won't let a man like Gideon break my heart."

When Delilah replied, her tone sounded unusually quiet. "You're letting fear of a broken heart keep you from grabbing hold of something that could be special. You won't ever have great joy unless you are willing to risk your heart. There are no guarantees in life, but even if you end up with a broken heart, you've still gained something. I loved Gideon Bryant and he did break my heart, but I never regretted a moment of that time because I got you, didn't I?"

"It was hard for you, Mom."

"It was, but it was worth it. I'd never felt more alive than I did during my time with your father. That alone made it worth it."

Emery shook her head. Maybe there was something to what her mother was saying, but she'd have to think about it later.

"What happened last night?" Delilah prompted.

"Shane was adamant I come back to the ranch, and since I didn't want to stay in my apartment alone, I agreed. I feel safe at the ranch. Shane's here, and so are Gage and Harding. I'm safer here than I'd be anywhere else." She thought Delilah would pounce on the knowledge of how protective Shane was being.

Instead, she said, "He's keeping you safe, and that makes him a good man. I can't wait to meet him."

"He is a good man, but meeting him will have to wait. I need to find out if there's any news. Maybe the police have already caught Gerald's murderer and we can all stop worrying."

"That would be good, but until you know for certain, you be careful. I'll rest easier knowing Shane's watching out for my girl."

Emery thought Delilah was laying it on a little thick, but she said, "Right. I'll talk with you later. Love you, Mom."

Shane was passing the mom test without ever having met her. Wouldn't it be nice if from now on everything else went so smoothly.

She walked to the window to pull up the shade. The bedroom was on the east side of the house. A gray sky heavy with sullen clouds obscured all but the closest mountain slopes. Last night, when she'd arrived at the ranch, she'd caught the glitter of a star-strewn sky. The weather must've changed in the early morning hours. She saw the wind tossing the tops of pine trees, and even the cattle in the distant pastures were huddled together.

With a last look out the window, she gathered up her clothes from her suitcase. She needed to get dressed, then coffee and breakfast were the next order of business. She hoped she'd be ready to face whatever the new day had to throw at her.

***

"Those girls are wily an' always think there's better opportunity on this side of the fence. Get inside and close that gate fast as you can."

The minute Emery opened the gate the hens made a beeline to her. Chickens moved *fast*. She did as Harding directed and slipped through, Bruno following, then fastened the latch behind her.

"Do you ever let them out of their yard?"

"We do sometimes. Bruno helps round them up. Gotta watch out on account of coyotes. Bastards would love to get a fat hen for dinner." Harding motioned with his hand. "Now toss that scratch out so they'll be busy pecking and won't be a bother when you collect the eggs."

Emery cast the grain mixture in a wide arc and soon the hens—some a coppery red, some black and white, others tannish—began pecking in the dirt.

She took a deep breath of mountain air and scattered more feed, feeling tension ease from her shoulders. She added a chicken coop and hens to her fantasy tiny house in the meadow.

She took the handled basket to the back of the coop and, reciting Harding's instructions in her head, lifted a door. She found the hook to hold it open, exposing a row of nests. A grin split her face and she felt like a miner striking gold. Brown eggs, blue eggs, speckled eggs, all nestled in beds of straw. After carefully placing the eggs in the basket, she closed the door and returned to the gate.

"Look at these, Harding. They're beautiful." She picked up a light brown egg covered with dark speckles. "This one is the prettiest."

She figured she had city slicker written all over her but didn't let that keep her from feeling delight at the bounty. A gusty breeze had her hair blowing in her eyes. She glanced at the sky where dark clouds obscured the sun.

"Those girls." Harding pointed to hens with beautifully patterned black and white feathers. "They're called Wyandottes, and those speckled eggs are theirs. The light-colored birds are Ameraucanas. They lay the blue eggs, and the Rhode Island Reds lay brown eggs."

"What are their names?"

Harding tugged on his beard, dark eyes gleaming. "Well now, I never got around to namin' them. Maybe you could do that."

If he was laughing at her, he hid it well.

"Maybe I will. What will you do with these eggs?"

"What do you think of egg salad sandwiches for lunch?"

"That sounds great, but I'm supposed to go to a meeting in town."

The thought of seeing Vance had dread settling on her shoulders. She'd much rather make egg salad sandwiches with Harding, but hiding from her employment situation would work for only so long.

And Gerald had been murdered.

She was the closest thing to a witness, which made her feel like a target had been painted on her back.

Whatever the identity of the man who'd killed her boss, she was convinced Gerald's death had something to do with the Norris Group.

Even if she ended up having to move back home until she got a job offer, and maybe getting a part-time job, she could no longer work for Vance Norris or his company.

Harding narrowed his gaze as he studied her, though when he spoke, his tone remained unhurried. "Accordin' to the boy, you had a rough night. You need time to recover yourself. Maybe your meetin' can wait."

By "boy" she figured Harding meant Shane, though "boy" was far from accurate, especially when she thought of the man who'd been her rock the night before.

She hadn't seen him at all that morning. He'd sent her a text before dawn, saying he'd be out for the morning and would touch base when he returned.

Being in his home and around his things made her restless. She missed him, which was stupid because only hours before she'd been in his arms. But she felt steadier with him nearby. Instead of letting her sleep, she'd rather he'd woken her, even if it was simply to say good-bye before leaving to wherever he'd gone.

When she'd descended the stairs to the kitchen that morning, Harding had been sitting at the table with a cup of coffee and a newspaper propped in front of him. He'd insisted on preparing her oatmeal and tea, and they'd spent a quiet half hour sharing the paper while she ate her breakfast. She could almost pretend it was a normal morning and Gerald hadn't been murdered the night before.

Carrying the egg basket, she asked Harding, "Are you keeping an eye on me?"

He gave his beard a tug. "Well now, not so much keeping an eye on *you* as makin' sure no one *else* is keepin' an eye on you."

"You mean you're worried about me being safe here at the ranch?"

"Bossman found tracks on the road up near the reservoir. None of us have been up that way since that cloudburst a couple of nights ago. The rain woulda wiped out any tracks from before that time. Means someone was up there who's not one of us."

The hairs on the back of her neck twitched. "Maybe it was a hiker."

"Maybe," he agreed. "We get them sometimes."

Which wasn't much of a reassurance. Going on instinct, she came to a decision. She didn't know if the things happening to her were related, but she needed to play it safe. Meeting with Vance wasn't playing it safe. "You're right. My meeting can wait. I'll text my boss and tell him." Earlier, she'd texted Vance telling him she couldn't meet with him until noon, but now she'd go ahead and cancel. Sending him a formal resignation via email would be good enough.

Harding nodded in approval.

Once she gave notice she could respond to her professor with a clear conscience. He'd sent another email asking if he sent a team, would she meet them to show where she'd made the frog recording. He'd also sent a draft letter asking permission from Shane to allow the team on his property with a request that Emery speak with Shane to pave the way.

Vance would be pissed, which would no longer be her problem. She had no idea how Shane would react to the request.

Back in the guest bedroom, she was opening her tablet when a text from Vance appeared:

Need to go to Sac and deal with GS death. Fucking inconvenient. We still need to meet but we'll do dinner. Meet me at 6:30 at hotel bar.

Vance had to *deal* with Gerald's death? And it was *fucking inconvenient*? His callousness knew no bounds. She closed her eyes, rubbing her forehead with the base of her thumb where the calm of the morning had been replaced by a tension headache.

Going with her earlier decision, she found a letter of resignation template online, made the necessary changes, and sent it to Vance.

***

"That's a lot of egg salad."

Harding had hard-boiled a dozen eggs. Not the ones she'd collected that morning as he'd claimed shells stuck most to the freshest eggs. With his beard braided—to keep it out of the way, he said—he was now dicing celery with rapid-fire strokes. "Could be company'll want to be fed."

"What company?"

At that moment she heard a series of sharp barks. Harding tipped his head to the window over the sink and she followed the gesture to look out.

"Oh."

Two vehicles had parked in front of the garage. Gage stepped out of Shane's truck and leaned down to pet Bruno. Then her attention zeroed in on the man exiting from the driver's door.

Tall, self-assured, broad shoulders seemingly capable of bearing any burden. He settled the black hat on his head as rain pelted from low clouds. Then he glanced at the house and went motionless as his gaze locked on hers.

Her heart gave a hard thud.

Why did it feel like he could see deep into her soul?

She rubbed a hand over her heart. How was it possible for one man to simply look her way and her brain went haywire?

It'd been that way the moment she'd first laid eyes on him all hot-cowboy gorgeous at Easy Money, but now the attraction was layered with so much more than his physical appearance.

Gage said something and Shane looked away as another vehicle pulled in behind his. Emery looked at the loaf of bread she'd been holding like she didn't know what to do with it.

"Well now." Harding's brown eyes gleamed as he dumped celery into the bowl with the chopped eggs.

"Well now what?"

"Well now, I guess the boy's smitten." He hummed under his breath.

Emery didn't know what to say to that so she took bread slices from the bag and stacked them on a cutting board.

The outside door opened bringing a low rumble of voices. A minute later, Bruno led the way into the kitchen, toenails clicking. The testosterone level in the room ratcheted up as four gorgeous guys entered, having shed hats and coats in the mudroom.

"Preliminary finding from the coroner's office confirms strangulation without evidence of defensive wounds on Slater," Sawyer was saying. He was in uniform, holstered gun on his hip, a shiny badge on his chest. "That's unofficial, mind you, but it's doubtful the findings will change."

Gage leaned against the counter, phone in hand as he tapped out a message. Walker, his dark hair looking finger-combed back from his forehead, stood with feet planted and arms crossed over his massive chest, his gaze locked on Sawyer. He said something to his brother, but Emery's focus shifted when Shane followed the other men in and strode directly to her side.

"You got a minute?"

Harding was stirring mayo and mustard into the egg mixture. She gestured to the stack of sliced sourdough in front of her. "I'm supposed to toast the bread for egg salad sandwiches."

Shane took the bread she'd stacked, dumped slices into the toaster, pressed the lever, and took her hand. "Come with me."

Before she could articulate a protest, he led her through the wide door of the kitchen to the short hall where Harding's bedroom and Shane's office were located. Once around the corner he backed her against the wall, dipped his head, and, eyes open, took her lips in a kiss that made her knees buckle.

Sensations hit her in a flurry, the smells of wind and rain that clung to him, the gold of his eyes that looked like they were lit by a fire from within, and feeling like in his arms were where she was meant to be.

All that, plus the warm-chocolate slide of his tongue over hers, had her craving more.

He released her hand to spear his fingers through her hair, his other arm braced on the wall beside her head. It was like being hit by a bomb cyclone that laid waste to her emotions. The groan she let loose reflected equal parts desire and frustration.

He lightened the kiss, then shifted to press his lips over her cheekbones. He straightened to his full height. "Emery, we—"

"Uh-uh. No way, mister." With her un-splinted hand, she fisted his shirt at the collar and tugged, bringing his head back to where she wanted it. Lips, tongue, the taste of *him,* she couldn't get enough. Good thing he didn't resist because she wasn't allowing it.

It was minutes before they broke apart again, both breathing heavily.

"'No way, mister'?" One corner of his mouth curled with the hint of a smile.

"Don't look so smug. You started it. You can't go all warm chocolate on me then try to cut off the supply."

Heat flared and amusement vanished. He grabbed her hand again. "We're going upstairs where we can finish this."

"If that's what you wanted, why'd you come home with company?"

"Wasn't thinking. Hold that thought and I'll get rid of them."

"You can't kick out your friends."

"Wanna bet?" His dark gaze lasered into hers and she realized he was perfectly serious.

"Toast is burning, Keller." Walker rounded the corner of the hall and stood, hands in pockets, his brow lifted in a sardonic look.

Emery wanted to cover her cheeks as warmth surged up her neck.

"Harding'll kick your ass if you disappear upstairs with your woman."

"Don't give a damn," Shane growled. "Go away. All of you."

"Shane," she whispered.

"Not happening. I can't go upstairs with my woman, you can't go upstairs with yours." Walker's gaze rested on Emery. "Laney just showed up. She's not happy her sister witnessed a murder."

Shane's chest expanded as he drew in a deep breath. "Fuck. Okay. We'll be there in a minute."

Walker's look suggested he wasn't sure he could trust them, but he disappeared into the kitchen.

Shane rested both hands on her shoulders. "Things could get crazy over the next couple days."

She frowned at his serious tone. "I guess so."

"Before the craziness breaks out and we get dropped into it, I need to tell you something."

Sudden nervousness had her heart thudding heavily. He cupped her face, his thumbs stroking along her cheekbones almost like he couldn't *not* touch her.

"I'm falling for you, Emery. Hard." Everything around her disappeared, all sound muffled, objects in the periphery of her vision blurred. Only Shane remained in focus.

"I wasn't looking for a relationship, didn't want one. Until you." His warm lips moved over her brow, her eyes, her mouth, as he murmured words that made her heart yearn. "You've got me rethinking my life and how we might build a new one together." He pulled back until she could see the warmth of gold glowing at the center of brown irises. "Tell me I'm not in this alone, darlin'. Tell me you feel even a fraction of what I feel for you."

She closed her eyes, searching for a scrap of resistance to being sucked under by the force of nature that was Shane.

"Emery?"

Nope. No resistance. She was going under. "I do, Shane. I'm falling just as hard and fast." She opened her eyes. "But I'm scared."

"Of what?"

"Of your feelings. Of mine. Mine are so huge. It would kill me if you walked away like my dad walked away from my mom."

"Don't put me on the same level as that asshole Gideon Bryant."

"I don't. It's more about how it affected me. I'm not good at relationships because I never let myself feel too deeply. But I haven't been able to stop myself with you and that's what has me scared."

"Will you two lovebirds be joining us for egg sandwiches? 'Cause the other folk are already sittin' at the table and eatin'." Harding's voice carried from behind Shane.

She peered over his shoulder to where the old man stood, his lips twitching like he was having trouble keeping a straight face.

"Damn," Shane muttered, then spoke louder so Harding could hear, "We're coming."

When they were alone again, Shane said, "He's not subtle."

"No, but you love him."

Shane gave an abrupt laugh. "Yeah, I do." He tucked a strand of hair behind her ear. "About us, we'll deal with whatever comes up, Em, but you and me? What we've got going on is worth fighting for. I'm committed to that." He paused. "Are you?"

She nodded slowly. "Yes."

"That's good enough for now. Let's join the others for lunch and decide on the battle plan to deal with what's going on with you."

She couldn't hide her shock. "That's why everyone's here? For me?"

"Yeah. You're one of us now."

CHAPTER TWENTY
Emery

Emery followed Shane into the now crowded kitchen. A small dog with mottled brown and gray fur stood quivering, nose to nose with Bruno, who gave the little guy a lick.

"That's Bud. Walker's love before I arrived on the scene," Delaney told her.

Emery bent to let the pup smell the back of her hand. When she'd passed the sniff test, she stroked his head. "Oh, he's adorable. He's so ugly he's cute."

"He's just ugly," Walker muttered. "Don't try to make him better than he is."

"Walker treats that dog like a baby." Sawyer smirked at his brother. "The other day he had a little sweater on."

"Hey, he gets cold." Walker scowled.

Bud wagged what there was of his tail until Shane retrieved a box of dog biscuits from the cupboard. He gave one to each dog and they trotted into the living room with their snacks.

Harding set a plate of carrot sticks in the middle of the crowded table next to a bowl filled with potato chips. Walker rose, plate in hand, motioning Emery to the seat he'd vacated next to Delaney. "You can sit here."

"Oh, I'm fine. I'll wait until you're done."

Walker shook his head, and Delaney said, "You might as well sit because he won't change his mind."

Harding handed her a plate with a sandwich cut in a neat diagonal, and Emery sat.

"Shane told us what happened last night." Delaney crunched a chip, her expression troubled. "How are you doing?"

Emery shrugged. "I don't know. I feel bad because I was exasperated with Gerald more often than I wasn't. He was a jerk. When I told him Vance Norris was hitting on me, his solution was for me not to wear revealing clothing, which shouldn't matter even if my clothing had been revealing. Which it wasn't. I wish I'd been less frustrated with him the last time we spoke."

"Even jerks get murdered." Delaney poured tea over ice in a glass and set it by Emery's plate. "We have to live our lives with normal emotions, Em. You didn't know what would happen to him."

"Yeah, but I was *there*, literally down the hall from where Gerald was strangled, and I didn't do a damn thing to help him. I actually *saw* the killer. Now I'm the closest thing the police have to a witness."

Shane took the seat across the table from her. "Damn good thing he didn't know you were there or he'd have come after you too."

Which was exactly what Delilah had said.

Emery shivered.

Sawyer leaned against the counter, his plate in hand as he ate. "Couple things to catch you up," he told Emery. "First, early this morning a body was discovered dumped along an abandoned railroad spur in Sacramento. He's been identified as Sisters resident Dale Benson, a repeat petty criminal with a chronic meth habit. He'd been bludgeoned to death. Murder weapon was likely the crowbar found next to his body. He hadn't been dead all that long. Early estimate is he was killed sometime around midnight last night."

"That's awful, but he's relevant because…?" She already had a bad feeling about what Sawyer would say next.

"Because he matches the general description you'd given of the guy who'd stolen your phone, and his prints were found in the red Bronco abandoned out by Lost Lake. The paint left on your car where it had been hit from behind is a match to the Bronco."

"Oh."

"Yeah, oh. He might be our guy."

"Why do you think he was murdered?"

"Working on that. Interesting note, he's known to hang out with Bobby Finley."

Her expression must've been blank because Shane told her, "You saw Bobby at Easy Money when he and I crashed into your table."

"*That* I remember."

"Dale might have been hired to snatch your phone and decided giving your car a shove was his best shot," Sawyer continued. "He's not exactly known for his scholarship or common sense. If that was Dale, it's a step up the crime ladder for him."

"But why would someone kill him?" she repeated.

"To keep him quiet about who hired him?" Sawyer said with a shrug. "This morning we went down the mountain to meet with Sacramento PD. Dale being tied to a crime in our county, the sheriff wants to make sure we're part of the investigation."

While Emery digested that information, Sawyer continued. "We also met with the detectives assigned to Slater's murder and made it clear they aren't to release any information to the public about there being a witness. They aren't to identify you or mention your name publicly in any context."

"Who's the 'we' you're talking about?"

"All four of us." He gestured to the other men who'd arrived with him.

Shane spoke around the carrot he was chewing. "If they mention there was a witness, you could be in danger. We had to get ahead of them.

"We also wanted to make sure the asshole detective from last night wasn't wasting time trying to pin Slater's murder on you. Looks like he's pulled his head out since his investigation is no longer going in that direction. Regardless, this guy," he jerked a thumb at Gage, "is your lawyer, if needed. He's not practicing but he's got a law degree and can give you general advice if the situation arises. If it looks like you'll need someone licensed in California, we'll take care of it. In the meantime, Gage is your guy."

Emery held up her hand. "Wait." She didn't like being managed, however well-intentioned. If she didn't reclaim some control, important decisions would be made for her. They already had been.

She turned to Gage. "First, I appreciate the offer. Really, I do. But I don't have the funds to take on a lawyer. Down the road, legal representation might become important, but I'll figure something out if and when that becomes necessary."

"No charge for family, sweetheart."

"We're not family."

"You're with Shane, you're family."

That brought a lump to her throat, and she swallowed hard. "Thank you. I appreciate it, but I can accept only if you agree to speak with me before acting on my behalf."

"Done."

She swiveled in her seat to point a finger at Shane. "Listen carefully, cowboy. I'm a reasonably intelligent and aware individual. I will not allow a bunch of big, strong men to make decisions or act on my behalf unless I've given them explicit permission to do so. I expect to be a part of any discussion about anything that concerns me."

"You were asleep after a rough night. I wasn't going to wake you to tell you I was going to Sacramento to talk to the police."

"That's exactly what you should've done. It's nonnegotiable, Shane."

"You go, girl," Delaney cheered. "You have to hold your own with this group or they'll trample all over you and say it's for your own good."

"That's not true," Walker retorted. "We protect those we care about."

Delaney shot him a cool look and Walker shot right back with a lightning-fast grin. "You love me anyway."

"I do, but that wouldn't get you out of trouble if you went around me the way you all went around Emery."

Walker moved to stand behind Delaney's chair. He leaned down to kiss the top of her head. "Okay. I hear you."

She covered the hand he'd placed on her shoulder with hers. Tipping her head back, she mouthed, "Thank you."

Watching their byplay, Emery thought if she had anything close to that level of commitment and honesty in her own relationships, she'd be happy.

"You don't have to worry, Laney. My brother would cut open an artery for you if you asked." Sawyer wadded a napkin and tossed it in the trash.

"She's the love of my life, what can I say?"

Emery felt her message needed to be clear. "You two are adorable in a hot and sexy kind of way, but to the point I was making, I expect be included."

Shane lifted his chin in her direction. "Understood."

Delaney sighed. "Men can be such lunkheads, but at least our men mean well. I'd like to hear what happened last night, Em, but not if you don't want to go through it again."

She thought about her sister's request. "It might be good to talk about it now that it doesn't feel so immediate. Maybe I'll remember something else."

"If y'all are done with the eatin', move on out to the other room where you'll be more comfortable and let me straighten things here." Harding began gathering plates from the table.

"We'll all pitch in to clean up, Harding," Delaney said. "And thank you for lunch. It was unexpected and delicious."

"No need to worry about cleanup. Kitchen's mine. I know how I like things and it'll take twice as long with you all in my way. Shoo now."

Delaney pointed to a white bakery box on the counter printed with the Cider Mill Farm logo. "Cam sent over berry tarts. She says you're partial to them, Harding, so she sent extras just for you."

"You tell her thank you for me. I'll put some coffee on and we'll all enjoy berry tarts in a bit."

"How come he gets extra berry tarts? Cam never bakes for me," Sawyer grumbled as they trooped into the living room.

"Harding's nice to her. You're not."

Mouth gaping, Sawyer put a hand to his chest like he'd suffered a mortal wound. "Does she think I'm not nice? I'm always nice to her. When am I not nice?"

Emery couldn't help the smile. The day she'd visited Cider Mill Farm she'd had a front-row seat to the sparks between Sawyer and Cam, and suspected the cop had feelings for the baker.

Delaney hooked an arm with his. "You're protective of her, I'll give you that. Which just puts her back up. I also think you'd donate a kidney for her if she needed it." Sawyer opened his mouth, then shut it with a click. "But nice? No."

"She hardly says a word to me so I don't have much opportunity to be nice. Besides, I'm a cop, it's my job to be protective."

"If you say so." Delaney looked smug.

Sawyer had always seemed cool and unflappable, and Emery found it *very* interesting how flustered he got talking about Cam.

They all took seats, Gage and Sawyer on the wide brick hearth while Delaney took the spot at the end of the couch. Emery sat next to her with Walker at the other end. Shane leaned forward in a recliner next to the couch, forearms resting on his knees.

Delaney eyed Emery. "You still good with talking about last night? I can't imagine what you went through, so if you'd rather not, that's okay."

"I'm fine." She took a minute to gather her thoughts before speaking. She closed her eyes briefly against the kaleidoscope of images from the night before. The hulking man with the crooked nose, Gerald's eyes, blood red and vacant, the blue and red lights of the police vehicles.

The events of the evening seemed to stretch on forever, but the time between hearing the ping of the elevator and the police arriving hadn't been long at all.

With her voice low, she told the group about working on her computer in her office trying to finish the project, then hearing the elevator doors opening and voices carrying down the hall.

As she shared, many of the questions for clarification came from Gage. He moved to the coffee table in front of her, sitting on it facing her. He took his phone from his pocket and set it on the table beside him. "Do you mind if I record this?"

She was surprised but shook her head. "No, that's fine."

"Good. Tell me again what you remember of their conversation."

She repeated what she'd heard, finally adding, "Whoever Hulk was working for had some leverage over Gerald. But he was scared and refused to do whatever they were asking him to do. He said it was illegal."

"You didn't hear what that leverage was, why Slater was under obligation?"

"No, that wasn't mentioned."

"Okay, let's go back to when you saw them. You said the lights were off in your office, but the door was open?" he asked.

"Yes," she nodded. "The door was open about halfway."

"Is your computer screen visible from the door?"

She shook her head. "No."

"Wouldn't the glow have been visible?"

"I had it on dark mode, so there was no glow. The nurse had suggested doing that and keeping lights low or off as part of my concussion care. Gerald and Hulk walked by, but they didn't look into my office at all."

"Hulk?" Sawyer cut in. "You said he was a big guy, but calling him Hulk suggests a more than run-of-the-mill big guy."

"True. I started calling him that in my head because he was big, all muscley with hardly any neck. He's taller and wider than Walker, and that's saying something." She frowned, bothered by the faint sense he'd seemed familiar, but had nothing concrete to share.

"There something else?" Shane asked, his gaze intent. He must've picked up on her hesitation.

"I'm not sure. When he passed my office, his face was in profile and I felt like I'd seen him before. I didn't mention it to the detective. Maybe I should have."

Gage resumed his questions. "Let's go with the idea you might've seen the man before. I'd like to talk you through the past couple of weeks. What you did, where you went socially and professionally, who you talked to. Maybe it will jiggle a memory loose."

She had the fleeting thought that with his law background and questioning technique, there was more to Gage than being a friend of Shane's who worked on the ranch.

"Let's start with your time in Sisters." He asked questions and she responded, relaying what she could remember from the first day she'd arrived in Sisters and walked the boardwalk, meandering through shops in town.

He had her recount details of her initial meeting with Vance at Three Sisters Bakery, then her visit to Cider Mill Farm. She told him about being waylaid by Vance in front of the hotel after spending Saturday afternoon at the ranch with Shane.

"I didn't want to go with him to the bar, but he said he wanted to hear more about my ideas for the project and he wasn't staring at my boobs, so I finally agreed. We went to the bar in the restaurant across the parking lot from the hotel."

"Anyone there stand out to you?"

She shrugged, struggling to sift through the memories of what she'd seen that evening. "The place was busy, but I don't remember anyone in particular. We sat at the bar. The bartender was working, moving around a lot, making drinks. He was Hispanic and thin, and not the man I saw last night. Vance got a call and took it outside."

She shut her eyes tight as images flooded her mind. The murmur of conversation, her frustration that she was waiting in a bar for someone to return whom she didn't really want to talk to in the first place, taking out her phone to help pass the time. One image snagged her memory: sitting on a stool next to a very large man. A Hulk-size man with a crooked nose. "Oh my god. I was sitting right next to him."

"Who?" Shane asked, his tone sharp as a blade.

She opened her eyes again. "There was a man sitting at the bar. That's who Hulk reminded me of. We'd taken the stools next to his and I noticed he was a big guy."

"Vance had stepped out so I'd taken out my phone to pass the time. I played a video I'd taken earlier that day. I'd noticed the big guy looking at my phone. He asked what I was watching. The audio had come on loud, but it still struck me as odd because most people are pretty respectful about privacy and other people's phones. It's almost taboo to look at someone's screen without an invitation. Anyway, I remember hoping he wasn't trying to pick me up. Then Vance came back and I forgot about it."

"Did the guy stay seated next to you while you were talking to Norris?" Gage's demeanor hadn't changed, other than appearing more alert.

"Yeah, he stayed the entire time I was in the bar, which is also kind of odd because he was drinking soda."

"What struck you most about his appearance?"

She brought up the mental image again. "First, his size. Even sitting he was a big guy and had a rough appearance. Rough enough I thought he looked like a thug. Like one of those no-neck fixers in the movies. His nose was crooked like it'd been broken and not set straight."

Her stomach sank, because the more she considered it, the more obvious the implications.

"Hulk has a bump on his nose just like it. The guy at the bar could be the same guy who killed Gerald."

Shane surged to his feet. "If she's right and he's the killer, being in the bar with Vance is not a coincidence."

"We need to talk with the bartender." Sawyer dug out a small notepad and pen from a pocket and began writing as he spoke. "Find out if he remembers Vance and the big guy talking before or after you were there."

"I wonder if the big guy could have been saving seats," Emery mused. "The bar was busy, but Vance walked right to two empty barstools."

"That's another thing the bartender might remember."

"Wait." Eyes wide, Delaney turned to Walker, grabbing his hand. "Hulk could be No-Neck."

"No-Neck? Who the hell's No-Neck?"

"No-Neck, remember? Frank Dicarlo. Emery said he reminded her of a no-neck fixer. That matches exactly."

"Son of a bitch." Walker snarled the oath. "Dicarlo worked for Norris. If it's him, this ties Norris to the murder. He could be the guy who gave the order for Slater to do whatever he was refusing to do. That puts fucking Norris behind this." He whipped around to face his brother.

"I'm ahead of you." Sawyer's phone was in his hand. "I'll call the sheriff. We need Emery to make a positive ID on Dicarlo. Maybe we'll catch a break and he'll be in the system. Having a mug shot will make things a lot easier. If she IDs him, we can put out a BOLO."

"What's a BOLO?" she asked.

"Be On the Lookout," Sawyer responded as he tapped on the screen of his phone. "Goes out across law enforcement agencies to look for the guy."

"Okay, then who's Frank Dicarlo?"

Mug shots, a BOLO, Vance possibly being involved? Emery felt more than a little dazed.

Delaney leaned back against the couch cushion and let out a huff of breath before responding. "Earlier in the summer he was working for Vance. I think he's personal security in addition to basically doing whatever Vance wants him to do. Walker beat him up last summer."

"He hit me first. You're the one who laid him out across the pavement." Walker glowered at his fiancée. "You could've been hurt."

"I can't help if he tripped over my leg," she said primly. "And I didn't want him to hurt *you*."

Walker looked ready to argue the point, but Shane cut him off. "Can we focus?" He pinned his gaze on Emery. "Does Norris know you were working late last night?"

"No, I was finishing a project Gerald had assigned."

"So Slater knew you were working late."

"Not necessarily. I hadn't told him I was staying, and if my home computer hadn't been stolen, I would've finished the work from home."

"You didn't mention any of that to Norris."

"No, I'd texted with him to set up our meeting this morning, which isn't going to happen. I emailed my letter of resignation."

"Good," Shane growled. He swiveled to address Sawyer. "You putting out an alert on Norris too?"

"We'll get to him, but we need more evidence of a connection than the fuckers having been associates last summer and being in the same bar a week ago. Let me make this call." Sawyer strode into the kitchen, phone to his ear.

Gage leaned forward, attention on Emery. "Tell me about the video."

"You're a cop, aren't you?"

"The video, Emery. What made the guy so interested?"

After a quick glance at Shane, she said clearly, "Frogs."

If Gage was surprised, she couldn't tell. "Explain."

With a silent prayer that Shane wouldn't hate her, she told the group about her walk along Rock Creek. "In college I was part of a team studying the Sierra Nevada yellow-legged frog. Rock Creek is the kind of habitat they like. I was on the lookout for it, and when I heard the croak, I recognized it."

"You recognized the croak of a frog?" Walker sounded incredulous.

"I did because my job on the project was to sift through the recordings the rest of the team made in the field. That frog has a distinctive croak, kind of like a squeaky groan. I thought if I could prove the frog was present, it would be a barrier to development."

"Aren't those frogs endangered?" Delaney asked.

"Yeah, they were added to the endangered species list almost ten years ago." Emery shifted. "My first morning here I met with Vance, and he showed me a map of the proposed North Bench project. I told him the property might include critical habitat for endangered species. His response was basically that there are ways of getting around environmental restrictions, and a couple of damned frogs, his words, weren't going to stop his project. There's some family dynamics going on too, because he thinks if he's successful with a development he's nurtured from beginning to end, he'll have the support to take control of the company from his father."

"I've heard rumors Vance is trying to leverage control of the company," Delaney muttered.

Emery darted another look at Shane, trying to read his expression. "Despite what Vance said about getting around restrictions, I'm confident if we identify the habitat, we can stop development. I sent the recording to the professor I'd worked for and he confirmed my identification. He wants to send out a team to get a visual on the frog before making a definitive finding. Once he does, he'll get the ball rolling on designating the area as critical habitat needing protection."

She faced Shane's unwavering gaze. "I'm sorry, but this will mean you won't be able to utilize the land for cattle grazing, or anything else."

"That's not what's important right now."

Delaney frowned. "What if Vance already knew of the frog's presence in the creek? They meet and out of the blue, Emery mentions her concern. He freaks out because he has a lot riding on this project. The last thing he'd want is a positive verification. He wanted Cider Mill Farm, and when we wouldn't sell, he turned his attention to the Lone Pine Ranch. But an endangered species on Rock Creek blows the whole thing up."

Delaney turned to Shane. "Sorry, pal, but it impacts your land use as well."

Shane's expression wasn't giving much away.

"I'm sorry I didn't tell you sooner," Emery murmured.

"Like I said, that's not what's important right now. If the guy is Dicarlo, and he's the murderer and spoke to you at the bar, you're on his radar."

Gage glanced at Sawyer, who gave a slow nod in silent communication.

"What?" Emery looked from one man to the other. "What's that about?"

"Motive," Gage said.

CHAPTER TWENTY-ONE
Emery

Bright Sunday morning sunlight shimmered through Emery's eyelids as she rode the flood of sensation, her body lifting higher and higher. "Shane." His name left her lips on a gasp. "Oh god, *Shane*. I need, I need—"

"Yeah, darlin'? What do you need?" His gravelly voice was no more steady than hers. His forward thrust was long, smooth, and hard, the pleasurable tension coiling tighter and tighter.

She opened her eyes to a slit to gaze at the corded sinews and bulging muscles of the perfect male body braced over her.

Ranchers rose early and she'd roused briefly when he'd gone out before the sun had risen. He'd crawled back to bed sometime later and she'd woken that time to drugging kisses and clever hands. Oh so clever hands. Now those hands were kneading her breasts as hers grasped muscled buttocks to pull him in tighter.

"I need you to—"

"This? Do you need me to do this, darlin'?"

The rumbly sound of his voice spiraled the tension even tighter. Then he did it. With clever fingers and pistoning hips, he pushed her up until she launched over the edge, free-falling in weightless bliss.

His hot lips captured hers and Shane followed, a roar emanating from his throat, thrusting again and again as his release pulsed into her.

She still quivered with what felt like a thousand aftershocks when he framed her face with his wide palms. Mussed hair, scruffy beard, dark eyes locked on hers…in that moment she felt the cracks in her heart healing, like maybe here was the one person she could trust to stand with her.

She couldn't look away from the raw emotion in his gaze. His voice was gruff when he said, "I love you, Em. If you'll have me, I'm yours, heart and soul."

The words flooded through her like light, making everything around her suddenly brighter.

The fear she'd been holding on to didn't stand a chance against the onslaught that was Shane.

She cupped his jaw, the stubble of his whiskers making a crinkling sound as she traced his bottom lip with an unsteady forefinger.

"I wasn't expecting this." She cleared her tight throat. "I wasn't expecting *you*. But I'm exceptionally glad you crashed into my table." With a deep breath she took the greatest risk of all. "I love you, Shane. I'm yours, forever."

A grin split his face before he lowered his head.

Their lips met and she felt like the future was opening before them. The moment spun out and Shane's warm hands began stroking her rib cage and over the swell of her hips. The golden heat sparking in his eyes told her he was ready for round two.

Then his phone chimed with a text.

"Dammit. Who's texting at eight in the morning? Hold that thought, darlin'." He reached for his phone and read the text. "Damn. I gotta get up."

***

Emery yawned as the door from the mudroom opened and once again the kitchen filled with the people who were now her friends and family. She wouldn't've minded a nap after the mind-blowing morning nookie, but that wasn't to be.

Mid-morning Sunday and everyone—minus Harding and Gage—were back in the kitchen. The text interrupting potential round two had been from Harding, who liked nothing better than riding horseback in the early morning hours.

He'd discovered a section of fence down on the northernmost boundary of the ranch. Shane suspected Bastard was responsible, and thirty head of cattle were, according to Harding, headin' for the high country.

Harding and Gage were out looking for the herd, and Shane called Walker and Sawyer for help getting them rounded up and back on Lone Pine property.

Delaney arrived with Walker, declaring wryly the womenfolk would hang out at the ranch house while the cowboys did their thing. "I'd go with you, but I'm not the best on horseback so I wouldn't be much help."

The outer door slammed and seconds later, Sawyer shoved through the kitchen door ahead of a pissed-off Cam.

"I was *fine,* Lieutenant. I have work to do and you're keeping me from doing it."

Wearing a dark Stetson low over his eyes, a denim work shirt and jeans, and a holstered pistol low on one hip, Sawyer looked almost as cowboy hot as Shane. Almost.

A muscle in Sawyer's jaw twitched as he crossed his arms over his chest. Emery thought maybe to keep from strangling Cam.

"Look, you're not staying at the farm by yourself when it's closed and everyone else is gone.

"Yesterday, Emery positively identified Dicarlo, and he's disappeared. Vance Norris has dropped out of sight too. I don't trust either one of them, so no way in hell am I letting you stay alone. Plus, you work too hard."

Emery wouldn't be surprised if steam came out of Cam's ears.

Sawyer held up a hand like he already knew he'd said too much.

Cam leaned toward him. "You're not the boss of me so you don't *let* me do anything. I would've been *fine* alone. I like being alone. And how hard I work has nothing to do with you."

"What's so bad about spending time with Emery and Delaney?"

An expression Emery couldn't decipher crossed Cam's face. "Nothing, and you're deflecting, Lieutenant. You practically kidnapped me."

"You're exaggerating. If you'd been reasonable, I wouldn't have had to *almost* kidnap you. Not that I did. And why do you call me lieutenant all the time? I don't think you've ever called me by my name. It's irritating."

"Because you're always acting like a cop, *Lieutenant.*"

Sawyer reached out both hands and Emery thought he'd reached the upper level of his bullshit meter. She wasn't sure what he'd do to Cam—shake some sense into her or kiss her senseless.

The space between them crackled with tension and Emery held her breath until Shane growled, "Kids, can we stop bickering? We've got a job to do."

Sawyer breathed deep and took a step away from Cam, fisting his hands and dropping them to his side.

"Aw," Delaney said, "don't make them stop. I like watching. It's more entertaining than reality TV." Grinning, she turned to Shane. "But on to the matter at hand. How can we help?"

"Gage and Harding are already out there. Walker and Sawyer will ride with me, and that's as many horses as I have. We need to round up the cattle before they wander into some of the canyons. There are steep drop-offs and other dangers, and I don't want animals hurt."

They all trooped out to the front porch. The horses were saddled and lined up at a rail. The rifle hanging in a scabbard from Birdie's saddle brought Emery up short. Shane stopped beside her, his hand running down her arm before giving her fingers a squeeze.

"You're taking a rifle?"

He nodded, his gaze steady. "Yeah. There's no telling when or where Dicarlo or Norris will show up."

"Be careful, cowboy."

"I'm always careful." He gave her a crooked grin and she remembered when she'd told him the exact same thing.

He strode with the other men to the horses. She felt like Marion in the movie *Shane,* watching the man she secretly loved riding into danger. She continued watching until they'd ridden out of sight. Bruno whined like he wanted to follow, but being a good boy, he stayed with Bud.

Emery had some thinking to do. Biggest, hugest, and most important was her relationship with Shane. He loved her. He *loved* her. The thrill from when he'd first spoken the words hadn't faded, and she hugged the knowledge close, wrapping it around her heart like a warm blanket.

Her other reality was she was currently unemployed. If the suspicions of the group were correct and Dicarlo was working for Vance, then Vance was implicated in Gerald's murder.

Even if it turned out they were wrong and Vance wasn't involved, she didn't see how she could ever trust him, much less return to work for the Norris Group.

She was keeping her fingers crossed the application she'd sent in for the county planning department would at least land her an interview. It was a start, but she needed to seriously ramp up her job search efforts.

Opening the door for Bruno and Bud, she followed Delaney and Cam into the house.

A half hour later the three women were in the kitchen. Anytime she could hang out with her sister was a win, but Emery also liked Cam and thought they could become friends.

Delaney had decided the men should be rewarded for their cowboy work with pie, and after much discussion, they'd decided on lemon meringue and pumpkin.

Delaney and Emery assembled ingredients while filling Cam in on the events of the past few days.

"Motive for *what*? That's what I don't get." Cam paused, pastry knife in hand, her brows bunching over gorgeous blue-green eyes. Emery envied Cam's easy skill making the pie dough without even looking at a recipe.

"For what's been happening to Emery," Delaney took a bowl of eggs from the fridge and set them on the counter. "Sawyer thinks the guy who tried to push Emery's car over the cliff, and then stole her phone, was the same guy who broke into her apartment and stole her computer."

"The working theory," Emery took up the narrative, "is that Frank Dicarlo still works for Vance, and Dicarlo reported to him that he'd seen me playing the frog video. Which, in retrospect, was stupid for me to do in a crowded bar.

"We figure he told Vance, to whom I'd already expressed concern about the North Bench development impacting possible frog habitat, who then hires the Dale guy who rams my car."

"That doesn't explain pushing your car off the road. Wouldn't mugging you in the parking lot have been easier?" Cam glanced at Emery. "Not that I'd want you to be mugged in the parking lot."

"I'd wondered about that too. Maybe there was a greater risk of witnesses in town. I don't know."

"Sawyer thinks the goal was to get Em's phone and the recording before she could send it to anyone. Stealing her computer from her apartment could've been redundancy in case she'd sent the video to herself." Delaney shook her head. "If that's true, we're dealing with criminals who aren't up to date on technology."

"And who are also willing to kill to keep their schemes going," Cam added. "I wonder what Gerald was being asked to do. From what you said, he seems like a yes-man and not the kind of guy to stand up to whoever he was indebted to, so whatever it was must have been bad."

"Or it had too much risk for him." Emery shrugged. "I'm not saying he had a finely honed moral compass, but I think doing something overtly illegal would've been difficult for him from the perspective of self-preservation more than anything else."

Cam glanced at Emery. "All this has been awful for you. I hope it doesn't make you feel Sisters is too dangerous a place to live. That is, if you're planning to relocate here."

"Me too." Delaney gave Emery a side hug. "There are two dead guys out there. We want you to stay safe." Then she grinned. "I think Shane would be heartbroken if you left now. But enough of that. Let's set the nastiness aside for a while and focus on pie."

"I can go out to the chicken coop to collect eggs for the meringue," Emery volunteered.

"Eggs that are at least a few days old are better for meringue, but fresh eggs will be great for the pumpkin filling," Cam told her.

Retrieving the basket used for eggs from the pantry, Emery headed outside.

The previous day's storm had blown through, and now the sun shined brightly in a deep blue sky forming the perfect backdrop to the dramatic Payback Mountain.

She crossed the yard to the chicken coop. She'd brought watermelon rinds Harding had set aside for the hens. Inside the enclosure she latched the gate, and with the hens busy with their treat, she went around to the back of the coop. She lifted the door and hooked it open, and bit her lip when a fluffy red hen occupying one of the nests turned to give her the side eye. She gathered the eggs from the other nests, then stood contemplating the hen.

"Do you have eggs in that nest? Am I supposed to get them?" Emery thought the side eye meant *Try me.* Since she had enough eggs in her basket, Emery told the hen, "You can keep your eggs, friend, because I'm not fighting you for them. I'll close the door to give you privacy."

Loud cackling erupted from the chickens at the front of the coop. Emery circled back to their yard to find the hens agitated, flapping their wings and running around the enclosure. "What's got you girls so upset?"

Not surprised when they didn't answer, she exited the enclosure, latching the gate behind her, the basket of eggs clutched in her hand. From the house she could hear Bruno barking. She stood motionless, scanning her surroundings. The barn door, left slightly ajar, creaked as it opened slowly as if pushed by a breeze.

Except there was no breeze.

Alarm had the hairs at the back of her neck standing on end. Not questioning her instincts, she broke into a run. But her hesitation cost her. He was out the door in a flash, moving fast for such a big man. She caught a brief glimpse of a face distinguishable by the poorly aligned nose.

Instinctively she swung the basket. Hulk caught it and sent the eggs flying. The hens set up a din of squawking. Emery got about three steps before the grip on the back of her sweatshirt had her stumbling to her knees. A rough hand clamped over her mouth and nose.

Hulk swore as she bit down on a finger. Hard. "Fucking bitch. You'll pay for that."

Emery was a tall woman, but Hulk was huge. In seconds he had a knee in her back, holding her down as he wrenched back her arms.

Face in the dirt, she gave a muffled cry when he tore off the splint and tightened what felt like a zip tie around her wrists. On his feet, he picked her up and slung her over his shoulder like she weighed nothing.

She gasped, struggling to get the breath to scream. She jerked her body and kicked, but he kept his grip tight and carried her behind the barn.

Fighting the paralysis of terror, her breath coming in panicky gasps, Emery kicked again, aiming for his balls. But hanging over his shoulder and with his arm clamped around her knees, she couldn't get leverage.

"Fuck," Hulk growled. "Where are the keys?" He dumped her unceremoniously onto the back bed of the Gator, the side of her face scraping against the rough floor. Hulk searched under the seats and in the storage bin.

She tried to get her legs over the side of the Gator. Then he grabbed her by her hair, shoving his face close to hers. "Where are the fucking keys?"

She wanted to snarl that she wouldn't tell him even if she knew, but thought she was in too vulnerable a position to risk provoking him. "I don't know."

He swore again, then seemed to come to a decision. Hauling her up over his shoulder again, he took off running down the dirt road. Emery could only hope the women in the ranch house realized she'd been taken.

CHAPTER TWENTY-TWO

Shane

Shane urged Birdie faster. They'd finally reached the ranch road and the mare was able to fly on the hardpacked dirt. A diversion. The break in the fence had been a fucking diversion. Yeah, Bastard had probably been the first of the cattle through the gap, but finding size fourteen footprints in the dirt and barbed wire severed clean by wire cutters told the real story.

Gage had figured it out, but cell phone coverage being spotty in the hills, he hadn't been able to get word to Shane.

He'd met Gage riding breakneck down a rough trail with the news the break in the fence was man-made. Now they were racing back, the sound of horse hooves like thunder behind him. Shane had been duped and they'd left the women defenseless.

The ranch house came into view, his gaze drawn to the front door left wide open. He pulled Birdie to a stop and he was off the horse and across the porch, rifle in his grip, before the others had brought their mounts to a stop behind him.

"Shane, wait."

He ignored Sawyer's command and strode through the doorway. The dining room, the kitchen, the back rooms, all were empty. Bowls, measuring spoons, cans of evaporated milk on the counter told him the women had been cooking something.

A whimpering sound came from the pantry. Walker came in, Sawyer behind him, and strode to the pantry to fling open the door. Bud scampered out, wagging his stubby tail. Walker scooped him into his arms.

"Why the hell was he locked in the pantry?"

Shane could hardly think past the voice in his head urging him to find Emery before something terrible happened to her.

"Delaney would've put him in there to keep him safe. The women aren't here." The same fear grabbing Shane by the throat echoed in Walker's voice.

He had his phone in his hand, swiping to find Emery's number, when Sawyer came down the stairs. "Upstairs is clear." He held up a phone in his hand. "This your woman's phone?"

Shane nodded and jammed his phone back in his pocket in frustration. "What about Cam? Can you call her?"

Sawyer was already shaking his head. "She doesn't own a phone."

Shane didn't have time to wonder why a young woman in the twenty-first century didn't own a phone. Walker put his phone to his ear and immediately a ringing sounded from Delaney's purse on the kitchen counter. He swore ripely and disconnected. "None of them have phones on them. I guess we do this old school."

Gage stood in the open doorway, sidearm holstered at his belt. "There are signs of a scuffle over the chicken coop. And this." He held up the splint that thirty minutes ago had been wrapped around Emery's wrist. "Looks like Emery was grabbed there. There are broken eggs on the ground."

They moved out of the house, Sawyer snapping out orders over the phone as he called for backup.

Harding had arrived and dismounted.

Near the barn, shattered eggshells and dirty yolks littered the dirt. What felt like an iron fist had Shane's heart in a vise, twisting it in his chest.

Gage joined him. "Big boot prints in the dirt. They match the ones up where the fence was cut and those we found by the reservoir." He pointed. "See here and here? Not so deep. But here? The prints are deeper."

"You're saying he was a big guy we all know is Dicarlo, and he was carrying something heavy, like a person."

"Yeah, that's what I'm saying."

Shane tried to think past the fear and seething anger to formulate a plan.

Walker crossed the yard to his truck, returning a moment later with his holster strapped onto his belt.

"Bruno found them."

Shane jerked his head to where Harding held the reins of three of the horses.

"What are you talking about?"

"Take a breath and listen, boy."

At first he didn't hear a thing. He had to make an effort to calm his inner voice urging him to move, to do *something* to find Emery and the other women. He cocked his head and focused.

Then he heard it, faint, but there. Bruno's raising hell bark that meant he was pissed about something. Shane turned to the other men.

"Dicarlo's grabbed Emery. She can ID him and he wants to get rid of his witness. Our best hope is if Delaney and Cam saw him and gave chase and took Bruno with them."

"That's solid," Gage said.

Bruno had quieted, worrying Shane. He addressed Sawyer and Walker. "Barking was coming from over by Rock Creek. You know the ranch road that goes along the creek and through the meadow?" At Sawyer's nod he went on. "You and Walker circle around to Mill Creek Road and take the ranch road from the south. Gage and I will come from this direction. If we're lucky and that's the route he took, we can trap the fucker in the middle. There's no place to go from there except off road, and he'd have to have a four-wheel drive for that."

"We're all armed," Sawyer warned. "Any one of you fire your weapon, you better know what you're shooting at and hit it. I don't want one of us caught in the cross fire."

Shane gave a curt nod. "We need to move. *Now*."

He faced Harding, who lifted his chin in a *get going* gesture. "I'm already ahead of you. I'll stable the horses and stay in case they come back. You go on now and find those women. None of you will be any good without them."

Shane drove as fast as he dared, his truck bouncing over ruts and dips in the road.

"You holding it together?"

He spared Gage a glance. "Yeah."

"Good. We end up in a hostage situation, you let me take lead. You can't go in guns blazing."

Shane was a damn good shot with a rifle, but Gage had FBI training behind him. "Got it."

The road crested a ridge, and from the elevation he could see across the meadow. A plume of dust rose from the area of Rock Creek. Sawyer and Gage were closing in.

Shane braced himself for the battle ahead.

The truck sped through a shadowy stand of pines then broke into blinding sunlight. He blinked and pulled down the visor.

The meadow stretched in front of him, serenely beautiful like there wasn't a fucking murderer threatening the woman he loved.

Across the meadow he caught the glint of the sun off the windshield of a dusty gray car parked in the shadows of tall pines lining Rock Creek. Not wanting to hit the women or the dog, he was forced to slow down. They reached the far side of the meadow.

"Holy shit. There they are."

The disbelief in Gage's voice was mirrored by Shane's distrust of what his eyes were telling him.

He slowed, then brought the truck to a stop.

Coming from the opposite direction, Walker's truck skidded to a stop behind the gray sedan, dust rising into the air. The four men stepped from their vehicles to survey the scene Shane was still having a hard time processing.

Walker's voice carried over Bruno's furious snarling. "What the fucking hell?"

Shane gave a disbelieving laugh. Frank Dicarlo lay face down in the grass bordering the road. His jeans were torn, and blood saturated the shirt he wore and was seeping into the ground. His arms were bound behind his back with what looked like shoelaces.

The three women were *sitting* on him, Delaney squarely in the middle of his shoulders, Cam on his butt, and Emery on his legs near his feet, cradling her injured wrist against her stomach.

Bruno was crouched, nose inches from Dicarlo's, his lips curled as a menacing growl emanated from his throat.

"Thank god you're here."

The tension in Emery's voice, and an abrasion on her cheek, had fury all but blinding him.

Shane grabbed on to some control before he lost it and did something illegal.

"Hey," Dicarlo wheezed. "I'm bleeding out. I need medical aid. Call off this fucking dog before it bites my face."

"Shut the hell up, asshole. Gage, you want to take custody of Dicarlo before I beat the shit out of him?"

"Got it."

Shane grasped Emery's uninjured arm and helped her to her feet. His arms went around her. A deep breath helped bring his ragged emotions under control.

He spoke into her ear. "You want to tell me what happened?"

"Yeah," she said. "I will. But can you hold me a little longer?"

He gave a short laugh in relief. "Sure. Fair warning, though. I might never let you go."

***

Emery

Emery pressed the uninjured side of her face to Shane's chest. Strong, solid, safe—he was her anchor. The knit shirt he wore felt soft against her skin. His arms wrapped around her, and she felt her muscles loosen as tension drained from her battered body. She breathed him in on a shaky breath, letting go of some of her fear on the exhale.

Cam and Delaney were safe. She was safe.

They were going to be okay.

She watched Walker lift Delaney to stand in front of him. Her sneakers, sans shoelaces, loose on her feet. Walker cupped her face as he rested his forehead against hers. Eyes closed, they held each other.

"You want to give me that knife, Cam?"

Cam rose to her feet next to the immobilized Dicarlo.

Sawyer had one hand on her shoulder, the other resting over Cam's rigid fingers gripping a long kitchen knife smeared with blood.

She stared at it like she didn't know how it came to be in her hand.

"You're safe now," Sawyer murmured.

Her pale face contrasted with the vivid aqua of her eyes, which were locked on his. "I stabbed him."

"I know, sweetheart. It's going to be okay."

She dropped the knife like it suddenly burned her to hold it. Then she reached for Sawyer, her arms going around his shoulders as she buried her face in his neck, her eyes screwed shut.

Without hesitation he pulled her close and turned the side of his face to press against hers. He murmured something Emery couldn't hear, his hold on Cam so tight she thought their bodies might fuse together.

Several long minutes later, Cam let out a shuddering breath and opened her eyes again. Looking like she was steeling herself for a herculean task, she loosened her grip on Sawyer. "Sorry," she muttered.

To Emery it seemed like she was rebuilding her defenses one shield at a time. With a frown of obvious reluctance, Sawyer let her go.

A siren wailed, the sound drawing ever nearer, and a plume of dust foretold the arrival of emergency vehicles.

Still facedown where they'd left him, Dicarlo sneezed, then howled in pain as he sneezed again. Ahhh, too bad. Sneezing must make stab wounds hurt.

"Get me out of this grass, assholes. I'm allergic. And I need first aid before I bleed to death."

Gage tested the security of the binding Delaney had tied around Dicarlo's wrists, then knelt beside him to read him his Miranda rights.

Dicarlo sneezed again. "I don't fucking care about that. Get me out of the fucking grass. I'm gonna pass out."

"Nah, dude. I think we're good." Gage retrieved the knife and laid it on the hood of Shane's truck. He scanned the women. "Backup will be here in a minute and we'll be swarmed. One of you want to give us a quick rundown on what happened?"

With her hand still grasped in Shane's, and feeling steadier, Emery spoke. "Dicarlo was hiding in the barn. He grabbed me when I came out of the chicken yard. I'd like to say I put up a good fight, but he overpowered me pretty quickly."

That rankled.

"He put me in the back of the Gator and kept asking where the keys were. He was pissed when I told him I didn't know.

"I guess carrying me was Plan B 'cause that's what he did. He slung me over his shoulder and took off running. I was trying to kick, scream, anything I could do to upset his balance or slow him down, but I couldn't get leverage.

"He pulled off the splint and tied my hands behind my back. I was hanging upside down over his shoulder. I couldn't even get the breath to yell."

Bruno had given up snarling at Dicarlo and came to rub against her leg.

"We'd come down the road and just gotten through the trees to the meadow when Bruno caught up with us." She let go of Shane's hand to scrub the dog's face and drop a kiss on his nose. "This guy is a hero."

Delaney took up the narrative. "Bruno started barking and I looked out the window to see what was up. I thought Emery was behind the chicken coop collecting eggs, but then I noticed the basket on the ground. I knew something bad had happened to her so I got Cam.

"It was a group effort. I let Bruno out and he was off like a shot, racing down the road. Cam grabbed a knife and then *she* was off like a shot. I shut Bud in the pantry and ran after them." Delaney eyed her friend. "You run fast."

"I ran cross-country and distance on the track team in high school." Cam shrugged. "I guess I still got it."

"I'd say," Emery stated. "Bruno caught up to us. He latched on to Dicarlo's pants and wouldn't let go. I think it was hard to fight off a dog at the same time he was holding me. It slowed him down, and then all of a sudden Cam was there. She's badass. She stabbed Dicarlo." Emery shook her head in admiration. "Thank you."

Cam's throat worked as she swallowed, her face still devoid of color.

"I didn't know what else to do. I could see the car up ahead and thought if he got you in a car, we'd be sunk. I'd grabbed the knife so I…just…stabbed him."

Her voice wavered and she gulped in a breath.

"Then Delaney was there and we both kind of tackled him." She faced Sawyer, a resigned expression on her face. "Will you have to arrest me?"

She clenched her hands into fists.

Emery guessed to keep them from shaking.

Sawyer gave a snort. "Hell no. The sheriff might want to give you and Bruno medals for heroism, though."

Cam shook her head. "No, no, no. No medals. I don't want the attention."

Sawyer narrowed his gaze, but any argument was forestalled by the arrival of three sheriff's department cruisers and an ambulance.

CHAPTER TWENTY-THREE
Shane

Shane was beat. Neighbors had helped round up the cattle, and he'd spent the last hours of daylight repairing the fence. That was after two sheriff's deputies had photographed the cut wire and taken impressions of the footprints. As much as he hated it, he'd had to trust Sawyer and Gage to take care of Emery while he'd dealt with the fence. Then he'd gone to the sheriff's office to give his statement and bring Emery home.

When Shane followed Emery into the ranch house, it felt like a lifetime had passed since they'd spent an amazing half hour that morning tangled up with each other in bed.

He shut the door behind them.

It seemed like a repeat of Thursday night when they'd come back to the ranch after Gerald's murder.

And the time she'd been discharged from the hospital after her car had been forced through the guardrail.

He turned the lock on the door and pulled her into his embrace, backing her against the door. Her wrist was back in a splint, the scrape on her cheek had been cleaned, but hadn't needed a bandage.

Too many close calls.

He was done.

"That's it."

"What's it?" she murmured, her face buried in the crook of his neck, where she'd be putting it for the next fifty years or more if he had anything to say about it.

"You're marrying me."

"What?" The shock in her voice might not be a good sign.

Okay, so he needed to be convincing.

He'd been on edge ever since discovering her missing that morning, and he was done with her being vulnerable.

"You're marrying me. That's the only way I can keep you safe. You're moving to the ranch and I'm putting security cameras everywhere."

A hard poke in the ribs had him hissing out a breath. "What was that for?"

"Back up, cowboy."

"I don't want to back up. I like being with you like this."

Another hard poke accompanied by a push forced him back a step. "Ow." He rubbed a hand over his ribs.

"I'm not marrying you."

"Why the hell not? I love you and you love me. We'll get married."

"That's not how this works." Blue eyes fringed by dark lashes skewered him. "You can't order me to marry you to protect me."

"Us not being married obviously isn't working to keep you safe so we're changing the playbook."

This wasn't going the way he'd thought it would go.

Somewhere in the back of his mind he'd imagined her being thrilled, maybe kissing him like crazy as she accepted his proposal.

He felt a stab of panic that maybe he'd blown it.

He was even more convinced of that when her expression shifted from pissed to hurt.

She muttered something that sounded suspiciously like *jerk,* and he was pretty sure her checking him with her shoulder as she sailed past with her jaw set hadn't been an accident.

A minute later a door slammed upstairs, and he'd bet the ranch it wasn't his bedroom door.

He climbed the stairs.

Yep, she was in the guest room.

He scrubbed a hand over his face. It felt like every emotion he possessed had been wrung out of him, and he'd fucked up royally and wasn't even sure how.

***

The day had been a study in frustration. Somewhere around midnight, when he'd been lying awake staring into the dark, he had an epiphany.

Yeah, he'd screwed up.

She'd said he couldn't order her to marry him so he could protect her.

He still thought the argument was valid, but he'd played it safe and taken the easy way out by not laying it out for her.

It wasn't enough to admit he loved her. That was huge and he'd done it, but she needed more.

If he wanted her to marry him, he needed to make their marriage about love, not protection or obligation.

He'd shied away from opening himself to women because he'd learned love ultimately led to hurt.

But now, he had to take the risk or he wouldn't get what he wanted more than anything: her.

Emery not being in his life wasn't an option.

To change her mind, he'd have to lay his heart bare. And ask, not order. That might get him the result he wanted.

Somehow, he'd slept, and had risen early to take care of feeding the livestock with the plan he'd return to the house as soon as possible so he could make his case.

That plan had been shot to hell when he'd come back to find vehicles missing from the parking area and a quiet house.

A note from Harding said he was going into town because Martha Watkins had promised him pancakes. Harding's note also stated Emery had gone to visit Delaney at the farm and wouldn't be back for several hours.

Dammit. Restless, Shane forced himself to sit in his office and deal with paperwork.

It was well after noon when hunger had him searching the refrigerator for something for lunch. With a scrabbling of nails on the hardwood floor, Bruno raced to the front door, barking his head off. Seconds later the doorbell chimed.

He opened the door to a middle-aged couple. A clue to their identity came from the teenage boys with identical smiles and bright blond hair.

The woman, who held herself with the same poise as Emery, wearing a dress of vivid greens and blues, gave him a big smile. "Hello, Shane. I'm Delilah. We're Emery's family."

"Yeah, we're her brothers," the less wild-looking of the two boys said. "We want to make sure she's all right. Where is she?"

"Dude, you have horses. Can you teach us to ride? And can we drive your Gator?" his twin asked.

The thin man with dark blond hair tied back in a ponytail, Dustin, Shane assumed, said, "Rowan, save it. We're talking to Emery first."

"Sure, but *after* maybe we could do something cool."

The sound of tires crunching on gravel had the people crowded onto his porch pivoting. Emery got out of the car and there was a loud whoop. He didn't know if it came from Emery or one of the boys already racing across the yard. But an instant later Emery was engulfed by the towheaded boys and then her parents.

The afternoon was spent with the unexpected visitors and Shane didn't think Emery had spoken more than a dozen words directly to him.

He didn't know if that was because she was pissed at him or she was engaged with her family.

Rowan and Griffin peppered him with questions about the ranch and requests to ride horses until he took them out on the calmest of his mounts.

Harding had returned and been pleased he had a crowd to feed. He'd figured out his guests were vegetarian so they were all sitting around the table eating a spinach lasagna that was surprisingly good.

"What are your intentions toward my daughter, cowboy?"

Shane paused, fork midair.

"*Mom*."

Delilah raised her brows at her daughter's warning tone. "How else am I to know if he plans to marry you? You don't tell me anything."

Emery's cheeks reddened and she gave a strangled sound that had the brother seated next to her, he was pretty sure it was Griffin, thumping her back.

This was her family. He got it. They cared about her.

When he and Emery got married, they'd be his family too. Best to start out right and be up-front with them. "I intend to marry her, if she'll have me. I asked her last night, but she turned me down."

"Awesome," Rowan crowed. "Say yes, Em. We'll get to visit and ride horses."

Griffin gave him a narrow-eyed look. "You have to treat her right. You can't be an asshole."

"Griffin, I'll smother you in your sleep if you say another word." Emery's cheeks were bright tomato red.

"Griff's right, Em." Dustin might have been talking to Emery, but his gaze was locked on Shane. "Dude can't be an asshole."

Since there was no way to argue the point, he gave a brief nod. "Understood."

Emery huffed out a breath and turned to him, giving him her full attention for what felt like the first time all day. "You didn't ask me to marry you, you told me I was marrying you. No, you *ordered* me to marry you."

"Oh man, you messed up. You gotta have game," Rowan lectured. "I *asked* Liliana to go with me to the Homecoming dance, I didn't tell her. I made a big sign and got her flowers. Even I know better."

Harding gave a cackling laugh and Shane wanted to kick him under the table.

"Even if you make a sign and ask, she doesn't have to say yes if she doesn't want to," Griffin pressed.

"No, she doesn't, but I'm hoping she will. I'll ask right the next time."

"Oh, will you." Emery's voice was cool enough to give him frostbite.

"Yeah, I will."

Not that he had a chance to do that, because nothing went the way he wanted.

He could hardly get her alone, what with her family spending the night.

She'd given up the room next to his to Delilah and Dustin.

The twins slept in the third upstairs bedroom.

He thought that would work out well because Emery could sleep with him, but she'd opted for the couch.

Okay, he got that.

They weren't married—yet—so she didn't want to share his bed with her family around.

They'd stayed up late after the boys went to bed, the four adults talking.

Delilah had asked pointed questions about ranching, and he'd explained the program he was working on with UC Davis to lessen the environmental impact of cattle ranching.

All very well and good, but he wanted time alone with Emery.

He thought he had his chance the next morning after feeding the livestock. The house was still quiet when he returned. He found her sitting up on the couch where she'd slept, phone in her hand, the blankets she'd used neatly folded.

"Hey." He leaned over to kiss her, gratified when she didn't hesitate to respond. He'd meant to keep it brief, but couldn't pull back.

His arms were braced on the back of the couch as he leaned forward. Her hand went to the back of his head as the kiss deepened. Her mouth tasted of minty toothpaste.

She gave a little hum in the back of her throat that told him she wanted this as much as he did.

God, he'd missed having her close.

He was breathing heavily when he finally straightened. "You still mad at me?"

"No, not really."

"Good."

She gave a surprised yelp when he scooped her up in his arms and settled on the couch with her on his lap.

"Oh yeah, baby."

She straddled his hips and dove into another kiss that had him rock-hard and wanting more.

But first things first.

He broke the kiss with a last bite to her lower lip, then cupped her shoulders to hold her in place when she leaned forward like she wanted his mouth again.

"Em, I'm sorry. I screwed up the other night."

She gave a heavy sigh. "Yeah, you did. You told me I had to marry you because you were frustrated and wanted to keep me safe."

"I should've done better." He grasped her hands in his. "I love—"

A door opening and footsteps overhead had her leaping off his lap like a startled gazelle.

He swore under his breath.

Seconds later Griffin and Rowan were trooping down the stairs and that was that.

Shane liked Emery's family. He truly did. And he got why they'd shown up at the ranch.

Emery's life had been in almost constant danger, and they wanted to make sure she was okay.

But he wasn't unhappy when Delilah announced they needed to get back to Santa Cruz. The boys had been off school for quarter break and teachers' professional development, and classes were set to resume the next day.

Maybe now he'd have a chance to really talk with Emery without being interrupted.

Dustin was arranging duffel bags in the older-model van they'd arrived in when Emery, who'd gotten a notification on her phone, let out a squeal.

"I got an interview."

Delilah also let out a squeal. "For the county position you applied for?"

Shane felt left out of the loop. "What county and what position?"

"El Dorado with the planning department."

"That's so exciting, Em." Delilah gave her daughter a hug. "When's the interview?"

Finger scrolling as she read, Emery said, "Day after tomorrow." She looked up at Shane. "I need to go to my apartment and make sure I have clothes to wear to an interview."

"You've got clothes here."

"Yeah, but not the *right* clothes."

***

Emery

Emery parked her car next to Shane's truck in front of the garage. It amazed her how fast Lone Pine Ranch had begun to feel like home, and how much the apartment in Sacramento no longer felt like her place. She still didn't know what would happen between her and Shane, but he'd asked her to come back to the ranch after her interview with the county so here she was.

In the few days since Frank Dicarlo had been arrested—the word was he was looking for a plea deal—her life had been a whirlwind.

After her family's unexpected visit, she'd gone to Sacramento, where she'd managed to get her hair trimmed, put together what she'd wear to the interview, got her mail with the insurance check in it, and made the internet negotiations to purchase a car.

She'd driven back to Sisters in a sporty hybrid she hoped would last a couple hundred thousand miles.

She stepped out of the car, inhaling the mountain air tinged with the chill of early autumn. The setting sun cast long shadows behind the pine trees as the sky purpled in the west. The thunder of horse's hooves had her looking up and the next minute Shane was there, dismounting from Birdie's back.

Hat low on his forehead, his plaid shirtsleeves rolled up to reveal his sinewy forearms, and his long legs encased in denim were all great viewing, but the smile that lit his eyes when he saw her made her heart trip in her chest.

"Hey, cowboy."

He kept moving until she was backed against the car and his lips were on hers. When he shifted to nibble along her jaw and then nuzzle the soft skin under her ear, all she could manage to say was a shaky, "Wow."

"Missed you."

"I like the way you show it."

He stepped back but kept his hands on hers. "How'd the interview go?"

"Well, I think. The panel seemed impressed with my education and job experience. I was honest with them about why I won't get a recommendation from Northwood."

"They said they're interviewing four candidates. I hope they offer me the position, but until that happens, I need to continue looking." She shrugged, then laughed. "I'm trying to play it cool, but I really want this position and hope, hope, hope they like me. I now know what that expression of waiting on pins and needles feels like."

"They'd be foolish not to offer you the job. When will you know?"

"They said by early next week. By that time, I'll have gained ten pounds from stress eating."

"Then there'll be more of you to love. Listen, darlin', I need fifteen minutes to take care of Birdie, but then will you sit out on the porch with me?"

"Of course."

If she hadn't already fallen for him, that comment about more to love would've pushed her over the edge.

She was on the curvy side and it truly didn't matter to him.

She knew he wanted to marry her, and despite his boneheaded proposal earlier, she wanted to marry him.

But from the first time they'd met, he'd felt a sense of obligation toward her and marrying her for protection wasn't a good foundation for a successful marriage.

He'd said he loved her, but she wondered if that meant the same to him as it did to her.

He admired her car, carried her suitcase into the house and up the stairs, then was out the door again. She watched from the guest room window as he grabbed Birdie's reins to lead her to the barn.

He hadn't assumed they were sharing a bedroom and she didn't know how to feel about that.

She took a few minutes to change into leggings and a sweatshirt, then jammed her feet into shearling-lined boots before stepping out onto the porch again.

Crows flew across the darkening sky, and she figured they were looking for a place to roost for the night.

Shane's boots thudded on the treads as he came up the steps. He set his hat on a low table and joined her on the loveseat, taking her hand as he sat.

She brought up her knees and turned toward him.

The fading light brought a warm glow to his skin. He opened his mouth to speak, then closed it with a curse as a vehicle pulled into the yard.

The white SUV had El Dorado Sheriff's Department markings and she wasn't surprised to see Sawyer behind the wheel. Bruno gave a happy bark of greeting as Sawyer came up the steps to join them.

Shane's frustrated sigh had Emery grinning.

Sawyer raised a brow at Emery. "Heard you had an interview with the planning department today."

"How did you hear about that? *What* did you hear about that?"

"I don't want to get your hopes up."

"Tell me what you know, mister, before I hurt you."

He gave a bark of laughter. "I wouldn't want that on your conscience." His expression sobered. "This is on the down low, but word is you nailed the interview."

"Really? Did someone really say that?"

"Yeah, one of the panel members said it. They have one more interview tomorrow, but you're a strong contender."

Shane squeezed her hand and said, "But that's not why you came by."

"No, it's not. I wanted to confirm Dicarlo's trying to get a plea deal. He's spilling his guts about Vance Norris to avoid a life sentence."

"What's he got on Norris?" Shane asked.

"For one, that Gerald Slater had gambling debts he wasn't able to pay. We verified the guy played poker on an underground circuit and was in debt to the wrong people. Norris paid off those debts, which meant he had Slater by the balls."

"So Slater owed him and Norris sent Dicarlo to collect the debt," Shane surmised.

"Wow." Emery felt a chill snake down her spine that had nothing to do with the cool of the evening. "I wonder what Vance wanted Gerald to do."

"Poison Rock Creek and the Lone Pine reservoir."

Shane went still. "You're shittin' me."

"I'm not. Norris gave Dicarlo a list of chemicals he was supposed to buy to put together a cocktail to kill the frogs and kill your cattle. Dicarlo refused to do the job. Something about him not liking nature and allergies. Norris figured since Slater owed him, he'd make him do the deed. Two birds, one stone. There'd be no endangered frogs to get in the way of development, and with your herd dead and the water supply fouled, Norris figured he could get the ranch for a song."

"What's the second thing?" Emery asked.

"Second thing is apparently Norris flipped out when he learned you had video evidence of the endangered frogs in Rock Creek. Not that he's an upstanding citizen, but if Dicarlo's telling the truth, and we'll need verification, Norris came up with the plan to steal your phone.

"Like Slater, Dale Benson owed a debt and he paid it by stealing the phone. Norris was hugely pissed that instead of a simple robbery, Benson nearly killed you. Norris figured if the police nabbed Benson, he'd point a figure at him."

"Sounds like a motive for Benson's murder," Shane commented.

"Dicarlo swears on his mother's grave he wasn't the one who bludgeoned the SOB to death." Sawyer gave a wry smile. "I did a little digging and learned Frank's mother is alive and living in a condo in Orange County so I'm not sure how much his oath is worth."

"What about Dicarlo kidnapping me?"

"He claims he was under orders from Norris, but I'm betting he figured out you were at the Northwood office and wanted to eliminate you as a witness."

"You arrest Norris?" Shane asked.

"Not yet. Warrant's been issued, but the fucker's disappeared." Sawyer paused. "He's as slippery as they come. Nothing's stuck to him before, but he's not skating out of this one."

The story sounded like the plot to a TV murder mystery Emery used to watch with her grandmother. "I can't believe Vance would go that far. But as bad as he is, killing Gerald was all on Hulk."

"Yeah, about that, Dicarlo is claiming self-defense. He says Slater attacked him. You'll be called to testify at the trial about what you heard." Sawyer rested his hand on his utility belt. "You two keep an eye out for Norris. DA thinks he's unstable and there's no telling how he'll react to his world falling apart. I won't rest easy until he's behind bars." He raised a hand in salute. "Talk to you later."

They both thanked Sawyer for coming by, then watched as the taillights of his cruiser disappeared down the dirt road.

Bruno settled himself next to the loveseat with a heavy sigh.

The screen door opened and Harding stepped out, crossing the porch to settle into a cushioned chair.

Shane shoved his fingers through his hair and Emery smiled.

She was kind of having fun watching Shane deal with the frustration.

CHAPTER TWENTY-FOUR
Emery

Emery walked on the boardwalk across the pools of light cast by rustic lampposts flanked by Delaney and Cam. Not many people were out this late in the evening on a weeknight. They were making their way to Easy Money where they were meeting Shane and Walker. She wouldn't be surprised if Walker convinced Sawyer to join them as well.

She nudged her sister with her hip. "Thanks for setting up the video chat with Clara this afternoon. It was nice talking with her."

"Clara isn't exactly warm and fuzzy with emotions," Delaney said. "But it's obvious she's happy you're here."

Their grandmother was due back from her world cruise within a few months and Emery couldn't wait to meet her in person.

"I think it's awesome you and Shane found each other," Cam stated.

Emery gave Cam the side eye. "What about you? I can't help noticing the sparkage between you and Sawyer."

"There's no sparkage," Cam denied.

Delaney choked out a laugh. "There's enough sparkage between you two to power a small city. You can't be that blind."

Cam shook her head. Emery frowned when she caught the hopeless expression on her friend's face. "No, no sparkage. There can't be."

Before Emery could ask why, Delaney gripped her arm.

A man stepped out from an alley and approached them on the boardwalk.

"Is that Vance?"

Where before his determinedly stylish clothing had always been impeccable, now he looked like he'd slept in his clothes.

His shoes were scuffed, his shirt wrinkled, and his sport coat had dirt on one shoulder. He pushed unkept hair from his forehead and the scruff on his jaw was days old.

"Emery, I wondered where you'd gotten to." His voice was overly loud in the still evening air. "I want you to join me for dinner. We have business to discuss."

Emery blinked. Vance Norris was a wanted man and was acting like nothing had changed since the first time they'd met.

"Ah, I no longer work for you," she said carefully. There was something off about him, like he was one foot to the left of reality.

She stepped back, pulling the other women with her like she was easing away from a ticking bomb.

An ugly expression crossed Vance's face. "I haven't accepted your resignation. I'm still your employer, I'm still in charge." His gaze took in the women flanking her, pausing on Delaney. He sneered. "You should pick better friends, Emery. Delaney here is nothing more than an ex-con's whore."

Before she could respond, he took a swift step forward and grabbed Emery's elbow. "Come with me and we'll discuss our business in private."

"Stay away from me." She backpedaled, wrenching her arm away. Cam latched on to her other arm like she would keep Emery from being kidnapped.

Delaney gave Vance a solid shove. "Take your hands off my sister or you'll find yourself on the ground with your balls in your throat. You remember what happened when you put your hands on me last summer, don't you, Vance?"

"Your sister?" Vance straightened his coat, his gaze traveling from Emery to Delaney, then back again. "I should've seen it," he sneered, anger lacing his tone. "You should've told me you were related, Emery. If I'd known, I would never have tapped you for this project. I might have to reconsider your employment with the Norris Group."

Before she could process the ridiculousness of his statement, he reached into a pocket of his sport coat. When he withdrew his hand, light gleamed dully on a gun. Emery sucked in a breath.

Beyond being delusional, Vance was dangerous.

He waved the gun at the women. "Emery and I are having a simple conversation. But I've brought a little incentive in case our conversation doesn't go the way I want it to go."

"Delaney, Cam, you should go on. This is between me and Vance." The last thing she wanted was for them to be in danger because of her.

"Not a chance," Cam muttered.

"We're not letting you go anywhere with him," Delaney confirmed.

Vance spoke directly to Emery. "You've done nothing but challenge me since our first meeting. I'll ignore your defiance for now. Feisty girls turn me on so we'll see if we can channel your *energy* into more satisfying avenues."

Emery swallowed against the bile rising in her throat as he continued.

"Norris Group supports positive relationships between key personnel. We want our best and brightest to develop personal relations that will benefit the company. Of course, those relationships can also be, ah, personally satisfying." He put the gun back in his pocket and beckoned her like she would simply follow along.

"Are you insane?" She knew her tone was incredulous. "A warrant's been issued for your arrest for setting your henchmen on me, and you think I'll go anywhere with you?" Only the gun in his pocket stopped her from delivering a swift kick in the balls.

"How's it going this evening, folks?"

She'd been so focused on Vance, Emery hadn't noticed Sawyer's approach. His easy question belied an underlying steel to his tone.

Shadows behind Vance formed into Shane and Walker, who approached Vance from behind.

"None of your business, McGrath," Vance snarled. "You're not in uniform and have no business interfering with me and my employee."

"Sawyer, he's got a gun in his right pocket," Cam spoke clearly.

That was all it took for the two men behind him to take action.

They rushed forward as Vance thrust his hand in his pocket. Walker was on him in an instant.

Grabbing him from behind, the big man threw Vance to the ground. Sawyer spread his arms to push the women back as Shane scooped up the gun from where it had skittered across the boardwalk.

Sawyer produced handcuffs and tossed them to Walker, who cinched them snugly around Vance's wrists.

The whole thing was over in under a minute.

Sawyer's sharp tone carried as he used his phone to call for assistance.

With Delaney on one side of her and Cam on the other, the three women stood in unity. Vance's eyes were open in a blank stare, all fight seemingly gone from his body. "It's done now, isn't it?" Emery asked.

Shane passed the gun to Sawyer and settled an arm over her shoulders. "Yeah, it is."

Walker pulled Delaney into his side, his stance protective.

Sawyer disarmed Vance's weapon, shoving the clip into one pocket, the gun in another. His gaze was on Cam when he asked, "You okay?"

She nodded, her expression impassive, but her gaze was locked on Sawyer.

The process that followed was becoming all too familiar.

Once again there were police cars and officers swarming the area, followed by a trip to the sheriff's department. Through the questions and statements, Shane remained glued to Emery's side.

Hours later, they returned to the ranch. Walking hand in hand to the porch under a starry sky, Emery tipped her head back to take in the swath of the Milky Way. "I finally feel like we're safe. Vance is in jail, Dicarlo is in jail. I may be unemployed, but I don't have to worry my life is in danger."

Shane turned her into him until all she could see was his face in shadowy darkness. Then his mouth was on hers in a kiss that wiped away the stress of the past few hours with the delicious feeling of belonging with the man she loved.

"Let's sit for a minute."

He tugged her hand to follow him up the steps of the porch where they settled side-by-side onto the cushioned loveseat.

"Will you marry me, Emery?"

"Wait, what? You're asking me to marry you now?"

Shane's eyes glittered in the glow of the porch light. "Yes, now. I need to get it out before something else happens and we're interrupted."

He lifted her with easy strength so she straddled his lap.

"I need to see your face when I do this." She opened her mouth to respond, but he set a finger on her lips. "Wait a second. I don't have a sign like Rowan, but let me lay it out for you."

He grabbed her hands, always careful of her wrist, took a deep breath, then spoke in his low voice.

"I love you, Emery, like I've never loved another living soul. I hope to god you feel the same way about me." His grip tightened. "When you're not with me I feel like I've lost a limb, like a part of me is missing. I want to marry you. I want to have a family with you. I want to grow old together. Will you marry me?"

A tidal wave of emotion she recognized as sheer joy swelled inside her. She rested her forehead against his, tugging her hands free to rest on either side of his face.

She could feel the grin splitting her face. "Yes, Shane, I'll marry you. I love you, so yes to everything." She wrapped her arms around him, burying her face in his neck. "I love you so much. My heart's beating so hard it's going to burst out of my chest."

He gave a shuddering sigh. "Thank god."

He held her, their breaths in sync, until he straightened his leg and nudged her knee aside so he could dig something from his pocket. "I've been carrying this around for days so I'd be ready." She straightened and he held a tiny box between them. He flipped open the lid to reveal a perfect solitaire diamond gleaming in its velvet cushion.

"You got me a ring?"

"Of course. I'm trying to do it right, but I don't like the whole down-on-one-knee thing."

"I'm not a fan of that myself."

His gaze hadn't wavered. "Would you wear my ring, Emery?"

"Oh yes. The ring's beautiful. I'd be honored to wear it."

He took the brilliant solitaire with its platinum band from the box and held it up between them. "I know next to nothing about jewelry. I thought this one looked nice, but if you want something different, the guy at the store in town said we can exchange it."

"No, it's perfect because you picked it out for me. I love it." Emery held up her hand, fluttering her fingers in front of him.

Shane kissed the ring, then slipped it easily onto her finger. "Damn, it's a little loose. We'll need to get it sized."

She closed her hand in a fist. "Okay, but I want to wear it for a while first."

His gaze caught hers and his lips spread in a wide smile. "We're really going to do this. We're getting married."

"You got that right, cowboy. We're getting married."

"Will you move in with me here at the ranch? Or if you'd rather live in town we'll figure out a way for that to happen."

She shook her head, smiling. "I fell for your ranch maybe not as fast as I fell for you, but it was close."

"Oh yeah?"

"Yeah. That day you rescued me from Bastard, I'd found the meadow and thought I'd never seen a more beautiful place in the world. My fantasy was to build a tiny house there where I could live with a dog named Tucker. I hadn't met Bruno yet or he could have been the dog in my fantasy."

Bruno's tail thumped when he heard his name.

"Guess I should tell you I already knew yellow-legged frogs were in Rock Creek."

"You didn't."

"I did. The guy I'm working with at the university came up a couple years ago and brought his girlfriend. She was a wildlife biologist. She convinced me to keep cattle out of the meadow and creek to protect the habitat. I was way ahead of you. There was nothing official, but I would've made it official if I needed that leverage against Norris."

"Oh my god. I should have told you right away. I thought you were going to hate me."

He snorted out a laugh. "There's not a chance of that." His gaze sharpened. "Can I kiss you now?"

"Yes, please."

He pulled her to him and their lips met in a kiss that swelled with the promise of forever.

She'd roped herself a cowboy and she was never letting him go.

ABOUT THE AUTHOR

USA TODAY Bestselling Author, Diane Benefiel has been an avid reader all her life. She enjoys a wide range of genres, from westerns to fantasy to mysteries, but romance is her favorite. She writes what she loves best to read—emotional, heart-gripping romantic suspense novels. In her stories, she puts the heroes and heroines in all sorts of predicaments that they have to work together to overcome. Her novel, *Solitary Man* was a National Readers' Choice Award winner.

A native Southern Californian, Diane enjoys nothing better than summer. For a high school history teacher, summer means a break from students, and time immersed in her current writing project. With both kids grown and gone, she enjoys her leisure time camping, especially in the Sierras, and gardening, both with her husband.

Diane loves hearing from her readers.

Website: dianebenefiel.com
Twitter: twitter.com/dianebenefiel
Instagram: @diane_benefiel
TikTok: @diane_benefiel_romance
Pinterest: diane_benefiel
FB: /DianeBenefielRomance
BookBub: /authors/diane-benefiel
Goodreads: /author/show/8075321.Diane_Benefiel
Newsletter: https://landing.mailerlite.com/webforms/landing/n1i2u8

Sign up for Diane's newsletter for sneak peeks and inside info on her new series.

www.BOROUGHSPUBLISHINGGROUP.com

If you enjoyed this book, please write a review. Our authors appreciate the feedback, and it helps future readers find books they love. We welcome your comments and invite you to send them to info@boroughspublishinggroup.com.

Follow us on TicTok and Instagram, and be sure to sign up for our newsletter for surprises and new releases from your favorite authors.

Are you an aspiring writer? Check out www.boroughspublishinggroup.com/submit and see if we can help you make your dreams come true.

Love podcasts? Enjoy ours at www.boroughspublishinggroup.com/podcast

www.ingramcontent.com/pod-product-compliance
Lightning Source LLC
Chambersburg PA
CBHW021959170626
46808CB00001B/216